P9-CET-864

Miracles in Maggody

Other books by Joan Hess

The Maggody Series

MALICE IN MAGGODY

MISCHIEF IN MAGGODY

MUCH ADO IN MAGGODY

MADNESS IN MAGGODY

MORTAL REMAINS IN MAGGODY

MAGGODY IN MANHATTAN

O LITTLE TOWN OF MAGGODY

MARTIANS IN MAGGODY

The Claire Malloy Series

STRANGLED PROSE

MURDER AT THE MURDER AT THE MIMOSA INN

DEAR MISS DEMEANOR

A REALLY CUTE CORPSE

A DIET TO DIE FOR

ROLL OVER AND PLAY DEAD

DEATH BY THE LIGHT OF THE MOON

POISONED PINS

TICKLED TO DEATH

BUSY BODIES

Miracles

in

Maggody

An Arly Hanks Mystery

Joan Hess

A DUTTON BOOK

DUTTON
Published by the Penguin Group
Penguin Books USA Inc., 375 Hudson Street,
New York, New York, 10014, U.S.A.
Penguin Books Ltd, 27 Wrights Lane,
London W8 5TZ, England
Penguin Books Australia Ltd, Ringwood,
Victoria, Australia
Penguin Books Canada Ltd, 10 Alcorn Avenue,
Toronto, Ontario, Canada M4V 3B2
Penguin Books (N.Z.) Ltd, 182–190 Wairau Road,
Auckland, New Zealand

Penguin Books Ltd, Registered Offices:
Harmondsworth, Middlesex, England

First published by Dutton, an imprint of Dutton Signet,
a division of Penguin Books USA Inc.
Distributed in Canada by McClelland & Stewart Inc.

First Printing, November, 1995
10 9 8 7 6 5 4 3 2

Ⓐ REGISTERED TRADEMARK—MARCA REGISTRADA

LIBRARY OF CONGRESS CATALOGING IN PUBLICATION DATA:

Hess, Joan.
    Miracles in Maggody/Joan Hess.
        p. cm.
    "An Arly Hanks mystery"—CIP data sheet.
    ISBN 0-525-94051-0
    I. Title.
PS3558.E79785M565 1995
813'.54—dc20   95-14561
                                                      CIP

Printed in the United States of America
Set in Palatino
Designed by Eve L. Kirch

PUBLISHER'S NOTE

This is a work of fiction. Names, characters, places, and incidents either are
the product of the author's imagination or are used fictitiously, and any resemblance to actual persons, living or dead, events, or locales is entirely co-
incidental.

To the 1992–93 AAAA State Basketball Champions
Fayetteville High School Lady Bulldogs

Carrie Braker, Carrie Cawthon, Wendy Cook,
Emily Corrigan, Heather Cullers, Cher Gabbard,
Anita Hampton, Melissa Hayden, Becca Hess,
Dawn Jenkins, Ashley Jones, Erin Kirkpatrick,
Melissa Levesque, Jennifer Masters,
Marika McKinen, Laura Neeley, Sharon Neeley,
Melinda Polk, Catherine Reynolds, Sharlie Reynolds,
Melissa Simpson, Cherry Starling, Cari Tanneberger,
Paige Thompson, Laura Todd, Cherie Tyree,
and Lindsey Wagner.

Although each and every character
in this book is fictional,
your accomplishment remains very real.

1

THE so-called extraterrestrials who'd visited Maggody a few months ago had found no sign of intelligent life, and I doubted anyone else could, either. Maggody's tucked up in the northwest corner of Arkansas, but it's not some picturesque little town with storybook houses, quaint cafés, and carefree, college-bound children flying kites in a field of wildflowers. Maggody is more a hodgepodge of rusty mobile homes, uninspired tract houses, shacks, a dirty barbershop and a dirtier pool hall, and snotty children playing serial killer in an illegal dump. There may be more cars and trucks set on concrete blocks than cruising the roads. There certainly are more Buchanons; they're strewn across the county like rabbits. As a rule, rabbits are smarter than Buchanons, with damn few notable exceptions. You can spot a Buchanon a mile away by his or her yellowish eyes, simian forehead, and thick-lipped, repugnant sneer. Most of them are related to each other in more ways than one. Mayor Jim Bob Buchanon's my least favorite, with his wife, Barbara Ann Buchanon Buchanon (aka Mrs. Jim Bob), running a real close second.

It's hard to explain why I, Ariel Hanks, had come limping back home to this oasis of poverty and incest. The primary catalyst was the collapse of a disastrous marriage to a hotshot Manhattan advertising executive. It had taken me a while to realize his office was the only one in the agency with a sofa that made into a bed. The divorce had been far from amiable; it was the one time he'd really gone out of his way to screw me. Now it was taking me a while to convince myself that my head was on my shoulders instead of in a place where the sun don't shine (as we say in Maggody—we're partial to euphemisms).

I was entertaining all these gloomy thoughts as I drove past the town limits sign (pop. 755), past a peculiar metal structure known as the Voice of the Almighty Lord Assembly Hall, past a lot of storefronts with boarded-up windows, and into the gravel lot in front of the Maggody Police Department. When I first accepted the job as chief of police, I considered putting out a sign reserving the prime parking spot. However, it didn't take long (maybe twenty minutes) to realize that the citizens weren't exactly fighting for the privilege of parking by the door. I'd twiddled my thumbs for seventeen days before someone came in to report a stolen lawn ornament (a concrete garden gnome, I seem to recollect).

The pace had picked up, though. Tourists driving through on their way to the crowded country music theaters and go-cart tracks of Branson, Missouri, would never suspect the bizarre happenings that put everyone in a tizzy and me in bed with a pillow over my head.

There'd been kidnappings, murdered movie stars, booby-trapped marijuana patches, feminist rebellions, a downright psychotic period when Maggody had been the hometown of a famous country singer, and fairly recently, the most absurd string of incidents imaginable involving crop circles, aliens, and dueling tabloid reporters. And let's not forget the Bigfoot sightings.

Somehow or other, we all kept muddling along. My mother, the infamous proprietor of Ruby Bee's Bar & Grill as well as maven of the grapevine, might go so far as to switch the daily blue plate specials or serve popcorn instead of pretzels at happy hour, but only when she's feeling risqué. Most of the time she sticks to the traditions, one of which is to make pointed remarks about my lack of promising beaus and my biological clock, which as far as I can tell is still ticking away at thirty-four. She's more enamored of the idea of grandchildren than I am of an icy cold beer on a sultry August afternoon.

It being a sultry August afternoon, I wasn't all that thrilled as I dutifully went into the PD, glanced through the mail that had accumulated in my two-week absence, and debated calling the sheriff's office to notify the dispatcher that I was back. I finally decided against it, since there was a real danger that Sheriff Harve Dorfer actually might have something that would interfere with my immediate objective. He seems to believe I'm the only officer in the county capable of writing up a really juicy accident report or intervening in a domestic dispute out on some remote dirt road. He may be right. A goodly number of his deputies are Buchanons; I can eat an ice-cream cone without anything dribbling down my chin.

I wasn't in the mood for anything but that beer I mentioned earlier, and maybe a grilled cheese sandwich to tide me over until supper time. I made sure my bun was firmly affixed to the back of my head, applied a layer of lipstick, took my badge from a desk drawer and stuck it on my T-shirt, and walked down the road to Ruby Bee's.

There were more pickup trucks and cars in the lot than had graced the PD parking lot in the last three years. I squinted at Jim Bob's SuperSaver Buy 4 Less across the road. Heat was shimmering on the asphalt, but business was far from booming. There were a few people trudging in and out of the Suds of Fun Launderette (also part of the Jim Bob Buchanon financial empire), and the old coots were nodding on the bench in front of the barbershop. Roy Stiver was sitting in a rocking chair by the door of his antiques store, playing the redneck for a couple of tourists ogling a pie safe. My amazingly inefficient efficiency apartment is above the store; at some point down the line I was going to have to drag my suitcases upstairs and start shaking sand out of my unmentionables. The sand was likely to enhance the decor.

No one appeared to be committing any crimes, so I continued inside the bar and paused to allow my eyes to adjust to the dim light before I ambled across the dance floor. The jukebox was blaring some nasal lament of lost love, and the booths were filled with familiar (but not necessarily attractive) faces. Estelle Oppers, Ruby Bee's best friend and co-maven of the grapevine, was perched on her stool at the end of the bar. She's tall and as scrawny as a free-range chicken. The only thing different about her was her hairstyle; most of the time she piled her fire-engine red hair into a daunting beehive, but today it shot out like a frizzy explosion.

"So you're back," she said as I selected a stool far enough away from her to give me a chance to take cover should her hair begin to flicker. Her tone was accusatory, but this was not extraordinary. She and Ruby Bee are pretty much always convinced I'm doing something wrong—like not subscribing to *Modern Bride* magazine.

"Looks like it." I picked up a menu on the off chance it might be a chicken-fried steak day and Ruby Bee had leftovers in the kitchen. "What happened to your hair?"

She sniffed haughtily. "If you must know, I have been experimenting with a new product. What would the clientele of Estelle's Hair Fantasies think if I tried it on them and all their hair fell out?"

"Is all your hair going to fall out?"

The kitchen door opened and Ruby Bee came out, wiping her hands on a dish towel. "Might be a blessing if it did, Estelle. It looks like you were roosting on a utility pole in an electrical storm." She turned her gaze on me. "Well, are you gonna sit there and insult Estelle, or are you gonna tell us about your vacation down in Florida?"

Decisions, decisions. I put down the menu and said, "May I have a beer, please?"

Ruby Bee is often mistaken for a grandmotherly sort because of her chubby cheeks, stocky body, and starchy apron, but she's more akin to a stevedore in drag. At the moment, her eyes were snapping below several layers of undulating pink eye shadow, and her expression was sour enough to curdle milk as she banged down a mug of beer in front of me.

"At least you remembered to say *please*," she said. "Sometimes you act like you were raised in a barn. Last month Eula Lemoy told me you walked right past her in the produce section and didn't so much as ask about her arthritis. She's been feeling real poorly."

Estelle opted to butt in. "She told me she can't do any needlework on account of her knuckles swelling up like gnarls on a branch. When I happened to mention it to Elsie McMay while I was giving her a perm, she had the nerve to ask me if I thought Eula would be entering a quilt in the county fair this year! How's that for Christian charity?"

"I ain't surprised," Ruby Bee said as she filled a pitcher from the tap and took it to a bunch of good ol' boys in a corner booth. When she returned, she positioned herself in front of me, crossed her arms, and said, "So?"

"Is Eula entering a quilt?" I said, pretending to misunderstand her simply to amuse myself. Maggody's not a place where you find yourself rolling on the floor all that often.

"What about your vacation with that man who pretended to be a tabloid reporter just so he could snoop around town? Is he coming to visit anytime soon? Did you stop spitting out smart remarks long enough for him to get a word in edgewise?"

Estelle gazed slyly at me over the rim of her glass of sherry. "You didn't find out he was married, did you?"

"Don't be absurd!" snapped Ruby Bee. "Arly wouldn't have gone off like that with a married man— not after the awful time she had with that philanthropist of an ex-husband."

If sperm counted, he'd have been right up there with Carnegie and Mellon. I took a swallow of beer, steeled myself for the inevitable counterattack, and said, "Jules and I had a perfectly nice time. We had dinner with his friend from the tabloid, spent a lot of time on the beach, drove through the Everglades one day, and bought each other incredibly tacky souvenirs. When we were ready to go our separate ways at the airport, there was some discussion of seeing each other again. But he lives in Washington, D.C., and works for the IRS, which is kind of spooky. One night while he was asleep, I started wondering if he was dreaming about widows in bankruptcy court and bond daddies in federal prisons."

"Just exactly what were you doing in *his* motel room, missy?" said Ruby Bee. Bear in mind she owns the Flamingo Motel out behind the bar, and although she doesn't rent rooms by the hour, she herself will admit there are rarely any cars parked in front of the units at sunrise.

Estelle waggled a finger at me. "Men don't respect girls who take a trip to Memphis with every man they meet—particularly on the first date. You might keep that in mind if you intend to catch yourself a husband in the next month of Sundays."

"Oh, I will," I said as I finished my beer. Instead of trying to wheedle a grilled cheese sandwich out of Ruby Bee, who was huffing and puffing, I slipped off the stool. "See y'all later. I need to unpack and run a few loads at the launderette."

"That doesn't mean you ought to go running off to Washington, D.C.," Ruby Bee began. "You don't know anything about this Jules fellow except for what he told you. He didn't have any reluctance when it came to lying to me about how there was a government conspiracy to keep folks from finding out the truth about flying saucers." She was going to elaborate (at length, no doubt), when the door banged open and all three hundred pounds of Maggody's most recent bride, Dahlia (née O'Neill) Buchanon, thundered into the room. Her more typical bovine expression had been replaced with wide-eyed agitation, and her hands were flapping. Underneath her voluminous tent dress, everything quivered.

"You got to come see!" she shrieked.

"Now, Dahlia," Ruby Bee said soothingly, "you're in no condition to get all worked up like this. Why doncha sit down right here and have a nice glass of skim milk?"

Dahlia flapped harder, although her chances of becoming airborne were poor. "It's the most unbelievable thing I've ever laid eyes on! Y'all come see for yourselves!"

A few dedicated beer drinkers stayed where they were, but everybody else followed her out to the parking lot. For the first time in ages, she was right. Driving up the road at a decorous rate were, in order: a gold Cadillac, a massive motorcycle driven by a figure clad in black leather, a recreational vehicle only slightly smaller than a tennis court, a white Mercedes, a bus with darkly tinted windows, and four trucks the size of moving vans. The bus, trucks, and RV were emblazoned with the logo "Hope Is Here" in swirly gold-and-silver letters.

"It's Malachi Hope," Estelle breathed over my shoulder. "Smack-dab here in Maggody!"

"Who?" I asked as the last truck rolled by and the customers drifted back inside to discuss what they'd seen.

Dahlia's jaw dropped, squashing two or three of her chins. "You don't know? Malachi Hope is this really famous preacher who used to be on television on one of those cable stations. He had this show where he healed blind people and made cripples get right out of their wheelchairs and walk across the stage. Kevvie and I used to watch him every Sunday night, but then his show went off the air and we took to watching reruns of *Gunsmoke*. Why do you think Marshal Dillon never married Miss Kitty, Arly?"

I ignored her question, which was distressingly earnest, and frowned at Ruby Bee and Estelle. "Do you know anything about this?"

Ruby Bee gave me an innocent smile. "I may have heard some rumors, but I didn't want to bother you when you have all this laundry to do. You might even feel obliged to go run a speed trap out by the remains of Purtle's Esso station so you can get your salary this month."

"Just tell me—okay?"

"I'll tell you, Arly," said Dahlia. "Malachi Hope's gonna have a revival out at the big pasture that belongs to Burdock Grapper. It starts on Sunday and will last for a whole week! He's gonna heal everybody and save all the sinners in Stump County. Then he's gonna build this humongous theme park, and thousands of people will—"

"Theme park?" I said, addressing Ruby Bee and Estelle. "On Bur's property? What's she talking about?"

Ruby Bee wiggled her eyebrows at Estelle, who snagged Dahlia's arm and propelled her inside. She paused to collect her thoughts, and said, "What I heard is he aims to lease a thousand acres with an option to buy if he works out his financing."

I stared at her. "Does Bur have that much property?"

"No, but next to the Grapper place is a two-hundred-acre tract that Jim Bob bought from Bimbo Buchanon's widow when she had to go to the old folks' home. Beyond that is the land that belongs to Lottie Estes's second cousin Wharton. All together there'd be in the range of a thousand acres, give or take."

"What's he going to do with it?"

"Build something called 'The City of Hope.' It'll be this amusement park, with a church, rides, water slides, restaurants, a campground, and I don't know what all. It's the most foolish thing I've heard since Perkin's eldest took that correspondence course in tap dancing and made everybody in town come to a recital, but Estelle keeps insisting this preacher's nigh onto a saint and we shouldn't be questioning his motives."

"Which are?" I said encouragingly.

"Did you ever see him on television?"

"I don't watch televangelists."

"Don't go thinking I do, either, Miss Masterpiece Theatre," she said, giving me an extensive view of her flared nostrils, "but a while back Estelle made me do it one night. This Malachi Hope was the smarmiest man I've ever seen, and I've seen a lot in my day. He was so oily I don't know why he didn't slip right off his stage and go flying into the laps of all those pitiful people in wheelchairs. After he got everybody all fired up, his wife floated down from the ceiling in a billow of smoke. She was dressed up like an angel and sang gospel songs. If she hasn't been to Memphis so many times she has a key to the city, then my name isn't Rubella Belinda Hanks!"

If you think I was getting all this, then you're sorely overestimating me. "This televangelist is going to build a thousand-acre religious amusement park in Maggody?"

"I said no such thing."

"Then what did you say?" I asked blankly.

"Burdock Grapper's property starts on the far side of the low-water bridge, and Jim Bob's and Wharton's are beyond that. It's all within spittin' distance, but not inside the town limits. I heard over at the launderette that Mr. Malachi Hope's people made real sure about that."

I wrinkled my nose as the last exhaust fumes wafted over us. "Did they?" I murmured under my breath.

"You want something to eat?" asked Ruby Bee.

"No, but I'll see you long about supper time. I think I'm going to look into this Malachi Hope business. It beats doing laundry."

"You never were much for doing laundry," she said as she went inside.

I seldom fool my mother.

Mrs. Jim Bob and Brother Verber stood in front of the Assembly Hall, watching the last Hope Is Here truck turn the corner and roll down County 102 toward the low-water bridge.

"I don't have a good feeling about this," she said as she brushed the dust off her navy blue skirt, then straightened up to give him a beady look. "What do you think?"

He thought she was as fetching as a little sparrow, with her yellow-flecked eyes and thin lips pursed into what sort of resembled a beak and her undeniably shapely calves and trim ankles. He didn't think that was what she wanted to hear, though. Sometimes—or even most of the time—it was hard to figure out what she *did* want to hear, but he always obliged her as best he could. "About this Malachi Hope fellow? Is that what you mean?"

"I wasn't asking if it was hot enough for you, Brother Verber. Do you know anything about him and his plans?"

"Just what I heard at the potluck," he admitted as he pulled out a handkerchief to mop his forehead. "He's looking into buying land out past the bridge so he can build some ridiculous park. I saw a flyer over at the barbershop about a tent revival next week. Do you reckon I should call off the Sunday evening service and the Wednesday evening prayer meeting so folks can go?"

"You are not thinking this through," Mrs. Jim Bob said, her impatience increasingly hard to miss. "Canceling a couple of services for the revival is one thing, but consider what'll happen if Malachi Hope goes through with this project. Where do you imagine most everybody in town will go on Sundays—to the Assembly Hall to hear Lottie Estes fumble through hymns on a piano, or to a big, glitzy church where they can wander around afterward, riding the Ferris wheel and eating cotton candy?"

Brother Verber sank down on the steps of the porch, his fat face all puckered up as he mulled over what she'd said. Lottie Estes got most of the notes right, but she was liable to loose her place in the refrain and they'd have to start all over. The Assembly Hall was hot in the summer, drafty in the fall, and colder than a witch's tit long about January. In the spring, most folks brought umbrellas. He himself always looked forward to the potluck suppers after the Sunday evening services, but the same green bean casseroles and gelatin salads showed up just about every week, and he'd heard some tart remarks lately. There wasn't near enough in the coffers for a cotton-candy machine, much less carnival rides.

Sighing, he looked up at Mrs. Jim Bob. "I reckon it's gonna be the end of the Voice of the Almighty Lord Assembly Hall, Sister Barbara. There ain't no way to compete."

"Once he gets it built, you'll be lucky to fill the front pew," she said without sympathy, "but this Hope fellow doesn't own so much as a square inch of land—yet. I don't know about Bur Grapper and Wharton Estes, but Jim Bob got a long letter a while back. Jim Bob happened to be off in Hot Springs at one of those municipal league meetings, so I took it upon myself to open the letter just in case it was important and I needed to call him."

"You are so saintly," Brother Verber said, shaking his head in admiration. "I would never have thought of that."

"Well, I did. The letter was from a man named Thomas Fratelleon, who claimed to be Malachi Hope's business manager. It was all a lot of complicated jargon about the southeast quarter of the northwest quarter, but as far as I could make out, he was asking if Jim Bob would sell that parcel for a hundred dollars an acre."

"Generous offer, I suppose. It's nothing but scrub and

rock out that way, and the only thing it's good for is chickweed. After ol' Mrs. Wockermann ran off to Mexico with Merle Hardcock, her nephew sold that pasture beside her house for more like fifty an acre."

Sometimes Mrs. Jim Bob wondered if he was exactly the right person to be the spiritual leader of the congregation. However, it was a thought unworthy of a pious Christian, and everybody knew she was the most pious Christian in town and maybe the entire county.

Brother Verber shivered like a wet dog. "Like I said," he continued in the sonorous voice he used for funerals and the till-death-us-do-part moment in wedding vows, "there's no way to compete with a cotton-candy machine. If I lose my congregation, I won't be able to take a modest percent of the offering to support myself. I might ought to write the seminary out in Las Vegas and see if they know of a vacant pulpit someplace else. It breaks my heart to think about having to leave my cozy little rectory over there under the sycamore trees." He was so choked up he had to clear his throat like a bullfrog. "And you, Sister Barbara. You are such an inspiration to us all, what with your soul as pure as the Lord's rain and—"

"Malachi Hope can be stopped," she interrupted, since he wasn't saying anything she didn't already know. "If you'd been paying attention, you'd have realized the significance of what I just said. He doesn't own any of the parcels as of now, and even if Bur and Wharton agree to sell theirs, Jim Bob's two hundred acres are in the middle of them."

"Jim Bob wouldn't turn down a hundred dollars an acre, would he? That'd add up to . . ." He tried to do the computation in his head, then finally gave up and said, "A right tidy sum of money."

"Twenty thousand dollars."

Brother Verber whistled through his teeth. "Nothing to turn up your nose at."

"It is if what's at stake is the salvation of the community. Jim Bob is the mayor of Maggody, and his first concern should be the spiritual well-being of his constituents. I watched some of Malachi Hope's television shows. He preached about how Jesus wants everybody to have themselves a good time in the here and now. From the way he carried on, you'd think Jesus was a camp counselor. I don't recollect him saying one word about eternal damnation. He had celebrities on his 'Hour of Hope' who talked about how they used to be miserable sinners, but as soon as they dedicated their lives to the Lord, they got rich and famous. He even had Matt Montana on his show one time. He sang 'You're a Detour on the Highway to Heaven,' and half the folks in the audience were bawling by the time it was over."

"I'll bet they emptied their pockets when the plates were passed," Brother Verber said, getting misty as he imagined the scene. "I wonder if I could get—"

"Jim Bob has a duty to this community, and he is not going to stand aside and allow this charlatan and his hussy to lure everybody away from the Missionary Society after all I did to win a third term as president. I'll have a word with him this evening. If I can't persuade him, you may have to throw in some words about Satan and the root of all evil."

"You think it'll work?"

Her expression was so fierce he cringed. "It will work, Brother Verber."

Burdock Grapper watched the trucks and buses rolling up the dirt road next to his house, then took a beer out of the refrigerator and sat back down on the recliner. He was sixty-three, which made him nearly twenty years older than his wife, Norma Kay. He was also two inches shorter than she was. His narrow nose was more crooked than his teeth, which had been aching so much he was thinking about having 'em yanked. He had a full head of brown hair tinged with gray; he dropped by the barbershop every six weeks or so for a trim, but mostly to hear the latest gossip. Not that he'd hear what gnawed at him night and day—the identity of the sumbitch Norma Kay was having an affair with. If and when he found out, the sumbitch and Norma Kay would both be real sorry.

"You're late," he said as she came into the living room. "It's almost supper time. Where were you?"

"At school. Where else would I be—over at Raz Buchanon's house gossiping with his hog?" Norma Kay went into the kitchen and took a pound of hamburger meat from the freezer. "I asked you this morning to defrost this, Bur. Is it too much trouble to get off your butt for one minute and help out? All you've done since the day you retired is watch those stupid soap operas and drink beer. One of these days you're going have a heart attack and die, and I won't even notice until you start to stink worse than you do already."

"Watch your mouth," he said, finishing the beer. He crumpled the can and tossed it onto the floor with the others. "Why were you at school so late?"

"The schedule's a real mess. We were supposed to play Hasty the week after Thanksgiving, but the coach canceled because her best players have to go to a choir competition down in Clarksville. She knows we'll whip their asses if they don't have that six-foot-tall center." She stuck the meat in the refrigerator and pulled out the remains of the previous evening's casserole. She did so with a smug smile, since Bur hated leftovers more than he did soap and water. "I was on the phone all day trying to line up another team. We might be able to play Emmet, but then I have to figure out how to get us there, since the boys are still playing Hasty. Cory's not about to let us take the bus."

"Talking to Cory, huh?"

She came to the doorway and glared at him. "Cory and I have to talk to each other because we have to transport both of our teams to the out-of-town games and we only have the one bus. For pity's sake, Bur, you were the basketball coach for thirty-three years. Did you ever tell your players to take a cab?"

Bur shrugged. "So you needed to talk about the bus. How's he doing as head coach while Amos is laid up over at the nursing home in Farberville?"

"I don't know. He just started off-season training today. Some of the first string are on vacation, but there's a new junior with promise, and the MacNamara boy must have grown two inches over the summer. He's going to make a good point guard."

Bur aimed the clicker at the television set, having lost

interest in basketball right after the buzzer went off to end the final game of his career. He'd never liked his players; the only pleasure he'd derived from coaching was being able to make their lives hell during practices and games.

Norma Kay returned to the kitchen to stick the casserole into the oven and fix herself a glass of iced tea. She never touched beer on account of her figure, which was holding up pretty good except for a broadening of her rump. She used a variety of expensive creams on her face and took pains to color her hair at the first sign of a dark root. Estelle Oppers was always giving her snooty looks, but Norma Kay was proud of its bright yellow color and the perky little flip like she wore when she was a starter on the Coffeyville varsity team twenty-five years ago. Nobody except parents had ever come to the games, girls' athletics being a joke back then, but the team always played as if the bleachers were packed and a championship was at stake.

Thinking about that was enough to keep her entertained as she sat down at the kitchen table and waited for the casserole to burn.

2

Dust was hanging in the soupy heat as I drove past the Grappers' house, bounced up a lane to a pasture, and parked behind the bus. Two dozen men in jeans and sweaty shirts were unloading the trucks. As I climbed out of my car, I was treated to wolf whistles that brought to mind a Manhattan construction site. It was not a warm memory.

"It's a cop," one of them said as he paused to stare. "Can I spend the night in your cell, honey? I'll bet you got the hottest little cell in town."

"Hey, cop," said another, "want to charge me with exposing myself in public?"

"If she saw your prick, all she'd give you is a ticket for loitering."

"I'd sure like to have the long arms of the law wrapped around me tonight."

"Enough of this," said an older man as he appeared from behind one of the trucks. "This is a pasture, gentlemen. It's going to be dark in two hours, and you will be unable to see what you're stepping in."

"Bullshit," said one of my admirers.

"Precisely." The man approached me with an apologetic smile. Despite the temperature, he wore a tweedy jacket and a dark tie; he looked so straitlaced that he might have been the headmaster of a prep school on Parents' Day. He was tall; expensive tailoring minimized his bulk. His face was benignly wrinkled and worn, but his eyes, alert behind wire-rimmed bifocals, focused on my badge.

"May I help you?" he asked with a trace of wariness.

"I'm Arly Hanks, the chief of police down the road in Maggody. Are you Malachi Hope?"

"No, I am not. Are you here in your official capacity, Miss Hanks? Has there been a violation of a local ordinance?"

"I'm not aware of any violations. I just dropped by to see what's going on." I stepped back as two men carried by a massive bundle of canvas. "If you're not Hope, who are you?"

"The drive from Little Rock was so tiresome that I have forgotten my manners. I am Thomas Fratelleon, the business manager of Hope Is Here, Incorporated. I handle all the paperwork, including whatever we might require in terms of local permits and variances. It's my understanding that we are outside the city limits, but we certainly desire to cooperate with the authorities in every way we can."

"Oh, really," I said, unimpressed. "I was told you're staging a tent revival out here. Where do you and all these gentlemen plan to stay for the next ten days?"

"Once they get the site prepared, they'll be at a motel in Farberville except when we need them here. Some of them will undoubtedly have encounters with the local police, obliging me to hire others of their ilk, but that should not concern your department. Our special-effects man and I will set up cots in an area behind the stage in order to discourage trespassing."

"And Malachi Hope?"

"He and his family will stay here, too, but in the RV until we can arrange for something more permanent. Once we get it hooked up to the generator, it's self-contained and more spacious than you'd suspect. It has a small bedroom, a bathroom, and a living room with a kitchen area. The sofa converts into a bed." He gestured at the residence under discussion. "Would you like to meet Malachi and Seraphina?"

I considered his question while I moved out of the way to allow another large bundle of canvas to be carried by. "Maybe at another time," I said. "Why don't you give me a tour of the site, Mr. Fratelleon? How big is this tent they're putting up?"

"Quite large," he said as he took my elbow and guided me between the trucks. "We can seat a thousand worshipers on benches, and another two hundred on folding chairs at the back if necessary. Our stage and equipment take up nearly eight hundred square feet, but we're hardly an old-fashioned tent show making its way around the salvation circuit. People are too sophisticated these days to be satisfied with a single charismatic preacher and a dozen choir members. Our special-effects man used to work for rock bands out in California; he's

21

a real wizard when it comes to adding elements of drama to the service."

In front of us an enormous tent was rising as if it were a sienna mountain. Hydraulic winches were stationed at strategic corners, and cables thicker than my wrist strained as the tent poles inched skyward. Canvas sagged, then snapped into symmetrical lines. The workers barked orders at one another, but the exchanges were perfunctory (and vulgar, even by Maggody standards). Other workers walked unconcernedly beneath the listing poles, intent on their own assigned duties.

"When do you bring out the clowns and elephants?" I asked.

Fratelleon gave me a wry look. "There is a certain similarity, I must admit, but selling religion takes showmanship as well as a calling. Don't make any stereotypic assumptions about Malachi until you meet him. You may be surprised."

"What about you, Mr. Fratelleon? Surely you haven't done this all your life."

"I was an accountant in a large manufacturing firm for more than thirty-five years. When I neared retirement, the board of directors chose to discharge me rather than give me a gold watch and a pension. I found it impossible to find steady employment and was doing menial temp work when I met Malachi two years ago. His offer was too tempting to turn down."

"Peddling miracles," I said.

"I was earning no more than fifteen thousand dollars a year as a temp. Now I earn a hundred thousand in salary and bonuses. I live frugally and invest prudently, and should the future unfold as we envision it, I will retire in five years as a multimillionaire. That, Chief Hanks, is a miracle."

I was about to ask him for the name of his broker, when an olive-skinned young man in jeans, a black T-shirt, and a black leather vest came over to us. His dark hair was combed back into a 1950s ducktail, and a pack of cigarettes bulged in a rolled-up sleeve that partially covered a tattoo. He obviously fancied himself as a latter-day James Dean—or a character from a production of *Grease*.

"I've got to go into the nearest big town and find an electronics store," he said to Fratelleon. "A fuse blew in the dimming-control panel. I was gonna take my bike, but if you want me to pick up other stuff as long as I'm there, I'll take one of the cars."

"Miss Hanks, this is Joey Lerner, the special-effects wizard I was telling you about a minute ago. Joey works some amazing miracles through electronics."

"Pleased to meet you," I said as I realized he'd been the black-clad motorcyclist in the caravan and that his bowed legs were not the result of years of riding the range. He had Harley-Davidson legs, as well as a cute derriere.

"Me, too," he said without interest, then looked back at Fratelleon. "So what do you want me to do, Thomas? I'd like to get the fuse right away so I can start fixing the panel."

"I haven't spoken to Malachi since we arrived," said Fratelleon. "If they need groceries or such, I shall send someone back to that supermarket we passed. Take whichever vehicle you prefer."

"Joey!" cried a girl as she came down the steps in

front of the RV that purportedly housed Malachi Hope and his family. Waving frantically, she stumbled across the weeds, ducking under cables and barely avoiding collisions with the workmen. "Wait a minute!"

"Shit," hissed Joey. Fratelleon looked no more pleased then he, but settled for a sigh.

I studied her curiously as she neared us. She was in her middle teens, with brown hair pulled into a sloppy ponytail and a scattering of acne on her forehead that the heavy pancake makeup failed to conceal. Her halter and skimpy shorts made no attempt to conceal a well-endowed bustline, a somewhat thick waist, and heavy thighs. With an afternoon at Estelle's Hair Fantasies and a supervised trip to a department store, she might have been attractive. At the moment, a scowl did nothing to enhance her appearance.

"I gotta get out of here," she said, grabbing Joey's arm. "It doesn't matter where—just any place but here."

"I don't know," he mumbled unhappily.

Fratelleon put his hand on the girl's shoulder. "Chastity, I'd like you to meet—"

She jerked away from him. "Did they tell you about my having to go to some gawdawful little high school? Were you in on this, too?"

"Malachi and Seraphina only want what's best for you. You don't want to put on a tinsel halo and sing to the unwashed for the rest of your life, do you? You need to finish high school so you'll have some options."

"Yeah," Joey inserted. "I mean, I had to go back to college and get a degree in electrical engineering before I could get any decent gigs. Before that, I was stringing lights in bars for minimum wage."

Chastity was not in the mood for career counseling. "Nobody's gonna make me go to some crappy school where everybody'll whisper about me behind my back and cut me dead in the halls. And it's all Seraphina's fault. Malachi was on my side at first and said something about getting some textbooks so I could study at home, but she dragged him back into their bedroom to talk, and when they came out he said he'd changed his mind. He didn't change his mind—*she* changed it for him!"

As the resident keeper of the peace, I smiled at the girl and said, "I can introduce you to some of the high school kids before school starts. That way you'd have some friends on the first day of class."

She glanced at me, then leaned against Joey and said, "Please take me for a bike ride or something. We could grab a blanket and a couple of beers, and find a nice, quiet place where we'd be all alone." He tried to back away from her, but she stuck to him like a thistle seed. "Come on, Joey. It'll be fun."

"Listen," he said, shooting a panicky look at Fratelleon, "you can ride into town with me, but all we're gonna do is get a few things at an electronics store and come right back here. We're not stopping anywhere else."

"We'll see," she said, her scowl replaced by a coquettish simper.

Fratelleon watched the two walk away and then said, "This is not good, but I could see no way to intervene. Despite his penchant for affectation, Joey is a decent young man. Chastity, on the other hand, seems destined for trouble. Seraphina may have erred when she took the child from a foster home and became her legal guardian last year."

"Seraphina is Malachi Hope's wife?" I asked.

"Yes, and Chastity is her younger sister. Ten years ago the girls were abandoned by their mother and put into foster care. Seraphina was sixteen at the time, and Chastity was only five. As soon as Seraphina felt as though she could offer a home to her sister, she tracked her down and petitioned the state to allow her to assume guardianship. The problem arises from the fact that Chastity deeply resents being taken away from her friends and obliged to participate in our revivals. She's not yet adjusted to a migratory life in the Bible Belt."

"Apparently not," I said. "Should I go ahead and call a couple of the local high school girls and have them come out to introduce themselves? I can't promise they'll keep her out of trouble, but it might help."

"She needs more help than any of us can give her," Fratelleon said, then forced a smile and extended a large, well-manicured hand. "Thank you for dropping by, Miss Hanks. There are countless details awaiting my attention, so if you'll excuse me, I'd better see to them. Will you be attending the first night of the revival? I'll gladly arrange front row seats for you and any guests."

I hadn't thought that far ahead, being more intrigued by the dynamics of what sounded like a full-blown family crisis. "Thanks, Mr. Fratelleon, but I wouldn't want any preferential treatment. If I come, I'm sure I can find a seat somewhere."

Such as in the last row, next to an exit.

Dahlia's face was blotchy as she trudged across the yard and into the house. She was wheezing something awful, too, which only increased her misery. The nurse at the clinic in Farberville had been right cheerful when she was dishing out the orders, but she wasn't the one that had to walk a dadburned mile every day—or try to get by on a half cup of boiled this and two ounces of baked that. The "this" and "that" weren't gravy and scalloped potatoes, neither. They were more like lettuce and brussels sprouts. Dahlia figured she was getting to the point where she was gonna throw up if anyone so much as mentioned yellow squash.

She wasn't even sure she believed all this nonsense the doctor had tried to explain about diabetes and how it was caused by having a bun in the warmer. (The doctor hadn't used that particular phrase, but she herself thought it had a nice ring, being fond of hamburger buns with peanut butter and grape jelly for lunch.) He'd spent a good fifteen minutes telling her how serious it might turn out to be if she didn't stick to a diet and an exercise program, and then he sent in the nurse to give Dahlia brochures and lecture her like she was back in school.

At least when she was in school, she could have a couple of pieces of pie and an orange Nehi when she got home. Now, according to the nurse, she was allowed celery sticks and a glass of water.

To make matters worse, Kevin had alerted everybody in town, so when she'd dropped by Ruby Bee's for a blue plate special, she'd been served green beans, plain rice, and a sliver of dry turkey. The cocky foreigner that ran the Dairee Dee-Lishus had flat-out refused to serve her a chili dog and offered her a free diet limeade. Even her own mother-in-law had turned on her and served such a dreary mess of vegetables and broiled fish that her father-in-law had jammed on his hat and left the house.

Of course she realized it was important if she and Kevvie were to be blessed with a bundle of joy with tiny fingers and toes and maybe a dimple. Then again, Dahlia thought as she hauled herself up and headed for the kitchen, it couldn't be too awful if she had a Twinkie every once in a while. A cookie when she was feeling blue, a little fried pork chop or two on Sunday after church, a scant handful of chips with onion dip while she and Kevvie watched television.

There was nothing in the refrigerator worth bothering to chew, so she went into the bedroom that would be the nursery and tried to distract herself by admiring the lacy nightgowns and crocheted booties all neatly set out in the pine crib that Kevvie's grandfather had made.

"Five more months," she said aloud, having taken to talking to her womb on a regular basis. "I'll tell you one thing, Kevin Fitzgerald Buchanon Junior, as soon as I get wheeled out of the delivery room, I'm orderin' a pizza. It'll be a supreme with everything but anchovies. They give me gas."

There was no response, but the doctor had said it was too early for the baby to start kicking.

Jim Bob Buchanon was in his office at the SuperSaver, frowning at the unpaid invoices and trying to decide if he could fire a couple of the checkers and one of the girls in the deli. It wasn't any big deal if the customers had to stand in line for a whole five or ten more minutes, he thought as he ran his fingers across his stubbly hair. It wasn't like they could go to another supermarket up the street. During the summer and fall, they could buy fresh produce in town, but the closest place to get toilet paper and laundry detergent and Kool-Aid was fifteen miles away.

Kevin Buchanon entered the cubicle and stopped on account of Jim Bob didn't like being interrupted when he was doing something important. When Jim Bob didn't start snarling at him, Kevin cleared his throat and said, "I was wondering if I kin take off tomorrow afternoon."

"Sure," Jim Bob said in a deceptively friendly voice. " 'Course I'll fire your ass before you're out the door, but other than that, I don't see any problem." He went so far as to smile at Kevin, who was as gawky and poorly put together as a widow woman's scarecrow. Kevin's membership in the clan was more obvious than some, and his Adam's apple had an unfortunate tendency to ripple so wildly it looked like it was trying to burst out of his slack mouth and go flying across the room.

"You'd fire me?" gasped Kevin, horrified. "I can't lose my job when Dahlia and me is gonna have a baby long about December. We're saving every penny so we kin pay the clinic and start paying on the hospital bill. Then there's groceries and electricity and—"

"Keep your tail in the water, boy," Jim Bob said before he was treated to the entire budget. "I haven't fired you yet. What's your dumbass reason for wanting the afternoon off when we've got a truckload of paper goods to unload?"

"I'm gonna take Dahlia to her appointment at the clinic, and then I thought I'd treat her to a picture show. She's plum run out of sap since the doctor put her on a real strict diet. Why, just the other day at supper, she took one look at the string beans and liked to burst into tears and—"

"Spare me the details. Yeah, I suppose you can take off tomorrow afternoon, but you'll have to work till midnight the rest of the week—and you ain't getting any overtime. I am running a business, not a charity. Got that?"

Kevin shook his head, thought better of it and nodded, then gave up trying to figure out how to respond and hurried out of the office before Jim Bob changed his mind.

Jim Bob went back to scowling at the figures and wondering how much longer he could get by with not paying the wholesale grocer, who had sent a pissy letter that very day implying he might turn the account over to a collection agency. When the phone rang, he gazed at it uncertainly. Most of the calls these days didn't end on a friendly note.

Finally he picked up the receiver. "Yeah?"

After listening for a minute, he said, "No, I didn't know you all were already here, Mr. Fratelleon. As soon as I can hunt down my good-for-nuthin' assistant manager, I'll hustle my butt right out there so we can talk about this deal you're offering. I got to warn you, though—property values have been going up since you wrote me back whenever it was. You and me may be in for some dickering before we make a deal."

He was grinning like a possum as he left the store. The two checkers abandoned their counters to watch him through the plate glass window, asking each other what in tarnation could have caused this minor miracle. Over by the door, Kevin leaned on the mop handle and imagined himself and Junior fishing at some secret spot on Boone Creek. He didn't even notice when the bucket tipped over and scummy gray water spread across the linoleum.

Back at the Maggody High School gymnasium, Cory Jenks sat in the dim locker room, thinking about how twelve years ago the team had cinched the conference title and had exploded through the door like a pack of coyotes. There'd been so much hooting and towel-snapping and ass-grabbing that Coach Grapper had cussed up a storm. Later they'd rounded up their girl-friends, a dozen six-packs of beer, a couple of jars of hooch, and gone down to a clearing next to Boone Creek to build a bonfire and do some serious celebrating.

Cory had been the high scorer in the game, and scored pretty damn well on an old quilt off in the bushes. He'd been a handsome kid, tall and muscular, with regular features, blond hair, clear skin with a few freckles. It was hard to recall the details, but he knew he'd made it with two of the cheerleaders and somebody's cousin from Mississippi. It'd been the first time he'd ever screwed a girl from out of state.

He was trying to remember what she'd looked like as he went back to the office, dropped the leather thong with a whistle on his desk, and picked up his keys. Not that the girl mattered, he thought with a smile. His nearly flawless performance during the game is what had really mattered, since it had earned him a scholarship at a junior college down by the Louisiana border. After two years, he'd been picked up by a second-rate college team and been able to hang on to the scholarship until he'd eked out a degree in physical education.

It'd been rocky after that. The coaching job at a junior high had ended when he was accused of seducing a girl in his driver's ed class, although everybody knew she was sleeping with every jock, even the sissies on the soccer team. Finding a job with that on his résumé was like trying to slam-dunk a bowling ball. After a couple of wretched years selling used cars and cemetery plots, he'd come home for his mother's funeral and found himself begging Grapper to hire him as assistant coach.

Now it was possible Cory might find himself head coach of the Maggody Marauders, what with Amos in a body cast (on account of not noticing his grandson's skateboard on the porch steps) and liable to retire. The other assistant coach had an edge, being Amos's nephew, but there were ways to make sure that didn't happen (like another skateboard). And Norma Kay kept swearing she put in a good word with her husband every chance she got. Bur was retired, but he'd reigned over the basketball program so long his opinion would matter when it came time for contracts in the spring.

Cory parked his truck in front of his house and switched off the headlights. From where he stood, he could see Norma Kay's car in her driveway alongside Bur's ancient truck. Light shone from behind drawn shades, but the porch lights weren't on to welcome unexpected guests.

His social life was no more exciting than theirs, he thought as he went inside. He'd learned his lesson and steered clear of the local girls—despite their provocative looks and wiggly bottoms as they cut through the gym between classes. There were damn few single women in Maggody, except for spinsters like Edwina Spitz and withered-up widows like Bethesda Buchanon, who was rumored to fry up one of her cats when she ran low on grocery money. Arly Hanks was always crumpy when he ran into her, leaving him to wonder if she remembered his reputation in high school. He cruised the bars in Farberville every once in a while, but the college girls didn't seem all that interested in his team's chances for a conference title—and he wasn't about to gabble about rock concerts or foreign films.

Instead of starting supper, he took a scrapbook off the mantel and lay down on the couch. Maggody was in the AA conference and therefore rarely warranted more than a paragraph or two in the newspaper. The year they'd won the conference was different: There'd been a long story and a photograph of Cory as he leapt into the air, the ball clutched next to his chest, his face contorted with concentration. At that moment, all he'd wanted was to make that one particular shot.

Now all he wanted was to be head coach.

It had been quite a day in Maggody, but by midnight everything had settled down. Ruby Bee's Bar & Grill had been the site of a lot of conversation about the Hope Is Here caravan, but all of it had been speculative at best, and now the pink concrete-block building was locked up tighter than bark on a tree. Ruby Bee was sound asleep out back in #1 of the Flamingo Motel, her alarm clock set to rouse her in plenty of time to get the biscuits started for breakfast. If her clock failed to go off, there were plenty of roosters to do the job.

Kevin Buchanon was snuggled in bed, snoring steadily as he dreamed of fatherhood. Dahlia tiptoed into the kitchen, peered wistfully into the refrigerator, and then found consolation of a sort in a late-night movie in which trustworthy American soldiers were bombing the wicked Japs into oblivion. Dahlia was mimicking the explosions, but real quietly so's not to disturb Kevvie.

Over in the rectory, Brother Verber was sitting at the dinette, working on a second bottle of sacramental wine while he considered how he was going to defend his flock against this slick-talking serpent with his cotton-candy machines and promises of milk and honey.

Out on Finger Lane, in the finest house in Maggody, Mrs. Jim Bob was staring at the shadows on the bedroom ceiling as she visualized how her position in the community would dwindle into nothingness if the members of the Missionary Society defected. She'd campaigned too long and hard to let that happen. Rather than count sheep, she began a mental list of Jim Bob's latest batch of transgressions. By the time she got to fifty (tracking mud on the living room carpet), she was fast asleep.

Jim Bob was across the hall, thinking of what he could do with the money from the sale of the acreage. None of his X-rated fantasies included his wife.

Earlier, Estelle had been hunting through her supply closet in hopes of finding a product to salvage her hair, but she'd given up and gone to bed. Sleeping on bristly hair rollers was a challenge she could meet with ease, having done so for forty-odd years.

In the field beyond the Grappers' farmhouse, the RV was dark and still. A few spotlights had been left on in strategic corners of the vast tent, but the two occupants were used to them, as well as to the cots and the persistent presence of hungry mosquitoes.

Dressed in a tired cotton robe and worn slippers, Norma Kay stood at the living room window, gazing at the top of the hill. In the back of the house, Bur was making his usual disgusting noises as he slept, but she'd long since given up hope she'd find his dead body in the morning (although she had a black dress in reserve in the coat closet). If she strained, she could hear the gentle hum of a generator behind the RV. It had been painfully tempting to rush up the hill to see Malachi, but she'd prayed for strength to wait for him to come to her. She was certain that he would.

A man of the Lord always kept his word.

3

"Guess who called this morning," Darla Jean Mc-Ilhaney said as Heather Reilly got in on the passenger's side of the station wagon. Both of them wore shorts and blouses that subtly complemented each other's, having worked it out beforehand on the phone. As soon-to-be seniors, they had an obligation to the sophomores and juniors to provide leadership in such matters.

"Elvis?"

"No, seriously."

Heather waited until they were out of the driveway, then took a pack of cigarettes and a lighter from her purse. "Brother Verber, because he wants you to play the Virgin Mary in the Sunday school pageant this year?"

Darla Jean did not appreciate the implication that she wasn't qualified for the role, even though she wasn't. "Arly Hanks called me," she said huffily. "She was all sugary on account of wanting us to do a favor for her."

"Us? You'd better not have—"

"I already did, so there's no point in having a hissy

fit. Besides, it might turn out to be interesting, and I don't seem to recall you having anything better to do. Just last night you were whining about how you were ready to dye your hair green out of boredom." She glanced at Heather, who didn't look convinced, and continued in a brighter voice. "There's a new girl in town named Chastity. She came with that preacher and his trucks, and she's all upset about having to go to high school here."

"Aren't we all?" Heather said as she let smoke dribble out her nostrils like an Italian actress she'd seen on a late-night movie.

"Arly thought it would be nice if we went over to where this girl's staying and introduced ourselves."

"And get dragged off to a tent revival? I don't think so, Darla Jean. Why don't you drop me off at the Dairee Dee-Lishus on your way to eternal salvation? I'd just as soon go to hell with a corn dog and a cherry Coke."

"Look, I owe Arly a favor because of her not telling my parents about certain things. If this girl is all snotty, we'll remember how we have to go get our hair cut or something and leave. I heard my ma talking on the phone this morning about the preacher and all the celebrities that appeared on his TV show. Maybe we can meet some if we pretend to be her friend."

"As long as you don't invite her to hang out with us," Heather muttered. "She probably doesn't approve of smoking or drinking. Wait till she finds out that's all there is to do in Maggody." She suddenly realized whose house they were approaching and jerked the cigarette out of her mouth. "Shit!" she said, stubbing out the cigarette in the ashtray and trying to fan the smoke out the window at the same time. "Why didn't you tell me we were going to Coach Grapper's? She'll kick my ass off the team if she sees me with a cigarette!"

Darla Jean downshifted as the station wagon lurched up the road. "She's over at the high school. I saw her car when I went there to talk to Miss Estes about the 4-H booth at the county fair next month. We're gonna do something about muffins . . ."

Her voice faded as the tent came into view. Neither of them had seen the arrival of the caravan the day before, having been at the mall in Farberville. It might have been discussed at supper in their respective houses, but so was a lot of other crap not worth listening to.

"Arly said to find the RV," Darla Jean said bravely. "I reckon that's it behind those trucks." Despite the urge to turn around and race down the hill, she cut off the engine. "Come on, Heather. It's just some girl with a dorky name. She can't make us do anything we don't want to do."

They climbed out of the station wagon and looked nervously at the tent looming over them. There were two trucks from the telephone company, along with one from the electric co-op and another from a wholesale grocer. No one seemed to be around, though, and the only sounds were bugs whirring in the weeds and a truck grinding its gears at the low-water bridge.

"Now what?" whispered Heather.

"I'm not exactly the Welcome Wagon lady, you know. I guess we ought to knock on the door."

"So knock on the door."

"I said *we*, Heather, as in *we* ought to knock on the door."

"I never agreed to this. You're the one that—"

The door opened and a woman came out to the top step of a concrete-block porch. She was wearing shorts and a blouse, but her hair was a pale blond cloud, all puffed out so her face was barely visible. Her figure was hard to miss, though. Although Darla Jean had never seen a Las Vegas showgirl, this was what she figured one would look like: big breasts, small waist, rounded hips, and legs so long she could kick somebody in the teeth from six feet away.

"Hi," she said, her bright red lips curving into a smile. "Isn't this a pretty morning! I just love waking up to the sound of birds singing. It makes me want to spread my wings and go flying into the sky. Can I do something for you girls?"

Heather was standing there like a fence post, so Darla Jean took a deep breath and sputtered out an explanation for their visit.

"You two are so sweet," the woman said. "I'm Seraphina Hope, Chastity's big sister. She's been feeling a mite lonely since we got here, and I know she'll be tickled pink that you came out just to meet her. You wait here and I'll fetch her."

Darla Jean and Heather were too dumbstruck to do more than stare as Seraphina went back inside. They hadn't so much as caught their breath when a girl appeared in the doorway, her hands on her hips and her mouth twisted into a sneer that reminded Darla Jean of Miss Estes when she caught Andrea Sicklepod cheating on the personal hygiene quiz.

"I don't need anybody's help," said Chastity. "You've done your good deed for the day, so beat it, okay?"

Darla Jean bristled. "Okay with us. We got better things to do. Come on, Heather, let's go see who's hanging out at the Dairee Dee-Lishus."

Chastity glanced over her shoulder, then stepped onto the stoop and growled, "What's that?"

"Nothing that would interest you, I'm sure." Darla Jean shoved Heather toward the station wagon. She had to admit the blond woman had flustered her, but she was used to dealing with slutty girls on account of having lived in Maggody for seventeen weary, dreary years.

Chastity closed the door behind her. "Maybe I'll go have a look at it. Gawd knows there's nothing to do around here."

"You don't know the half of it," Darla Jean said as she pointed ungraciously at the backseat. Once they were heading down the hill, she poked Heather. "Gimme a cigarette."

Heather finally found her voice. "You'd better wait until we're past Coach Grapper's house. She liked to have throttled Traci when that story came out about the party behind Purtle's Esso the week before the post-season tournament. All Traci ever does is ride the pine, anyway. It's not like she's ever scored a basket."

"Who's Coach Grapper?" asked Chastity.

Darla Jean grimaced. "Remember that witch that tried to poison Sleeping Beauty? Compared to Coach Grapper, she was a nun."

"She's the basketball coach," said Heather, making a rude gesture at the farmhouse. "According to her, we're all half-blind wimps. If we win, we should have won by more. If we lose, at the next practice we have to run a lap around the track for every point we lost by. When Hasty beat the shit out of us, I thought my legs were gonna fall off and my lungs were gonna burst."

"Quit the team and tell the bitch to kiss your ass." Chastity leaned forward and plucked the cigarette pack and lighter out of Heather's open purse. "There's no law that says you have to play basketball, is there?"

Heather giggled. "No law, but there's a reason for being on the team. Actually, there are fourteen reasons, some better than others."

"Yeah?" said Chastity.

Darla Jean was giggling, too. "Coach Grapper has this thing for Coach Jenks, who's acting head coach for the boys' team. She's all the time gazing at him like a cross-eyed cow, practically drooling—and she's got to be ten years older than him. It's unbelievably nauseating. Anyway, the girls' and boys' teams ride on the same bus. We also stay at the same motels at tournaments."

"Some of the tournaments last four days," said Heather. "We have a blast. The way the coaches carry on, we might as well not have any chaperons. Last year a couple of the guys got some whiskey, and we played strip poker half the night."

Chastity hung over the back of the seat. "Where are these tournaments?"

"Oh, all over the place," Darla Jean said as if the Maggody Marauders had been dribbling from California to Calcutta. "You really ought to go out for the team. Coach Grapper's a pain in the butt, but you just have to mind your mouth around her, act like you're listening, and not snicker when she comes out of her office in a jogging suit the color of Pepto-Bismol."

"I'm not any good at basketball. I had to play in phys ed classes and I used to shoot baskets with some dumbshit little kid at one of the foster homes, but that's about it."

Darla Jean glanced in the rearview mirror. "There's not exactly a long line outside the gym every fall. If you go out, she'll put you on the team. You may not get to play much, but you'll still dress up and go to all the games and tournaments."

"And the retreats," added Heather. "There are three of those a year—one before the season starts, one about halfway through it, and one afterward. We stay in cabins at one of the state parks and supposedly set goals and strengthen team spirit. Mostly we goof off."

Chastity sat back and thought about what she'd heard. Seraphina refused to let her drive and made sure the car keys were never lying around. Nobody who worked for Malachi would risk losing his job by helping her run away, not even Joey. When school started, she could probably sweet-talk some redneck into taking her to a bus station, but Malachi would hire a private detective like he'd done in the past. She'd be dragged home and catch holy hell for months.

But if she went out of town with the basketball team, she could get a good head start—especially if the two girls in the front seat would cover up her absence for a few days.

She was imagining herself back in Milwaukee when the station wagon splashed across the low-water bridge and Heather yelped, "Who was that?"

"Ruby Bee Hanks and Estelle Oppers," answered

Darla Jean. "Do you think they saw us smoking? My pa'll whip me silly if he finds out."

Heather groaned.

"Who was that?" asked Estelle.

"Darla Jean McIlhaney, Heather Reilly, and some girl in the backseat I didn't recognize right offhand. Maybe one of them has a cousin that's visiting." Ruby Bee turned off the pavement and started up the hill, clinging for dear life to the steering wheel. "You'd think now that Bur's retired, he could do something about that scraggedy yard, but Norma Kay told Lottie Estes that all he does is lie around all day in his underwear, watching television."

"He's an ornery little cuss. I don't know how Norma Kay puts up with him. If you ask me, she ought to—"

"Will you look at that!" Ruby Bee said, gasping. "That tent's bigger than the new Wal-Mart in Farberville! I swear, I can't think when I've ever seen a tent so big."

Estelle would have mentioned having seen a bigger tent if she could have. She was obliged to settle for a snort as the car came to a stop. "I ain't sure we should be doing this," she said. "Maybe we should wait for a few days so they can get all settled in."

"We are merely being neighborly," Ruby Bee said, although she wasn't exactly leaping out of the car like the seat was on fire. "What would they think if nobody came out to welcome them?"

As they sat bickering at each other, a young man in a leather jacket and jeans came out of the tent and walked right past them without so much as a nod. Ruby Bee waited until he disappeared between the trucks, then said, "You don't reckon that was Malachi Hope, do you?"

"You saw him on TV," Estelle said in a snippety voice. "He didn't look like some two-bit hoodlum, did he? I hope this doesn't mean you're turning into another Virella Buchanon and will commence to accusing everybody of being your evil twin sister."

Ruby Bee thought of a lot of comebacks, some of them real jewels, but she decided to be magnanimous this one time. "Well, are we gonna sit here till the cows come home or are we gonna be neighborly?"

She picked up the offering, got out of the car, and waited until she heard Estelle coming before she approached the door. Breathing a tad unevenly, she opened the screen and knocked just like visiting televangelists was something she did every day.

"Maybe nobody's home," murmured Estelle.

"Maybe you got a yellow stripe down your spine," Ruby Bee said as she raised her knuckles to knock more sharply. She snatched 'em back real fast as the door opened and she found herself staring at a man wearing nothing but a towel around his waist. She looked back at Estelle, whose eyes were popped out like a stomped-on toad frog's.

"Yes?" he said nicely, if a shade impatiently.

Ruby Bee turned around and took a deep breath. Despite her stupefaction (and his wet hair), she recognized him. "Mr. Hope, I'm Ruby Bee Hanks and this is Estelle Oppers. We just wanted to drop by and say welcome to Maggody." When he didn't say anything, she thrust forward the foil-covered dish. "We brought you a little something for your supper. It's a green bean casserole. Estelle said I should have made a pie, but I always think it's nice to have something solid and filling after a long trip."

"Thank you," Malachi Hope said as he took the dish from her hand and stepped back. "As you might have guessed, I was in the shower when you arrived. It was very kind of you ladies to come all the way out here, and I hope I'll see you at the first night of the revival. God bless you."

The door closed, leaving Ruby Bee and Estelle standing on the little stoop like a set of andirons. After a minute of stunned silence, Estelle took Ruby Bee's arm and pulled her toward the car, saying, "See? I told you he wouldn't want to be disturbed on his first official day in town. He must be awful busy getting ready for the revival, and the last thing he wants is to—"

"Let's have a peek," Ruby Bee said as she veered toward the tent opening.

"That's trespassing," Estelle said, trying to sound virtuous but following right on Ruby Bee's heels just the same.

The tent didn't seem so big on the inside because there were navy blue curtains blocking off the back part. There was still plenty of room for benches and chairs, though, although they were going to be unsteady until the grass was trampled flat. In front of the curtains were a metal scaffold holding up a stage and more scaffolds on either end that weren't doing anything at the moment.

"Look at those," whispered Estelle, pointing at enormous black amplifiers with enough wires to run electricity to every house in Maggody. "Whatever happened to a choir all dressed in black robes?"

"Same thing that happened to horse-drawn buggies and milkmen."

The young man in the leather jacket came out onto the stage, a screwdriver in one hand and slinky black cables in the other. "Help you?"

"No, thank you," Ruby Bee said, speaking politely even though she could see the tattoo on his hand plain as day. "We were just leaving."

She stepped on Estelle's foot in her haste to live up to her words, and pretty soon they were in the car, going down the hill.

I was a bit proud of myself as I drove by the Dairee Dee-Lishus and spotted Darla Jean, Heather, and Chastity standing at the window. They weren't chattering like starlings, but they appeared reasonably amiable. Some of the other kids were perched on a nearby picnic table, so it seemed likely Chastity would do okay on the first day of school. If Hope Is Here was still here, of course. I'd spent half the night unsuccessfully trying to imagine a thousand-acre Christian amusement park in this particularly desolate corner of the Ozarks. Then again, I don't think anyone ever dreamed that Branson could become one of the hottest tourist attractions in the entire country. The last time I'd been duped into going, traffic had been creeping along at a snail's pace and the preponderance of polyester had given me a rash that lingered for a week.

And there'd been Heritage U.S.A., too. Jim and Tammy Faye Bakker had raked in millions of dollars before the roof caved in—and the cell door slammed on one of them. If Malachi Hope was of the same species as other well-known evangelical predators, I was in for some deep shit. Religion seems to bring out the worst in mob mentality.

For lack of anything better to do, I decided to drive into Farberville and see what I could find at the library about Malachi Hope. After that, I'd drop by the state police barracks to inquire about outstanding warrants and requests for his extradition.

From someplace like Bosnia.

Norma Kay was wrong about her husband. Most of the time, maybe as much as ninety percent of the time, he sat around in his underwear and watched television. But that left ten percent for doing such things as hanging out at the barbershop, buying six-packs of beer, flipping through fishing catalogs, and his most favorite hobby—searching through Norma Kay's possessions.

He'd been through her dresser drawers so many times he could tell at a glance which bra she was wearing on any given day. He'd read and reread all the letters from her mother in a Wichita nursing home and her sister in Coffeyville, but he'd never found a hint that might lead him to the identity of the sumbitch.

After getting a beer, Bur went into the bedroom and checked the pockets of all her clothes on the off chance she'd forgotten to throw away a damning note from her boyfriend. He felt a flicker of excitement when he found a matchbook from a motel in Pine Bluff, but then he remembered the girls had played in a tournament there the year before.

He replaced the matchbook and stomped into the living room, his blood simmering as he envisioned her on sweaty sheets with some faceless man, her tongue hanging out like a slobbery dog's. He was certain there was someone. He could tell by the dreamy look that sometimes crossed her face when she didn't know he was watching her. A couple of weeks ago, he'd called her late one night at her office in the gym to tell her to bring home some ice cream, and she hadn't answered. He'd let her know about it the minute she stepped into the house, but she'd had some glib story about having to hunt up the janitor to fix a backed-up toilet.

For a long while, he'd suspected Amos Dooley. Amos wasn't much to look at, and he was far from being a rocket scientist, but he was a bachelor. Norma Kay had passed along a couple of jokes Amos had told her and even suggested they have him over for supper sometime, but Bur had made it clear he wasn't gonna sit at the same table with a man who was probably a faggot.

Cory Jenks was an obvious suspect these days. The problem was there was no hard evidence, and Bur wasn't about to confront her until he was sure he could nail her. Otherwise, she'd deny it and go to further extremes to keep the affair secret.

And he wasn't ready to rule out Lewis Ferncliff, who owned a body shop on the road to Farberville, or John Robert Scurfpea, who was as crooked as a dog's hind leg when he played dominoes at the pool hall. Or Jim Bob

Buchanon, who made a point of speaking to Norma Kay whenever she came into the SuperSaver. Or Fergie Bidens, who drove by every now and then, peeking at the house out of the corner of his eye. Fergie was married and had a whole passel of brats, but everybody knew he spent some afternoons at the Pot 'O Gold mobile-home park when he was supposed to be at work. Eddie Joe Whitbread wasn't above that sort of thing, either.

Bur covered his face with his hands as the names rolled through his mind like movie credits. It was Norma Kay's fault he was tormented like this day in and day out, he thought as he collapsed onto the recliner. He shouldn't have married her to begin with. Sure, he'd felt sorry for her after what she'd been through with the pompous pricks on the school board, the angry parents, the pious lawyers, the reporters—everyone had been quick to turn on her. He was the only one who'd tried to defend her, and when that didn't do much good, he'd offered her a fresh start in a different state.

Perhaps he needed to remind her of that more often, Bur decided as he picked up the clicker and aimed it at the television set. Instead of whoring around, she ought to be home remembering how grateful she'd been back then.

A talk show host came onto the screen and pointed at a row of people sitting on stools. "Today we're going to meet transvestite mud wrestlers who had near-death experiences, and the men who brought them back."

Bur opened a beer.

Thomas Fratelleon sat at a table in the RV, studying a surveyor's map of Stump County. He'd loosened his tie, but he was wearing a coat and neatly pressed trousers. He glanced up as Seraphina came out of the bedroom.

"This appears to be the only reasonable site near a highway," he said, gesturing at a rough square outlined in red ink. Blue lines divided it into three unequal sections. "If we want to suck in the tourists from Branson and Eureka Springs, we have to be within an hour's drive."

Seraphina sat down across from him and turned the map around. "So what's the problem, Thomas? Malachi wants to kick off the revival with a presentation of the project and a real emotional plea for donations to build phase one of the City of Hope. There won't be a dry eye in the tent. By the final night, we should have close to a hundred and fifty grand to option the property and launch a major fund-raiser." She propped her elbows on the table and leaned forward, her face aglow with exhilaration. "It's gonna be something, isn't it?"

"It's going to be a gold mine," Malachi said as he entered the room and took a bottle of apple juice from the refrigerator. He wore a discreetly expensive jogging suit and outrageously expensive athletic shoes. His hair, now dry and styled, hung to his collar in gentle brown curls. His high forehead was unwrinkled and his cornflower-blue eyes were as guileless as a baby's. "I can pack the Cathedral of Hope with five thousand Christians, all of them eager to assure themselves of prosperity in the here and now and eternal bliss when the time comes. We'll net over fifty thousand dollars at every service, and once we get back on the air . . ." He took a drink of apple juice and let it trickle down his throat like the costliest champagne. "Even when the show was broadcast on only a dozen stations, we were receiving upward of a thousand letters a week, each with a check. By this time next year, we'll be on half the cable outlets in the country. The good Lord will provide."

There wasn't a dry eye in the kitchen.

4

"**W**HAT happened to you last night?" demanded Ruby Bee as I chose a stool. "Didn't you get the message I left on that infernal answering machine at your office? I didn't get a wink of sleep on account of imagining you in some awful car wreck out on the highway, lying in a ditch all covered with blood. And how was I to know if you'd decided to catch a bus to Washington, D.C., without having the decency to tell me?"

"Any biscuits and sausage gravy left?" I asked.

Ruby Bee folded her arms and stared at me. "I don't believe you answered my question, young lady. Once you see fit to do that, I'll answer yours."

My options were limited and my stomach was growling in expectation. "If you must know, I went to Farberville to talk to people, then went to the drive-in and watched a couple of particularly gruesome movies. The first was about this guy with hideous scars all over his face and hands from a chemical accident. He crawled into this teenaged girl's bedroom window, doped her, took out a ten-inch carving knife, and—"

"I'll see what's left," Ruby Bee said as she strode into the kitchen, "but you're pressing your luck. One of these days . . ."

The doors swished closed on whatever was going to happen to me one of these days. I was in more of a carpe diem mood, so I poured a mug of coffee and snitched a doughnut from under a glass dome. I was licking the grains of sugar off my fingers as the front door opened and footsteps thudded across the dance floor. The sound reminded me of the second feature at the drive-in, which had starred an extinct reptile with an attitude (so my taste in movies is no better than my taste in ex-husbands).

"Hey, Arly," said Dahlia as she hoisted herself onto a stool. She plucked a napkin out of a metal dispenser to blot the sweat off her forehead. "Hot enough for you?"

"No, it's not. I was sitting here thinking that I ought to move to the Sahara desert and get a job chasing camel thieves."

She blinked at me. "You were?"

Ruby Bee came out of the kitchen and slammed a plate down in front of me. "This should hold you," she said coldly, then managed a smile for Dahlia. "How about a glass of iced tea?"

Dahlia was staring at the plate in front of me, her eyes as rounded as full moons and her breathing ragged. "I don't guess you have any more biscuits, do you?"

"Now, Dahlia," Ruby Bee said as she scooted the napkin dispenser alongside my plate, "the doctor told you how important this diet is. You don't want to do anything that might hurt the baby, do you? It's not all that long until your due date." She gave me a pointed look. "Aren't you impressed with how Dahlia has stuck to her diet for two whole weeks now?"

In that my mouth was full of biscuits and gravy, all I could do was nod. I put my elbow on the bar to further deter Dahlia from a slavering attack on my breakfast—an idea that was written all over her face in big capital letters. "I truly am impressed," I said when I could. "How much weight have you lost?"

"I don't rightly recollect," she said distractedly.

Ruby Bee added another napkin dispenser and a plastic pretzel basket to the barrier. "The reason I called you last night was to tell you about Malachi Hope. I thought you might be interested." Her voice rose and her pace quickened as Dahlia's tongue slid out between her lips. "After all, everybody in town has heard of him, but nobody except Estelle and me has actually seen him. Some older man bought groceries at the SuperSaver, and Eula Lemoy saw that blond woman drive by in a white Mercedes, but Malachi Hope is a real mystery man. Estelle and I are the only ones who've met him in person."

I'd been shoveling down the food as fast as I could, but this caught me by surprise. "Where'd you meet him?" I said, my fork poised in midair.

This turned out to be a mistake. Ruby Bee snatched up the plate and slipped it into a sink of soapy water. "Up at the Grapper place," she said as if nothing had happened. "Estelle and I took it upon ourselves to drop off a casserole and welcome him to Maggody."

I put down my fork. "So tell me about him."

Amid wheezy sighs from Dahlia, who'd shifted her attention to the pyramid of doughnuts, Ruby Bee described what might have been a meeting of no more than thirty seconds' duration. "He looked different on television," she continued. "Wearing nothing but a towel, he looked like a regular person who mows his lawn every week and puts out the garbage. I expected him to be . . ."

I waited, but she finally shrugged and busied herself washing dishes in the sink. Dahlia gave up on the doughnuts and announced she was going to continue her walk, which she seemed to equate with the Long March in China. She was trudging away in the opposite direction as I headed back to the PD. Woe to those who crossed her path.

The telephone rang while I was making coffee in the back room, and after a short debate, I took the adult approach and answered it.

"Heard you was back in town!" boomed Sheriff Harve Dorfer from his office in Farberville. He's a real country boy at heart, as well as a slick politician and a fairly astute law enforcement agent. His primary passion seems to be cheap, foul-smelling cigars; I'm always careful to stay upwind from him when he takes one out of his shirt pocket. "One of the boys saw you at the drive-in last night. I wouldn't have thought it was so boring out your way that you'd actually pay money to sit through four hours of that kind of crap."

As soon as he finished guffawing at his wit, I said, "Why wouldn't you think it's boring out this way? There are days when I cruise around town, longing to catch some scoundrel tossing a beer can out of a car window so I can shoot him on the spot. Yesterday morning I went so far as to consider trying to find Raz Buchanon's moonshine operation up on Cotter's Ridge. I was halfway to the car when I remembered he and Marjorie went to visit kinfolk at the state prison. I think they have a family reunion down there every year about this time."

"I wouldn't be surprised," drawled Harve. "So what's this about the preacher and some theme park? What's he gonna call it—'Six Flags Over Jesus'?"

I propped my feet on the corner of my desk and leaned back in the squeaky old chair. "I did some checking on Malachi Hope and his corporation. He's pretty tame compared to some of the better-known figures with the gift of electronic tongues. About five years ago he got into a dispute with the IRS over what constitutes a charitable organization and was slapped with a bill for more than a million dollars. The corporation filed for bankruptcy, reorganized the debts, and stayed quiet for a spell. Then a year ago, he resurfaced and began staging revivals, mostly in Texas and Oklahoma."

"So what's he really doing in Maggody?"

I searched the ceiling for a water stain comparable to the image on the Shroud of Turin, but no manifestation was obvious. "I wish I knew, Harve. The idea of building a theme park out here sounds ludicrous to me."

"You met him yet?"

"No, and in all honesty, I have no desire to do so. The business manager assured me that Malachi Hope was not a typical evangelist, but I won't be surprised if he shows up with a pompadour, a sequined suit, and cowboy boots made from an endangered species. He drives a gold Cadillac, for pity's sake."

"Now, Arly, you shouldn't judge a man by his choice

of vehicles. It ain't professional. Maybe you ought to go out there and ask him real politely what the goddamn hell he thinks he's doing here in Stump County."

"I don't want to," I said with all the charm of a sulky toddler. "Besides, I haven't made much progress with all the busywork that accumulated while I was gone. I have to set an appointment to confer with the county prosecutor about the charges against Pegasus Buchanon, who failed to explain what he was doing in the cemetery behind the Baptist church—with a shovel and a gunnysack. I have to call the travel agent about flights to Cairo. I have to do laundry at the—"

"Seems to me you're gonna need some help with traffic next week," Harve interrupted smoothly. "If you want, I can scrounge up a couple of deputies to help you out. There are flyers posted all over the county about the revival, and the new fall lineup hasn't started. Folks may be getting bored with reruns and pilots that didn't cut the mustard. They might come out your way in droves to find salvation and listen to gospel music on a hot summer night. Course, you need to confer with this preacher and make sure he's figured out where everybody's gonna park."

I told Harve he was a bastard, then hung up and resumed my morose contemplation of the stains on the ceiling. An interview with Malachi Hope was less appealing than a cozy conversation with Raz's pedigreed sow. It was less appealing than a confrontation with the town council about my budget ("Please, sirs, could I have a new pencil?"). It was less appealing than a burrito from the SuperSaver.

I kept a running count in my head, and when I'd

thought of exactly one hundred things that were less appealing than doing my duty, I stood up. I may have been dragging my feet as I headed for the door, but I was moving in the right (and righteous) direction, when said door banged opened and Mrs. Jim Bob flew in like a Harpy from the bowels of hell.

"I should have known you'd be lounging around the PD," she said by way of greeting. Her smile was as warm as the iceberg that took down the *Titanic*. "Not that I blame you, of course. As I told Jim Bob, the town council had no business hiring you in the first place. It's getting more and more obvious that women aren't cut out to do a man's job. If you'd take time to read the Bible, you'd realize that your only hope is to mend your ways. Why don't you come to church before it's too late?"

I retreated behind the desk. "Have you ever thought about changing laxatives, Mrs. Jim Bob? I know it's none of my business, but whatever you're using doesn't seem to be working all that well."

She sat on the edge of the chair across from me, her hands clasped and her ankles crossed, her skirt carefully smoothed to cover her knees. Her lips were so pinched they were almost invisible, but they seemed to be functioning. "I was telling Jim Bob just the other day that I wouldn't be surprised to hear you spent your vacation on an island named Lesbos."

"Is it in Florida?"

"How should I know about something disgusting like that?" she countered without missing a beat. "What do you plan to do about this snake-oil salesman and his hussy? He's as slick as an eel in a barrel of slime, and she's—well! I have made too many sacrifices to see our town awash in godless heathens and tourists with more money than piety. I demand you run that man and his entourage out of town."

"You get the tar and I'll get the feathers."

"I do not find you amusing, Miss Chief of Police. Malachi Hope is a threat to our community. I for one will not watch decency go down the drain like so much bathwater."

I nodded earnestly. "Okay, I'll get the tar and you get the feathers."

"I have had it with you," she said as she snatched up her purse and rose to her feet. Outside of flinging her purse at me, there wasn't much she could do in the way of a physical assault, but I stayed where I was (being a pacifist and all). "I'm asking for the last time—what are you going to do about this man?"

"Okay, okay," I said, shrugging. "I'll get the tar *and* the feathers, but it doesn't sound like a fair division of labor. At the least, I think you should offer to heat the tar on Jim Bob's barbecue grill."

She went flying out the door, although probably not to buy a bag of charcoal. I leaned back in my chair, wiggled around until the cane stopped poking my fanny, and began a new list along the lines of: Would I rather be lectured by Mrs. Jim Bob or eat cold grits?

There was no doubt in my mind.

Thomas Fratelleon put down the receiver and gave Seraphina a smug smile. "Mort will start drawing up the option papers this afternoon. We should have them in hand by a week from Monday."

"That's great," she said with manufactured enthusiasm. "I was afraid we were going to have a problem with that creep who owns the middle parcel. Imagine him thinking we'd fall for his lies about escalating property values. The price of rocks hasn't gone up."

Fratelleon winced as he recalled the bargaining session with the mayor. "As long as he doesn't shoot off his mouth about what we're paying him, it'll be fine. But if the other two yokels learn that he's getting twice as much as they are, they'll refuse to sign the papers. If we don't have the options, there's no way we can get any long-term financing for the first phase."

"The good Lord will provide," Malachi said from the bedroom doorway. He was wearing a coat and tie, and carrying a hand-sewn leather briefcase. He looked like a history professor, the kind whose classes are always jammed with sorority girls listening in awed silence. "I'm going into Farberville to do a little politicking with my fellow ministers. I think I'll promise them each five percent of the contributions in exchange for encouraging their congregations to attend the revival."

Fratelleon gave him a puzzled look. "And if twenty churches take you up on this generous offer of yours, we end up with the net from souvenir sales. It won't cover the utility bills."

Malachi put his arm around Seraphina's waist and pulled her against his body. "Thomas, my literal-minded son, I said I'd promise them a cut. I didn't say I'd actually give it to them." He kissed Seraphina's cheek and waited for her to reciprocate before he released her. "Where's Chastity?"

Seraphina moved away from him. "I'm not sure. She left an hour ago with those two girls who came by in a station wagon the other day."

"Where did they go?" Malachi asked softly.

"One of them said something about shooting baskets at the high school gym. Chastity didn't look excited at the idea, but she went with them anyway. I doubt she can get into any trouble at a gym. Besides, she needs to get some exercise or I'll have to let out her school clothes."

Malachi's voice remained soft, but Thomas could hear an edge to it. "When we had our little conversation last night, I told you that Chastity could get into trouble in Mother Teresa's rec room."

"You were in the tent talking to Joey," protested Seraphina. "I didn't see any harm in letting her—"

"I also told you that as of that moment—a scant twelve hours ago, if I remember correctly—you were not to allow her to leave this area without my explicit permission. She is not to be trusted. In that I have assumed joint responsibility for her physical as well as spiritual well-being, I must insist you respect my position of authority within this family. Do you understand me, Seraphina, or should I repeat it in words of one syllable?"

"I understand you, Malachi," she said as she tried to ease past him.

He grabbed her arm. "Why don't you remind Thomas and me of what the Apostle Paul wrote to the Ephesians?"

"Ephesians, chapter five, verse twenty-two," she recited numbly. " 'Wives, submit yourselves unto your own husbands, as unto the Lord.' "

"Continue," commanded Malachi, his fingers still clutching her arm.

" 'For the husband is the head of the wife, even as Christ is the head of the church: and he is the savior of the body. Therefore as the church is subject unto Christ, so let the wives be to their own husbands in every thing.' "

"Very nicely done. Now then, why don't you put on a pretty dress and go down to that supermarket to do some shopping? While you're at it, drop by the office and have a friendly conversation with Mr. Buchanon about complying with our private arrangement. His dim brain was clicking like a cash register, and I'm afraid he's keenly aware of the significance of his parcel to the overall sale. Do whatever it takes to make sure he keeps his mouth shut until the deal is final. Whatever it takes."

Seraphina pulled herself free, turned, and left the room. Seconds later, a door slammed at the opposite end of the RV.

Thomas busied himself with the papers on the table, uncomfortable as always when these scenes occurred. In his opinion, they did so much too often—but marital mediation was not in his job description. "I hope we have a good take the first few nights of the revival," he said, trying not to fidget as he sensed Malachi's gaze on the back of his head. "We'll need fourteen hundred dollars for the three options, and we used most of our resources to cover transportation expenses and the utility deposits."

"I'll ask the local churches to pitch in to sponsor us,"

Joan Hess

Malachi said. "After all, the Lord giveth and the Lord taketh away."

"You're not the Lord."

"Are you quite sure, Thomas?" Without waiting for a response, Malachi went through the living room and outside to the gold Cadillac. The interior was worse than Satan's furnace room, he thought as he switched the air conditioner to high, then drove down the road to County 102. At the intersection with the main highway, however, he sat for several minutes, idly watching pickup trucks rumbling by while he considered his next move. As he reached a decision, he saw a stout man with a particularly red face come out of a trailer parked beneath a scattering of sycamore trees.

He touched a button that caused the window to silently slide down. "You!" he called. "Can you tell me how to get to the high school?"

It was not a difficult question, but the man froze in midstep, his face crinkled with bewilderment—or perhaps even terror. Malachi patiently repeated the question and then did all he could to sort out directions from the mostly incoherent sputters he received in response. Unwilling to cause any more anxiety, he nodded and turned in what might be the correct direction. One more turn led him to a sprawling yellow-brick structure with a sign proclaiming it to be the home of the Maggody Marauders. A football stadium to one side confirmed his theory that this had to be the high school; even in an alternate universe, Maggody would not have attracted a professional football team.

At one end was a two-story addition with a rounded roof. Malachi parked in front of it, locked the car, and pushed open a metal door. It proved to be the gym, but there were no players of either gender shooting baskets or even sitting in the bleachers.

Muttering a phrase that might have caused his more ardent followers to think twice about writing a check, he walked across the glistening hardwood floor to a door marked OFFICE.

"Hello?" he said as he eased it open.

A woman with yellow hair looked up from a pile of paperwork. The annoyed expression faded as she recognized her visitor. "Malachi Hope," she exhaled reverently.

"I'm looking for my wife's sister, a girl named Chastity Hope. I was told she was here, shooting baskets."

"I knew you would come to me."

Malachi stepped back, his hand still holding the doorknob. He was accustomed to reactions such as this, and at times went out of his way to encourage them when he could sniff a profit in the air. At this moment, though, he was intent on finding Chastity. "Have any girls been here today?"

"I'm Norma Kay."

"It's nice to meet you, Norma Kay. Have any girls—"

She stood up and leaned forward, her eyes glittering too brightly for his taste. "I realize you have millions of loyal followers, Malachi, but you surely remember me. I wrote you for the first time about ten years ago, when I was close to committing suicide. You wrote back with such compassion that I found the strength to carry on with my life. I've written you every month since then, sending every penny I could and begging for your prayers."

If possible, her eyes became even brighter. Droplets of foam accumulated in the corners of her mouth, and her fingers were splayed like talons. "I've taken every bit of advice you've given me, Malachi, even when I had trouble understanding why. I ordered your Bible study course and played the cassettes over and over again. I even went to one of your revivals, but the stadium was so crowded I couldn't get close enough to talk to you."

"Of course, I remember you, Norma Kay," murmured Malachi, easing out the door, "and it's a real blessing to meet you in person like this. I want you to know you're always in my special prayers for those who rely on my guidance in spiritual matters. Now, I'd really better see if I can find my wife's sister. She doesn't know her way around town and I'm concerned."

Norma Kay was close to toppling across the desk and undoing a morning's worth of organization. "You said in one of the letters that you'd be pleased to meet with me in private if we ever had the chance. My husband and I own the property where you're going to build your park. We live in the white frame house at the bottom of the hill."

Malachi froze. "Your last name is Grapper?"

"I married Bur almost ten years ago. When I heard you were putting on revivals, I wrote and told you all about the pasture and how perfect it would be for your City of Hope. Don't you remember?"

It occurred to Malachi that the option and subsequent sale would be determined by his reaction to this disturbed woman with unnaturally yellow hair. "Of course, I do," he said through a strained smile, "and I am delighted. I'm sure if we pray together we can iron out all your problems and get you aimed straight for prosperity. Why don't you call my manager and ask him to make you an appointment sometime during revival week?"

She stumbled around the desk, taking a jolting hit to her hip in the process, and grabbed his hand. Rubbing it against her damp cheek, she said, "Thank you, Malachi. There's so much I want to tell you. I've allowed lust to rule my heart, and you must counsel me until I have the courage to cast aside my sinful ways."

He freed his hand and patted her shoulder as he would a large dog. "Until then, you'll be foremost in my prayers, Norma Kay. Foremost."

To his dismay (but not his surprise), she burst into tears and flung herself at him. He was much too concerned with the deleterious effects of salt water on his silk tie to notice as a door at the back of the office closed with a soft click.

Brother Verber was sitting on the rectory steps when he spotted Mrs. Jim Bob coming across the lawn, marching along like a brisk drill sergeant, her arms swinging smartly and her chin leading the way. As always, an aura of conviction and dedication hovered about her, he thought admiringly, giving him as well as the rest of the congregation strength to aid in the battle against wickedness and fornication. Why, he'd put her in the ring with Satan anytime and never once doubt the outcome. He mentally dressed her in a short leather dress and a hood that came just below her eyes so her mouth would be free to tell ol' Satan what she thought of his wily attempts to lure good Christians into his den of iniquity. She'd pull out a whip and flail his buttocks until he whimpered for mercy. Then she'd put her foot on his chest and look down at him, her face distorted with anger—

"I was looking for you in the Assembly Hall," she called, interrupting his pleasant reverie. "We can no longer sit in the sunshine and allow this Malachi Hope to destroy our town. It's time to take action, Brother Verber."

Uncomfortably aware of a peculiar sensation in his privates, he stood up and held open the screen door for her. "Action, Sister Barbara?"

She continued into the living room and sat on the sofa. "Yes, action. I was tidying some papers on Jim Bob's desk when I came across some ominous scribbles."

Aghast, Brother Verber plopped down beside her. "Scribbles like pentagrams and hexes? Jim Bob isn't turning to devil worship, is he? I had a newsletter from the seminary that said it's happening more and more these days—especially among the youngsters. This newsletter said we're facing a worldwide Satanic Panic, and if we don't stop it, women will be dancing naked and engaging in lustful degradation with their very neighbors and kinfolk."

"All I said was that I found some scribbles," she said as she watched the sweat dribbling down the sides of his face and clinging to the tip of his nose. "In this particular case, they had dollar signs attached to 'em."

He tried to keep the disappointment out of his voice. "Was he working on the family budget?"

"No, he was not, Brother Verber. From what I could

tell, he's been offered two hundred dollars an acre for that land next to Bur's. That adds up to forty thousand dollars all together."

"That's a lot," he said, gripping her knee so she'd know he was as concerned as she was. "It's hard to imagine Jim Bob turning down that kind of money just to save the Voice of the Almighty Lord Assembly Hall from the likes of this Malachi Hope fellow."

She tried to keep her chin from quivering, but it was a lost cause. Her eyes were stinging and her throat was so tight she could hardly swallow back the bitter taste in her mouth. "We can't let this happen. I tried to talk to Arly, but she wouldn't listen to a word I said. She was— she was downright flippant, if you must know." She opened her purse and pulled out a lacy white handkerchief to dab her nose. "I don't know what to do, Brother Verber."

He was so touched by this unprecedented display of vulnerability that he allowed his hand to move to her thigh and squeeze her supple flesh. "Don't you worry about this, Sister Barbara. I have a plan—and a real fine one, if I do say so myself. When you showed up a few minutes ago, I was just running through the details to make sure I hadn't overlooked anything. Why, a week from now we'll look back at this and laugh ourselves sick at the way we was all worried."

"What's your plan?" she said, sniffling into the handkerchief.

"I can't tell you until I've prayed to the Lord for approval. Sister Barbara, why don't we both git down on our knees and thank the Lord for sending me a plan to save our little town?"

"If the Lord sent the plan, why do you need his approval?"

Brother Verber clasped his hands together and slid to the floor. "The Lord moves in mysterious ways," he murmured as he started praying more fervently than he had since he'd been asked to explain in front of most everybody in town why he owned a life-size inflatable doll named Suzie Squeezums.

This was a true test of faith.

5

"YOU'LL never guess what Lydia Twayblade told me," Elsie McMay said as she reached for another slice of pound cake. She and Mrs. Jim Bob were sitting out on the sunporch, where they could admire the results of the latter's undeniable gardening prowess. The impatiens in particular were thriving along the wall at the back of the yard. Elsie was a mite jealous, having never had much luck with impatiens.

Mrs. Jim Bob was looking in the same general direction, but she was thinking of neither the flowers nor the challenge submitted to her. The last two days Jim Bob had flat out refused to discuss the pending sale and stayed down at the SuperSaver from dawn until well after midnight. Brother Verber kept insisting he had a plan, but he was vague when it came to offering any hints. She had debated trying to talk some sense into Burdock Grapper and had gone so far as to drive out to his house, before she lost her resolve and kept on going until she ended up in Hasty.

"You know who Lydia Twayblade is, don't you?" Elsie said to prompt her hostess.

"I just find it hard to believe she said something of interest, Elsie. She is one of the most tiresome women in town, all the time acting high and mighty when she's nothing but a glorified nurse's aide out at the county home. It's no wonder the undertaker goes out there once a week; Lydia bores the old folks to death."

"Lydia told me that a woman turned up out there yesterday afternoon and said she was Seraphina Hope. Before Lydia could stop her, she was out on the porch inviting all the old folks to come to the revival."

"That hussy!" gasped Mrs. Jim Bob.

Elsie took a sip of tea. "Lydia said Seraphina was real sweet and lingered more than an hour asking the residents about their health and their families. She even sang for them. Ol' Petrol Buchanon got so excited his teeth fell on the floor right next to her foot. She just laughed and handed them back to him. Petrol is Diesel's youngest brother, or so I seem to think. He's eighty if he's a day, of course."

"May I assume Lydia Twayblade has enough decency not to allow the old folks to be carted out to some tent and made to sit for hours and hours on a hard bench?"

"Seraphina promised that they would all be settled in comfortable wheelchairs so they wouldn't get tuckered out by walking down the aisle."

Mrs. Jim Bob snatched up the cake plate and took it into the kitchen. When she returned, her face was pale but composed. "What else have you heard?" she said, forcing herself to sound only mildly curious.

"She was at the SuperSaver," Elsie admitted cautiously. "I was waiting in line when I chanced to see her come out of Jim Bob's office. Her blouse was so tight I wondered why the buttons didn't pop off, and her skirt barely covered her panties." She decided not to describe Jim Bob's expression and instead said, "I'd better run along. Lottie's picking me up shortly to go shopping in Farberville for something to wear to the revival."

After Elsie left, Mrs. Jim Bob went inside and tidied the kitchen, then sat down on her newly upholstered sofa in the living room and tried to think up a foolproof scheme that would send Malachi Hope and his wife slinking out of town like whupped dogs. Despite Brother Verber's assurances that he and the Lord had everything under control, she suspected her position in the community was in grave danger.

Ruby Bee tried to act casual as Estelle came across the dance floor and perched on her favorite stool. She even went so far as to pour a glass of sherry and scoot a basket of pretzels down the bar. "Heard anything new?" she asked as she began to wipe the pristine surface of the bar with a dishrag.

Estelle shrugged. "Millicent McIlhaney says Darla Jean's been spending time with Malachi Hope's wife's sister. I reckon that's who was in the backseat of the station wagon the other day when we saw it at the low-water bridge."

"I reckon so," Ruby Bee said, sucking on her cheeks to keep from blurting out her news.

"I think Millicent was relieved when Chastity wasn't

allowed to go riding around with Darla Jean anymore. She happened to overhear a snippet of conversation when the girls didn't know she was in the kitchen, and she said she was dumbfounded at some of the foul language."

"You'd think someone who lives with a preacher would mind her mouth."

Estelle gave Ruby Bee a condescending smile. "Millicent was referring to Darla Jean."

"Everybody in town knows she talks like a sailor," said Ruby Bee, shooting back an equally condescending smile. After a few more swipes, she tossed the dishrag in the sink. "I had a surprise earlier today."

"So did I. Millicent was on time for her appointment for the first time since Hiram's barn burned to the ground, and that must have been a good fifteen years ago."

Ruby Bee sniffed. "If you don't want to hear about it, that's just dandy with me. I've got more pressing things to do than stand here discussing Millicent's tardiness. Maybe I'll go start the chicken and dumplings." She headed for the kitchen door, but slowly, so she could be persuaded to stop before it was too late.

"So what's your surprise?" Estelle asked grudgingly.

Ruby Bee whirled around and pointed at the end of the bar. "Seraphina Hope came in and sat on that stool. You'd think someone who's been on television would be uppity, but she was just as nice as she could be. I couldn't help thinking of Dolly Parton—and she's the sweetest, most honest person that ever came out of Nashville. Seraphina said they enjoyed the green bean casserole the very day we dropped it off, and asked for my recipe. She was real interested in learning about Maggody. We were having such a friendly conversation that I liked to have burned the cherry cobblers."

"I wouldn't think there'd be all that much to talk about. What did she want to know—the details of Marjorie's pedigree or the tomfoolery that went on during the Missionary Society election last year?"

"Regular stuff about who all lives here and what folks do to earn a living. When I told her about your beauty parlor, she said she just might call and make an appointment to get a trim. Her hair's frizzier than yours, if you can believe it, but I gather hers is that way on purpose rather than the result of a disastrous experiment."

Estelle finished the sherry and banged down the glass. "I guess I'd better go home and hide under the bed until my hair grows out. It can't take more than six or eight months."

"She gave me special passes for the first night of the revival. They keep the first few rows reserved for invited guests. I can't see Jim Bob taking her up on the offer, or Mrs. Jim Bob, either. I hear her nose is bent way out of shape these days. Anyway, I asked for a pass for you, too, so we can sit together."

"Lucky us," muttered Estelle, who was trying to decide what she could do with her hair if everybody in the county was gonna be looking at the back of her head. It might be time to buy a hat, she concluded.

"What a bitch," Chastity said as she turned on the water in the shower and let the cool spray wash away what felt like an inch of sweat. She reached for a bar of soap, then decided it was too much effort and let her arm fall. "I'm already three-quarters dead, and this is only my first day of practice. I wonder if they'll bury me with my halo?"

"You have a halo?" asked Darla Jean from the next stall. Based on what Chastity had let drop, it seemed improbable that she was a candidate for any of the roles in the Christmas pageant. It was hard to tell how much of it was true and how much was so much hogwash, though.

"I don't want to talk about it!" Chastity snapped. "Mind your own damn business—okay?"

Darla Jean pulled aside the plastic curtain separating them, made a face, and yanked the curtain back into place. "Well, excuse me," she said, allowing her irritation to come through as loud and clear as a TV commercial. "I'm just a redneck from a pissant little town, and I ain't never seen no honest-to-God real live angel afore. Here I was planning to ask you for your autograph, Miss Hope. You got a pen in there, Miss Hope? If you do, you can sign my ass, Miss Hope."

There were a few giggles and snide remarks from the other stalls, but for the most part the dozen girls were too tuckered out to worry about anything other than sore muscles and bruises. Coach Grapper insisted they practice with the same intensity as in regular games. Anything less resulted in extra laps.

Chastity's eyes were narrowed to reptilian slits, but she adopted a penitent voice. "Sorry, Darla Jean. It's just so friggin' embarrassing, you know? By Monday morning, I'll be the laughingstock of the town. It happens every place we go."

"Nobody's gonna laugh at you," Darla Jean said. "If they do, they'll have to answer to me and Heather." She paused while she rinsed out the shampoo and then added, "What would happen if you refused?"

"No one says no to Malachi."

"That's stupid," Heather said from another stall. "What's he gonna do—spank you and send you to your room without supper?"

Chastity twisted the spigot and tried not to yelp as cold water splashed onto her face. They didn't understand, but she sure as hell wasn't gonna try to explain about Malachi. When she was shivering so hard her teeth chattered, she turned off the water and wrapped a skimpy gray towel around herself. It reminded her of the detention center where she'd spent three months after she was caught shoplifting; the woman from social services said it would teach her a lesson. The lesson Chastity had learned—don't get caught—may not have been what the woman had in mind.

As she came out of the stall, one of the girls whose name she didn't know said, "What's with that guy that rides the motorcycle? Is he as hot as he looks?"

"He's my boyfriend," Chastity said as she found a seat on a bench and began to dry her hair, "and he's a helluva lot hotter than he looks. If he ever bothered to even glance at you, you'd turn to ashes and go floating away in the wind. He has that effect on virgins."

"Who says I'm a virgin?"

"No one, Carlotta," said Darla Jean as she emerged from her stall. "According to Billy Dick MacNamara, you've made it with pretty much anything that wears a jock strap."

"Shut your mouth!"

"Make me."

To everyone's dismay, Coach Grapper's voice crackled through the intercom before the matter could be resolved in a thoroughly uncivilized fashion.

"Listen up," she said. "I want you all to get dressed and be out on the bleachers in two minutes. Anyone who's not there will do twenty-five sit-ups. Got that?"

The squeals from the stalls and subsequent activity indicated everyone had. Exactly two minutes later, Norma Kay strode out of her office, made sure no one was missing, and said, "You'll be glad to know we aren't going to be obliged to have a rummage sale or a car wash to raise money for the team. I just had a real interesting call from a man named Thomas Fratelleon."

"Oh, shit," muttered Chastity, then hunched down behind Carlotta as the coach glowered at her.

Norma Kay let it go and continued. "With the exception of Chastity, you all are going to be ushers during the revival. We'll get a hundred dollars a night, which means at the end of the week we'll have seven hundred dollars in the account. That's more than enough for the tournament in Pine Bluff, and we may be able to go to the one in Longspur, Texas, too."

Heather figured she was on real thin ice, but she raised her hand and said, "I can't be there every night, Coach Grapper. My family's going to Arkadelphia in the middle of the week to see my grandmother. She's so sick the doctors say she may die any day now."

"I told this man that all of you will attend every

night. Explain this to your parents and arrange to stay with one of your friends. This is a team project, as well as a service to the Lord. Now, you need to report to the tent at six o'clock Sunday evening, dressed in church clothes and low heels, to get your instructions. I'll be there to take roll."

Several of the other girls had objections, but nobody had the nerve to voice them and risk Coach Grapper's wrath. Once she was gone, however, one of the Dahlton twins jabbed Chastity and said, "Thanks a helluva lot, Angel Face. I was supposed to go to the drive-in Sunday night with Cooter Bogbean, but now I get to prance around a pasture, telling little old ladies where to sit and trying not to throw up when people start babbling about the Holy Spirit."

The other twin (no one could tell 'em apart, not even their parents) took a poke at Chastity, too. "And I had a date with Cooter's cousin, Lloyd. He told me this morning he already found someone to buy beer for us."

"This isn't any of my doing," Chastity protested, squirming as they glared at her. "Thomas always calls the local high school and arranges for some organization to be ushers." She did not add that the organizations rarely saw a check at the end of the week when the caravan rolled down the road.

"Why don't you have to be an usher?" asked Traci.

"I'll be there every night, same as you. Trust me."

There was a lot of grumbling in the locker room as they gathered up hairbrushes, sweaty shirts, and gym shorts, and began to leave. Chastity waited until she and Darla Jean were the only two left, then said, "I need to ask you something, but you got to promise not to tell anyone, including Heather."

Intrigued, Darla Jean dropped her bag and sat back down. "I won't tell a living soul," she said solemnly.

"Is there a place in Farberville where girls can go if . . . well, if they need a doctor to take care of things?"

"What kind of things?"

Chastity made sure the door to Coach Grapper's office was closed and then sat down next to Darla Jean. "You know what I mean."

"An abortion? Are you . . . ?"

"Maybe," she said, her voice so low and miserable it was almost inaudible. "I'm two weeks late, and that's never happened before. If I was still in Milwaukee, I'd know how to find a clinic."

"Is Joey the father?" asked Darla Jean.

"Yeah," she said. "Last month when we were in a gawdawful town in Texas, we took a sleeping bag out to the desert. The condom must have had a hole in it or he put it on wrong or something like that. Anyway, I don't want him to know about this 'cause I lied and told him I was on the pill. He'll be so mad he'll jump on his bike and take off for good. All I want to do is take care of it before Seraphina gets suspicious."

"You'll have to tell her on account of your age. Girls under eighteen have to have their parents sign a permission form."

"We are not talking about a goddamn field trip! Just get me the name of a doctor, and I'll figure out something."

Darla Jean gaped at her. "I don't know of a doctor right offhand, and I'm scared that rumors might start spreading about me if I ask around. Why don't you ask Joey to call places in Little Rock? It's only a four-hour drive, so you could go down and back the same day if you get an early start. I'll see if I can find a fake ID for you. After it's arranged, you can tell your sister you're spending the night at my house. I'll stay home to make sure my ma doesn't get to the telephone first if anyone calls to check on you."

"Get off it, Darla Jean. Malachi won't even let me ride to practice with you. He sure as hell isn't going to let me sleep over at your house."

"Did he adopt you?"

"Yeah." Chastity picked up her canvas bag and stood up. "He's waiting outside for me, so I'd better go. Maybe one of the local workmen knows somebody. If not, I suppose I can try a home remedy."

Darla Jean didn't know what to say, but she couldn't help thinking some gruesome thoughts as they left the locker room. Neither of them spoke as Chastity walked across the parking lot and disappeared into the gold Cadillac with the darkly tinted windows.

Darla Jean watched as it rolled away, then drove home and went upstairs to her bedroom. She did not call Heather but instead lay across her bed. When her mother came to the door half an hour later to tell her it was supper time, she pretended to be napping.

By Saturday morning there were enough flyers taped to windows and utility poles to wallpaper my apartment, assuming I'd even consider it. My idea of interior decorating is to scatter magazines on the linoleum so I don't have to look at the cigarette burns and patches of mildew. It had taken me most of a year to get up the nerve to buy a small houseplant; within days, its leaves had turned as yellow as a Buchanon's eyes.

Now I was sitting in my car, watching a couple of high school boys tape flyers to the window of a vacant building that at one time had been a New Age hardware store. I leaned out the window and called, "You'd better be prepared to take all those down at the end of next week. I don't want them littering the roads."

"Yeah, we will," one of them said.

"Are you getting paid for this?" I asked.

"Sort of," the same one said. "Some man called Coach Jenks and cut a deal with him. All the money goes to the team for tournaments and equipment. Some of the guys have to work during the revival, but me and Cooter volunteered to get in our hours aforehand."

I drove back toward the PD, but when I pulled into the lot, I realized I could no longer ignore the upcoming revival. It was tempting to get my gun and all three bullets and concoct a reason to run Malachi Hope and his entourage out of the county before he got his hands on skimpy Social Security checks and Mason jars filled with crumpled bills. However, Malachi had the law on his side—for the time being, anyway—so I gritted my teeth and headed out on County 102.

The pasture was clotted with trucks, vans, the RV, and a variety of vehicles. Men were unloading boxes and hanging banners that made it clear (to the literate) that Hope was here for seven days. Tables had been placed outside the tent for the convenience of souvenir shoppers; I suspected that at some point there would be a blue-light special on splinters from Noah's ark and genuine plastic replicas of the Holy Grail. Three men staggered by with a popcorn machine, their faces red with exertion. Praise the Lord and pass the salt.

I wandered around, ducking beneath cables and dodging deliverymen as I searched for Thomas Fratelleon. I looked inside the tent, which was now jammed with metal benches, folding chairs, stereo speakers, strings of paper lanterns, fans, and a large stage in front of a dark blue curtain. As I tried to imagine what the tent would be like when packed with passionate rhetoric and impassioned spectators, several spotlights came on and cast irregular circles on the curtain. Fog began to drift from under the stage, swirling mysteriously as it crossed the beams of light.

When the Rolling Stones failed to materialize, I turned around and found myself nose to nose with a man dressed in jeans, a gray sweatshirt, and grass-stained moccasins. He smiled and said, "It's impressive, but just wait until tomorrow evening. We're planning on a full house."

Annoyed with myself for failing to hear his approach, I stepped back. "Do you know where I can find Mr. Fratelleon?"

"I believe he went into Farberville to meet someone. Can I be of help, Miss . . . ?"

"Arly Hanks," I said, struggling not to smile back at him. He had a smooth, boyish face and ingenuous blue eyes, but so had the ex-person I'd married in the past. I may be guilty of a lot of things (trespassing included),

Joan Hess

but I'm not a slow learner. "Do you know when Mr. Fratelleon will be back here?"

"You're the local constabulary," he said as his smile broadened to expose even white teeth. "Thomas mentioned that you dropped by earlier in the week to check things out. I hope you found everything to your satisfaction?"

"It's outside my jurisdiction, so it doesn't matter how I found everything. Tomorrow night the traffic will spill into Maggody, though, and I want to make sure he arranged for ample parking. The county road's too narrow to have cars and trucks parked along it."

"By noon, these trucks will be out of the way and there will be space for all the attendees. Thomas has hired local teenagers to direct parking."

"Okay," I said, "that's all I wanted to know."

"I do hope you'll come tomorrow evening," he said, then frowned as Joey Lerner came trotting up the aisle.

"Malachi," he said, "we've got trouble in the van. Something's wrong with the power. I've tried everything I can think of, but it won't kick on. If I hook it up to the lines to the tent, fuses are gonna blow."

I took a harder look at the man with whom I'd been conversing. Thomas Fratelleon had warned me not to make any stereotypic assumptions, but of course I'd gone right ahead and conjured up an image of Elmer Gantry (okay, Burt Lancaster) with unruly hair, fiery eyes, and an aura of erotic energy. Malachi Hope possessed none of these traits—or at least he wasn't displaying them.

"Am I supposed to fix it?" he demanded. "Shall I

84

put my hands on it and beg Jesus to let there be light in the van?"

"I was thinking more along the lines of calling the electric company to check the installation."

"Then by all means do it." Malachi sighed as Joey trotted away. "It's a good thing Joey wasn't Edison's right-hand man. We'd be performing miracles by candle-light."

"What miracles do you perform under the glare of spotlights?" I asked.

He lifted his eyebrows. "Do I detect a note of skepti-cism in your voice, Miss Hanks?"

"It's possible. What exactly are you selling?"

"Oh, dear," he murmured, "you *are* a skeptic, aren't you? What I'm selling, to use your terminology, is pros-perity. I'm giving people the opportunity to find happi-ness in the here and now, instead of living in terror they'll commit an unforgivable sin, knowingly or not, and be doomed to eternal damnation. If the financing comes through, I'm going to offer families a Christian utopia, where they can have some fun, ride some rides, spend some time knowing their children are safe from drugs and evil. Do you have a problem with that?"

"I have a feeling it's not free."

"That depends on what you mean by 'free,' Miss Hanks. I presume you understand farming. A man doesn't go out into his field in the spring and cross his fingers that he'll have a good crop in the fall. He plants seeds. If he plants sickly seeds, he gets a sickly crop. If he takes a risk and does everything he can to plant the best seeds he can find, he can expect a healthy crop. As it says in the Scriptures, 'Beloved, I wish above all things that thou mayest prosper and be in health, even as thy soul prospereth.' "

"All this requires is a donation?" I asked dryly. "Or is a copy of the Burpee catalog adequate?"

"I'm offering salvation, joy, prosperity—and hope. The Lord came to me one night when I was lying in a filthy, wretched hotel room, trying to remember if I had enough money for another bottle of cheap wine. All of a sudden, I felt such a golden glow inside my heart that I walked out of that room, hopped a freight train, and rode it clear across the country, marveling at the majestic beauty the Lord has given us."

"I've seen the movie. Save it for your performance tomorrow night." I walked out of the tent. I felt a tingle in my back, but I didn't look over my shoulder to see if Malachi Hope was staring at me.

By the time I reached the county road, I became unpleasantly aware that I'd stepped on something common to pastures. I drove as quickly as I dared to the PD, and was scraping my shoe with a stick when I heard the telephone ringing. I hurried inside and picked up the receiver. "Arly Hanks."

"This is Jim Bob. I want you to get your ass over to the SuperSaver right this minute—and bring your handcuffs. I have caught myself a shoplifter."

In the background I heard a wail of despair. Suddenly the cow shit on my shoe was the least of my problems.

6

As I came into the SuperSaver, Kevin blocked my way, no doubt envisioning himself with a gleaming sword instead of a gray-headed mop. "I got to talk with you," he said. "Jim Bob cain't do this."

"That's for me to decide," I said as I pushed aside the lethal weapon and continued to the walled cubicle at the end of the row of checkout counters. I could hear no wails, but the expressions of the shoppers and employees implied I'd missed an extraordinary performance. I knocked and went inside.

Jim Bob was leaning back in his chair, his boots on his desk, his fingers entwined over his beer belly, and a cigar clamped between his teeth. "It's about time you got here. It's a good thing nobody was holding up the bank."

"We don't have a bank."

"I know that," he said, the cigar wobbling enough to send ashes trickling down his shirt like gray snowflakes. "Did you bring your handcuffs?"

Ignoring him, I looked down at the lumpy mountain of misery in a chair. "Dahlia," I said gently, "what's this about? Were you shoplifting?"

She raised her face to gaze so mournfully at me that I expected her to start howling. "Are you gonna arrest me, Arly? I don't want to go to jail."

I looked at Jim Bob. "So tell me what happened."

"I was on my way to the lounge when I saw that gallon bucket of lard"—he flicked a finger at Dahlia—"slip something in her purse. She was acting so sneaky that I followed her all the way out to the parking lot. Problem is, she forgot to stop at the checkout counter and pay for what's in her purse. That's your basic definition of shoplifting."

"What's in your purse?" I asked Dahlia.

"Nuthin'."

I held out my hand. "Then we'd better have a look."

She clutched the purse to her breasts. "You got to have a search warrant."

"You've been watching way too much television," I said, my hand still extended despite a niggling worry that she might bite it. "If you didn't steal anything, open your purse and prove it."

"Oh, she did," volunteered Jim Bob, who looked as if he was hoping I'd lose a finger or two in the line of duty. "I saw her do it, and you can bet your ass I'm filing charges. Now stop acting like a gooey-mouthed high school counselor and get busy upholding the law, Chief Hanks."

"Shoplifting is not a class A felony, Mayor Buchanon," I retorted coldly. "You're impeding my investigation, so why don't you step outside?"

Hizzoner blew a stream of noxious smoke at me. "This is my office, and I'm damn well staying right here."

I wrapped my fingers (as far as they would go) around Dahlia's wrist, although I could no more drag her to her feet than I could make major modifications to the landscape. "Okay, then I'll continue my investigation at the police station. If I learn anything relevant, I know where to call you. Get up, Dahlia."

It took Dahlia a moment to figure out that I wasn't taking her to the county jail. Sniveling, she allowed me to hustle her out of the office before Jim Bob could get his boots on the floor. Kevin must have been lurking behind the rack of tabloids; before we were halfway to the glass doors, he skittered into our path and said, "I ain't gonna allow this. You unhand my wife or I'll be obliged to—to—"

"Coldcock me with your mop?" I suggested.

He stumbled back as if I'd shoved him. "Golly, I'd never smack you, Arly. It's just that I have to defend my beloved wife, especially on account of her delicate condition. The doctor doesn't want her to get riled up."

I tightened my grip on his beloved wife's wrist. "Then let me get her out of here before Jim Bob calls in the FBI. I'll drive her home and make sure she's feeling better before I leave. Why don't you call your mother to come sit with her until you get off work?"

Kevin was trying to sort through the compound sentences as I propelled Dahlia out to the getaway car. Once we were at the edge of the parking lot, I said, "You can either tell me what's in your purse right here, or you can tell me at the PD. I'd better warn you that the air conditioner wasn't working this morning, so it may be hotter than a fire in a pepper mill by now."

"A package of Twinkies. They don't cost but seventy-nine cents. I was gonna leave the money on a counter, but then Jim Bob started prowling behind me like a rabid polecat, and I got so scared I hightailed it out of there. He can't do anything to me, can he?"

"Put the Twinkies on the seat." I realized I'd sounded like Dirty Harry confronting a murderous thug and tried to soften my tone. "This does constitute shoplifting, Dahlia, but I'll give Jim Bob your seventy-nine cents and make it clear that he'll be stirring up a lot of ill will if he files charges."

"Thanks," she said, snuffling into a wadded tissue.

"Why did you do it?"

"Kevin made most everybody in town swear they wouldn't let me stray off this gawdawful diet. When I go to the clinic in Farberville, Kevin or his ma always drives me and watches me like I was a pickpocket at the county fair. If I'd tried to buy the Twinkies, Winnella—she's the checker—would have yelled at Kevvie to stop what all he was doing and come lecture me." She sighed so vigorously the windshield fogged over, obliging me to switch on the defroster. "I'm gettin' pretty tired of lectures. All I wanted was two little Twinkies. How bad kin they be?"

I pulled into her driveway and stopped. "Bad enough to risk a fifty-dollar fine for shoplifting," I said. "I understand why you did it, but you absolutely cannot do it again. I want you to stay out of the SuperSaver until you have the baby, okay? Call Kevin and tell him what you need in the way of groceries, and he can bring them home after work. Do I have your promise?"

"I suppose so," she said, although without much conviction. After a wistful glance at the package on the seat, she handed me exactly seventy-nine cents and heaved herself out of the car. "I don't want Kevvie to git fired on account of his wife being a Twinkie thief."

I drove back to the PD, grabbed the radar gun, and retreated to one of my favorite spots out by the remains of Purtle's Esso station. If anyone dared to exceed the speed limit by so much as one mile per hour, he or she was going to make my day.

Norma Kay replaced the telephone receiver and stared blindly at the papers scattered across her desk. The man she'd been talking to had refused to do anything more than promise to call back next week to arrange a counseling session with Malachi. She couldn't wait that long. Sin was hovering around her, threatening to suffocate her with its evil stench. Only Malachi Hope could bring redemption and absolution.

She redialed the number, and when the man answered, said, "Listen, I have to talk with Malachi today. It's gonna be too late if I have to wait, and—"

Thomas Fratelleon cut her off, saying, "I sense your urgency, Mrs. Grapper, but Malachi has gone into seclusion in preparation for the opening night of the revival. He always does this, and he insists that no one—not even his family—interrupt him. Doing the Lord's work requires all his emotional energy."

"Yes, but—"

"I'm sorry, Mrs. Grapper. Malachi told me to schedule you in as early in the week as possible. I'll call you Monday morning."

He hung up and flipped through her uncommonly thick file. She'd written plaintive letters for years, each detailing the particulars of whatever personal crisis she was experiencing. Notations at the bottom of each letter indicated the amount of her donation and which form letter had been sent.

The form letters were masterful. Each was designed to address a specific problem such as marital conflict, unemployment, loneliness, poor health, and a myriad of minor complaints. During the corporation's most successful period, a dozen employees opened letters, removed checks, selected appropriate responses from the computer file, and made sure the correspondent's name was scattered through the letter like toppings on a pizza. Even though he rarely skimmed them, Malachi insisted on signing them himself. He'd referred to it as "the personal touch," and it had worked well; most of those on the receiving end seemed to believe Malachi had read their letters and written an intimate reply along the lines of: "I have prayed for you, [insert first name], and felt a glow in my heart when I saw Jesus standing beside you during this time of tribulation. Yes, [insert first name], your prayers will be answered." Those who sent a hundred dollars or more also received a booklet of daily meditations and a tiny plastic vial of water from the River Jordan (according to the enclosed card, anyway).

Thomas read Norma Kay's last letters, in which she'd acknowledged having an extramarital affair despite Malachi's gentle admonishments to study the Scriptures by purchasing—at a special discount—a genuine leather Bible with her name embossed in gold letters at no extra charge. Shipping and handling charges were another matter.

He was relieved that he was not the one who would have to maintain a sympathetic facade while she whimpered through a confession. In his youth, he might have enjoyed hearing the more prurient aspects, but he found his amusement elsewhere these days.

He was reviewing delivery invoices when Joey came into the kitchen. "Yes?" he said, peering over the top of his bifocals.

"Power's on in the van and I'm pretty sure the dimming-control panel will work okay. If Seraphina's not busy, we can test the harness now."

"She took Chastity into town to shop. Find one of the workmen who weighs one hundred forty pounds and test it on him." Thomas let his eyes slide to the papers in front of him to make it clear he was busy.

"Has Chastity really agreed to go to the high school?"

Thomas pulled off his glasses to massage the bluish pouches beneath his eyes. The days preceding the first night of the revival were always hectic, and the nights on the cot were increasingly hard on his sixty-year-old body. "That is what she has said. For some inexplicable reason, she has signed up to play on the girls' basketball team."

"She's acting pretty weird these days," Joey said. He glanced over his shoulder at the door that led to the master bedroom. "I think she's up to something. She usually pesters me to take her some fool place or other, but she hasn't even tried to talk to me for a couple of days."

"Count your blessings," said Thomas as he replaced his glasses and picked up a pencil. He began to hum a hymn that reiterated the platitude.

"From Psalm Seventy-four," intoned Brother Verber, who paused to look out at the faces in the congregation. Attendance was definitely down from the previous Sunday; it was likely folks were waiting for the revival to get their weekly dose of piety. Sister Barbara was in her regular seat on the second pew, but Brother Jim Bob was nowhere to be seen. Kevin and Dahlia were absent, though he wasn't surprised after her disgraceful behavior the day before. Norma Kay was missing, too, as were several other dependable members.

He realized everybody was waiting for him to continue, mopped his forehead, and plunged into the text. " 'They have cast fire into thy sanctuary, they have defiled by casting down the dwelling place of thy name to the ground. They said in their hearts, Let us destroy them together: they have burned up all the synagogues of God in the land.' "

He slammed down the Bible and gripped the edges of the pulpit. "Now I suspect you all are wondering who it is I'm referring to. You're asking yourself, 'Who is this mysterious *they* he's talking about? Are *they* some gang of arsonists intent on setting fire to the Voice of the Almighty Lord Assembly Hall?' I see the puzzlement in your eyes, brothers and sisters. I hear your unspoken questions. I smell your fear of being roasted alive." He gave them time to chew on this, then continued softly. "But we know who *they* is, don't we? We've seen their faces and nodded to them at the grocery store and the launderette. Some of us have chatted with them about the weather."

His pronouncement, which sounded more like an accusation, elicited anxious stirrings in the congregation as everybody tried to remember if he or she had been consorting with Satanists or Catholics during the week.

Brother Verber basked in their uneasiness for a melodramatic moment. "Maybe we did these things only because we're friendly folks who aren't used to thinking the worst of everyone we meet. We stick out our hands and say howdy and pleased-to-meetcha without thinking twice about it. Well, maybe that wasn't so bad—until *they* came to Maggody with their wicked scheme to destroy our modest services and our potluck suppers and our Sunday school picnics on the Fourth of July!" He leaned forward, his face turning red and his eyes bulging as the pulpit cut into his belly. His voice crackled with fervor as he roared, "Malachi Hope! That's the one doing everything he can to destroy us—him and that blond, painted floozy that runs around in clothes from Satan's own boutique. Just because she drives a Mercedes doesn't mean she ain't a modern-day Jezebel!"

"Amen," said Sister Barbara, making sure everybody heard her. Lottie Estes jerked around so hard she nearly fell off the piano bench, but no one else twitched a muscle.

Brother Verber beamed at her and then got back to business. "Malachi Hope thinks he can lure you all to his

tent and talk in a velvety voice until you pull out your
wallets and give him every last dollar you have, even
what you'd been setting aside so your little ones could
have new shoes for school. That's what he thinks, this
sly preacher from the big city. But maybe you're sly, too,
and can see right through his phony act. Maybe you can
see the dollar signs in his eyes and the stickiness on his
fingers. Am I right, brothers and sisters? Am I right?"
There were nods, mostly tentative but encouraging nev-
ertheless. "Of course, I am, and I believe I'll be looking
at every last one of you this evening when we gather for
our service and potluck supper out in the vestibule. I
have it on good authority that we'll be feasting on some
tasty new dishes, as well as enjoying the opportunity to
visit with one another and share news about our family
and friends in distant towns."

Elsie McMay stood up. "Only the other day you told
everybody you was canceling the evening services tonight and Wednesday so folks could go to the revival." She sat down real quick when Mrs. Jim Bob turned
around and glared at her.

He clung more tightly to the pulpit as his palms began to sweat like saturated sponges. He'd been worried
this was gonna come up and had prayed for the Lord to
suggest a suitable comeback. If the Lord had a response,
He had sent it parcel post instead of overnight delivery. And from the way most of the flock was watching
him, he could tell they wanted an answer.

"Well, Elsie," he said at last, "I may well have said
something to that effect—but that was before I realized
the depths of Malachi Hope's depravity. Only someone
with ol' Satan lurking behind him could buy your souls

with cotton candy. Is that all it takes to entice you to eternal damnation?"

He carried on in that vein for a while, wiping his forehead periodically and dropping veiled hints about the high cost of dentistry. There was an atmosphere of rebellion in the room, though, and he was on the verge of having to wring out his handkerchief and try a different tactic when Mrs. Jim Bob stood up.

"I have an announcement," she said. "I meant to give it to Brother Verber so he could read it before he started his sermon, but I forgot to bring a pencil. The Missionary Society has voted to make the evening services more appealing to our youth by holding bingo games afterward. You have to make a dollar donation at the door, but every penny will go to buying Bibles for the little heathens in Africa. There'll be cash prizes, as well as gift certificates from Jim Bob's SuperSaver Buy 4 Less. Tonight's grand prize will be a Mr. Coffee and a box of filters."

The rank and file of the Missionary Society began to whisper to one another, but Brother Verber told Lottie to strike up the opening chords of the offertory hymn, "Give Your All to Jesus."

Darla Jean and Heather walked across the pasture to join their teammates by the entrance to the tent. There was no sign of Chastity, but they figured she was in the RV getting dressed. There were men fiddling with a popcorn machine and muffled voices from within the tent. A banner flapped in the light breeze. A woman with gray hair pinned up in braids took T-shirts from a box beneath a table and set them in immaculate stacks. A younger woman did the same with paperback Bibles. A portable trailer advertised the availability of hot dogs and lemonade. On a big table was an elaborate model of the City of Hope, complete with a cardboard cathedral with multicolored windows and a soaring steeple, a glass lake lined with tiny trees, and all kinds of paths winding through fuzzy, green slopes to white buildings. A sign announced this to be Phase One. The girls agreed it was real cute.

"I thought Coach Grapper was gonna be here," said one of the Dahlton twins.

Darla Jean shrugged. "Yeah, she said that, but she wasn't at church this morning. I can't recollect the last time she missed a service."

"If she's sick," said Heather, "she might not find out if we kind of slip away as soon as everybody is sitting down. I'd like to watch the first part of a miniseries about a beautiful woman that's raised in an orphanage and doesn't learn she's really a wealthy heiress until—"

"Here you all are," said Seraphina as she came out of the tent. She was wearing shorts and a T-shirt that read: "Hope Is Here!" "It's just so wonderful of you girls to help us out all week. Not only will you be earning money for your team, but you'll also have a chance to hear Malachi speak of the true joy of dedicating your young lives to Jesus."

"Swell," muttered Heather.

Seraphina winked at her. "Oh, I understand about boyfriends and moonlight. I had my share of both when I was your age. You should be able to leave by ten o'clock every night, so you can still snuggle up on the porch swing with your guys." She let that sink in, then added, "I need all of you to come to the van parked out back. We'll give you your badges and some hints on how to make folks feel welcome as they arrive. That doesn't sound too terrible, does it?" Without waiting for their answers, she headed for the corner of the tent, crooking her finger to indicate they were to follow her.

Like lambs, they did.

"Please," moaned Kevin as he knelt in front of his wife, who was spread across the sofa like a load of topsoil, "please don't fret over what folks are saying about what happened yesterday. Everybody knows Jim Bob's meaner than his hide will hold. He had no business bullying you like he did, and iff'n you want, I'll just go back down to the store and punch him in the nose."

"He'll have *you* arrested, too."

"You wasn't arrested, my goddess. Arly brought you home and made you promise to steer clear of the store until you have the baby. If she'd meant to arrest you, she'd have said something about it." He took her hand and nuzzled it until she jerked it away. "You cain't lie here for five more months. Why doncha put on that pretty pink dress Ma made for you and we'll go to the revival? Do you recollect how we used to watch Malachi Hope and his wife on television? We don't want to miss the chance to see 'em in real life."

Dahlia turned her face to the back of the sofa. "I ain't never setting foot out of this house as long as I live."

He pleaded some more, but her only responses were

melancholy rumbles and an occasional despondent belch. He finally gave up and went into the kitchen to see what he could find to fix for supper. It wasn't hard to see why she was suffering; the refrigerator was nigh onto empty except for carrots, celery, and the dried remains of a piece of fish neither of them had been able eat. The cupboards were empty, too. He himself had cleaned them out and taken all the cookies and chips to his parents' house for safekeeping.

"I have an idea," he said from the doorway, hoping she'd at least look at him. "After the revival, we can stop at the Dairee Dee-Lishus and share an ice-cream soda. I know your doctor won't like it, but a few calories is better than all this heartache."

"What if folks at the revival start whispering about how I'm a shoplifter?"

"Why, I'll slap 'em across the face," he said gallantly.

Dahlia opened one eye to regard him. The pregnancy made her sick to her stomach in the mornings, but it was making him downright manly. She wondered if she ought to ask the nurse about it.

"Did you see the signs out in front of the Assembly Hall?" asked Estelle from the living room of the two-room unit at the Flamingo Motel. She'd arrived earlier than expected and was having to wait while Ruby Bee finished getting gussied up.

"Can't say I did," Ruby Bee called from the bathroom. "What do they say?"

"There's gonna be bingo games every Sunday and Wednesday evening, with prizes and free popcorn."

"Isn't bingo illegal?"

"I ain't a lawyer. Are you ready to go?"

Ruby Bee went into the bedroom and clipped on the earrings Arly had given her for her fiftieth—or fifty-fourth—birthday, the number having been disputed. "Wasn't there something on the news about the Veterans' Auxiliary down in Little Rock being ordered to stop running their bingo games?"

"It must have been before my time. What are you doing in there—giving yourself a manicure? If we don't get there early, we're liable to have to park in the back of the pasture. I'm wearing my new shoes, and I'm not about to go stepping in cow patties."

Ruby Bee tucked a scarf into her purse, hitched up her girdle, and came into the living room. "I told Arly about the passes to sit in the front row, but she turned up her nose and said she wasn't going. I don't know what's gotten into that girl. All she ever does in the evenings is mope around that pitiful apartment of hers, watching television and reading magazines. What kind of life is that, I ask you? That's not to say it isn't a sight better than living in Washington, D.C., of course, but it's got to be lonely."

Estelle was shaking her head as she stood up. "She sure isn't gonna find a husband that way. Maybe you ought to convince her to talk to Malachi Hope."

"Are you out of your mind? I'd sooner try to convince her to go on a date with Diesel Buchanon, for pity's sake!"

"Is he still biting heads off squirrels and rabbits up on Cotter's Ridge?"

"When he's not exposing his privates at the school yard."

Ruby Bee made sure the front door was locked and then climbed into the front seat of Estelle's car. Shortly thereafter, they were waving at a sheriff's deputy as they turned down County 102.

"I for one disremember voting to have bingo games at the Assembly Hall," Lottie said as she turned down County 102. "If Mrs. Jim Bob wants to give away a Mr. Coffee, she's welcome to do it."

"Just because she's the president don't give her the right to act like a dictator," said Elsie McMay.

"Bingo is just another name for gambling," added Eula Lemoy from the backseat. "And gambling is a sin."

Lottie hit the brakes as they arrived at the rear of a long line of cars and trucks that stretched clear to the low-water bridge. "You'd have thought Brother Verber would have objected to gambling in the sanctuary, but he didn't say a word."

The conversation grew louder as the participants expressed their outrage. The fact that Lottie's air conditioner wasn't strong enough to ruffle a gnat's hair was a contributing factor.

"I still say we should have gone to the Assembly Hall," said Eilene Buchanon as her husband turned down County 102. "We've been attending Sunday evening services for more than thirty years. We were married there, and Kevin and Dahlia were married there, too. You may not care all that much for Brother Verber's long-winded sermons, but we have to remain loyal—"

"The hell we do," said Earl. "Besides, there wasn't a single car in the parking lot. If everybody else is going to the revival, then so are we. Malachi Hope asked to give a presentation at Kiwanis next week. As the program chairman, it's my responsibility to check him out. Besides, I'm partial to cotton candy."

"Oh, Earl . . ." she began, then conceded defeat and sank back into the seat. Sometimes there wasn't any point in trying to reason with a Buchanon—and Earl was the product of third cousins once removed.

Norma Kay watched the traffic crawl up County 102 as she waited on the porch for Bur to join her. He'd refused at first, but she'd kept at him until he agreed to attend this one time. After that, he'd growled, she could do what she damn well pleased but he was staying home.

Not that she wanted his company, of course. It just didn't seem fitting for her to show up by herself and have to find someone to sit with who wouldn't ask where Bur was and was he sickly. Married women didn't do that, except for morning coffees and meetings of the County Extension Club and Missionary Society.

She was about to go back inside and holler at him when she saw Cory Jenks walking up the road. He looked real nice in a blue dress shirt and trousers; she didn't want to think how slovenly Bur would look in whatever he found on the floor of the closet or in the clothes hamper.

"Evening, Norma Kay," Cory said as he came across the yard. "You and Bur going to the revival?"

"If he gets his butt out here before it's over."

He stopped at the edge of the porch. "Where'd that bruise on your cheek come from?"

"I got all tangled up when I was pulling on my dress and lost my balance," she said evenly. "Before I knew what was happening, I ran into the closet door."

"Like last time?"

"Yeah, like last time." She turned her face so the bruise was less prominent. "I'm surprised you're coming to the revival, Cory. I'd have thought you'd be home working on game plans or devising new drills."

"I'm curious about this Hope fellow, and I hear his wife's a real looker. Besides, the boys are in charge of parking cars and handing out hymnals. I thought I'd better make sure they all showed up sober."

Bur came out onto the porch, clearly uncomfortable in a white shirt and tie. "Why, look who's here!" he said with facetious enthusiasm. "You and Norma Kay having yourselves a cozy little conversation?"

Cory's ears turned pink, but he held his ground. "Evening, Coach Grapper. Norma Kay and I were talking about the varsity team's odds on a conference title. Did she tell you about that transfer student that can slam-dunk on a good day?"

Bur slid his arm through Norma Kay's and yanked her into step. "I can't say she did, Cory. Why don't you tell me all about him while we walk up the hill together? Maybe if we all three pray hard enough, you'll be adding a big silver trophy to the case come next spring."

Norma Kay bit her tongue as they joined the parade heading up the hill.

7

THE telephone jarred me out of a dreamless sleep. I fumbled my way from under the sheets to peer at the dial of the clock. It was a few minutes past 1:30, I realized as I lunged across the bed and grabbed the receiver.

"What?" I demanded gracelessly.

"Is this Arly Hanks?"

"Except for the monsters under the bed, nobody else lives here. Who's this?"

"Malachi Hope. There's been an accident."

I rubbed the grit out of my eyes as I tried to assimilate his words. "What kind of accident? What are you talking about?"

"A suicide, I think, but you'd better get over here."

"Whose suicide? Get over where?" I said. "For that matter, how do I know this is really Malachi Hope?"

After a pause, he said, "I met you in the tent yesterday afternoon. I was wearing a gray sweatshirt and jeans, and you were visibly surprised when you found out who I was. You also express a certain degree of skepticism in regard to my healing powers."

I switched on the bedside light. "Okay, you're Malachi Hope. Now explain what you said earlier."

"I don't think I can explain much. I'm at the high school gym, using the telephone in the office. The girls' basketball coach is—well, I hope she's not a close friend of yours . . . because I don't know how to put this any other way. She's dead. Somebody has to do something."

"Are you sure she's dead?" I asked.

"I'm very sure, Chief Hanks. Otherwise I would have called an ambulance." He gulped like a clogged drain. "Should I call the sheriff's office?"

I was already on my feet, pulling on jeans and looking around for my shoes. "Just sit tight, Mr. Hope. I'll be there in less than five minutes." I replaced the receiver, debated calling the sheriff's office myself, and finally decided to see what the hell was going on at the gym before I called anyone. It was possible I'd fallen for a prank and would find myself in front of a locked building, cursing my stupidity while juvenile delinquents tittered in the brush.

Four and a half minutes later I parked between a gold Cadillac and a less majestic Toyota. The door to the gym was unlocked. I eased it open and squinted into the dark interior, but all I could make out were oblique shadows and corners darker than the inside of a cow. A light was on in a room at the far end, however, so I took a breath and walked briskly across the court.

Malachi Hope was slouched in a chair behind a cluttered desk, his forehead propped on his fists. Whatever evangelical finery he'd worn earlier had been replaced with a more secular sweater. As I stepped into the room, he stood up. "This is a nightmare, Chief Hanks. Nothing like this has ever happened to me before."

"Where's Norma Kay?"

"Come back into the gym and I'll show you. I almost feel responsible for this tragedy. If I'd known how desperate she was . . ."

He stopped outside the door to flick a switch. Overhead lights flooded the room with a harsh white glare that glinted off the varnished benches of the bleachers. Mutely he pointed at the basketball goal at the opposite end of the court. Below it dangled a body, toes just short of the floor. The bright yellow hair was distinctive, the bilious pink sweatsuit infamous. Nearby was an overturned stepladder.

"Oh, my gawd," I said. "Are you sure . . . ?"

"Yes," Malachi said, resting a hand on my shoulder to steady either me or himself. "I forced myself to take a closer look. There's no doubt she's dead."

I pulled away from him, ran across the court, and halted beneath the body. As he'd said, there was no doubt, and there was no point in disturbing the scene and destroying what evidence might be gleaned. Once my queasiness subsided and my knees stopped quivering, I returned to the office. "What are you doing here, Mr. Hope?"

"It's a complicated story. Maybe you ought to call someone before I get into it."

I edged into the room, keeping an eye on him, and felt behind my back for the telephone. His face was pale, his eyes imploring, his hair rumpled as if he'd been running his fingers through it continually since he'd called me. Then again, he'd yet to explain what he was do-ing in the gym—beyond discovering Norma Kay's body, that is.

It took a lot of willpower on my part to turn around and punch the numbers of the sheriff's office. After a cer-tain amount of incredulity, the night dispatcher agreed to call Harve at home and let him know what had hap-pened. I promised to wait by the telephone should in-structions be forthcoming, hung up, and turned back.

"Now, Mr. Hope, would you care to explain?" I said.

"Call me Malachi," he said in an unsuccessful at-tempt to evoke a sense of camaraderie. He gave me a minute to respond (I didn't), then sighed and said, "Nor-ma Kay Grapper has been writing me letters once a month for the last ten years, asking for spiritual guid-ance. I always tell my most loyal followers that I'll meet with them for a private counseling session should the opportunity arise."

"That happen often?"

"Not if it can be avoided," he said dryly. "I'd forgot-ten that Norma Kay lived here, so it was a bit of a sur-prise when she told me who she was."

Deciding he was not going to fly across the room and attempt to throttle me, I risked sitting down behind the desk. I'd have thought he would have been a garrulous witness, eager to dominate the exchange with long-winded speculation, but it looked as if getting informa-tion out of him was going to be like pulling dandelions out of sun-baked ground. "When was that?"

"Friday morning. Chastity supposedly came here to shoot baskets with some local girls. I needed to speak to her, so I drove over and ended up talking with Norma

Kay. She was overly emotional, I'm sorry to say, and I deeply regretted my presence."

"Was that the last time you spoke with her?"

He sat down on a bench and rested his head on the wall. "She wanted to schedule a counseling session, so I told her to call Thomas. She did, and according to him, she was almost hysterical. He made it clear he could do nothing until Monday morning and promised to call her back. That was the end of it until earlier this evening, just before the revival. Were you there?"

"No, Mr. Hope, I was not." And damned if I was going to apologize, either.

"I didn't think so," he said with a small smile. "Anyway, Norma Kay asked one of the ushers to deliver a note to me. In the note, she begged me to meet her here at midnight to discuss something of a critical nature."

"So you came here at midnight?"

"I wasn't going to come, but I started feeling guilty about her waiting for me in some dark, deserted building. I arrived about ten minutes late, came inside, and found her in the office, bawling her eyes out."

When he failed to continue, I said, "Why was she doing that?"

"Now that she's beyond caring, I don't suppose there's any reason to bring up the issue of confidentiality, is there?" he murmured, wincing as he glanced at the door to the gym. "She was having an affair with a local man. She'd been trying to end it for some time because she knew it was sinful, but he refused to leave her alone. She was also terrified her husband suspected something was going on. He doesn't sound like an amiable person."

"No, that he's not," I said as I found a very dull pencil and wrote "12:10" on a scrap of paper. "Who was the lover?"

Malachi shrugged. "She didn't mention his name, but I would imagine in a town this size . . . Anyway, she carried on for a while, moaning about her sin and begging me to absolve her. I finally told her that her only chance to find inner peace was to break off the affair, confess to her husband, and put her excessive energy into charitable work. I even offered to let her do some office work for us during the week, although I wasn't sure how Seraphina and Thomas would feel about that. When I left at 12:30, she was much calmer and seemed resolved to take my advice."

I dutifully scratched "12:30" on the paper. "You left her here by herself? Wouldn't it have been chivalrous to escort her to her car and make sure she got home safely?"

He stood up and came over to the desk, his face distorted with anguish. "Don't you think I realize that now? Of course I should have insisted that she leave at the same time! I suggested it, and when she said she had work to do, I offered several times to wait until she was ready to go home. She remained adamant that I leave. I drove back to the RV and watched for headlights in her driveway. I finally came back to make sure she was all right."

"The door wasn't locked?"

"No, but when I left the first time, she walked with me to the exterior door and locked it behind me."

I heard cars arriving outside the gym. Leaving Mala-

chi to assess his guilt, I went to meet Harve and whichever deputies he'd brought along.

"Hanged herself, did she?" Harve said, gazing at the
body. "What's that she used?"

"A cord," one of the deputies volunteered.

I pulled Harve aside and gave him a summary of
what Malachi had told me. We agreed further interrogation could wait while we dealt with the corpse. It was
time for photographs, fingerprints, telephone calls, and a
visit from McBeen, who was a long cry from Marcus
Welby. In fact, he was rumored to be the crabbiest
county coroner in the entire state.

Lucky us.

Long about sunrise, I knocked on the Grappers' front
door. Blistering heat would descend by mid-morning,
but now it was nippy enough to make me wish I'd
grabbed a jacket when I left my apartment. I stuck my
hands in my pockets and turned around to look at the
scruffy yard and neglected flower beds. Down the road
a piece was a weathered house set among scrub pines,
weeds, a pile of busted chicken crates, and tires (tradi-
tional landscaping in Maggody). Parked in front was a
dark pickup truck with a well-stocked gun rack across
the back window. After a moment of reflection, I remembered it was the Jenks place, currently occupied by the
prodigal son.

The door opened behind me. "Who are you and what
do you want?"

I gave Bur a minute to recognize me, identified myself when he didn't, and then said, "I'm afraid I have some bad news, Mr. Grapper. May I come in?"

"Hell, no. I ain't in the mood for company. State your business and be on your way."

"Your wife's body was discovered in the high school gym."

My blunt recitation gained me entry to the living room, although not an invitation to sit down. I did so anyway, waited until he'd taken a seat across from me, and studied his face for any flicker of emotion whatsoever. When none was forthcoming, I said, "She was hanging from the basketball goal. Her body will be sent to the state lab in Little Rock to determine if it was a suicide. Someone will notify you as soon as we hear anything."

"Suicide?" he said, curling his lip in surprise. "Why would she go and do a fool thing like that?"

"That's what we're trying to find out. Was she upset these last few days, acting strange, refusing to talk to you—anything like that?"

"She's been acting strange for ten years. But as for these last few days—yeah, she was all the time creeping around the house at night, mumbling to herself, forgetting she had clothes on the line, burning food in the oven, things like that."

"Do you have any idea what was bothering her?"

"That preacher up on the hill," he said without hesitation. "The day he arrived was when she took a turn for the worse. A couple of times I caught her out on the porch, wearing nothing but her bathrobe, staring up that way and saying his name over and over like she was praying. It liked to drive me up the wall, her carrying on that way. I told her I wasn't gonna put up with it anymore, but it didn't do any good. You'd have thought he was the goddamn Messiah come to Maggody!"

It did not seem the moment to mention who'd discovered her body. The emotion that had been missing when I'd told him the news was now evident; I decided to find out if it went any deeper than Boone Creek in July. "You and Norma Kay went to the revival last night, didn't you?"

"It was all her doing. I ain't one for sitting on a bench all night while folks gabble about being saved. Reminded me of the fans at the ball games, all squealing like hogs at a scalding."

"Did you happen to notice if Norma Kay spoke to one of the ushers?" I asked delicately.

"Spoke to several of 'em on account of them being on her team. I don't know any of their names, though." He stood up and gestured at the door. "You'd better go so I can start calling her family up in Kansas about the funeral."

"I'll let you know when the body can be released," I said as I obediently rose. I was halfway to the door when it occurred to me I was no longer a high school student without a hall pass. "I have a couple of more questions before I go, Mr. Grapper. We're trying to get a clearer picture of what happened last night. What time did you and your wife leave the revival?"

"About ten o'clock or so."

"And you both came straight home?"

He nodded impatiently. "I settled down to watch the news, but Norma Kay was flitting around the house like a damnfool moth. After a spell, she said she was going over to the gym to do some work."

"What time was that?" I asked, wishing I'd brought the stubby pencil and scrap of paper.

"Maybe eleven. I watched a movie for a while, then went on to bed about half an hour later, assuming she was capable of locking up when she got back."

"You weren't worried about her being there by herself so late at night?"

"I didn't like it, but she swore she always kept the gym door locked while she was in her office. She wouldn't have unlocked the door unless she was expecting someone." He gave me a such a pugnacious look that I expected him to drop into a boxer's stance and cock his fists at me, but instead he shrugged. "But she wasn't, of course. Anybody who says otherwise is a damn liar. Norma Kaye knew better than to cheat on me."

I suppose I should have asked to search the house for a suicide note, but it didn't seem likely that she'd have come back to the house to leave one on the kitchen table or taped to the refrigerator. Her office seemed a more feasible location, although the crime squad had searched it carefully and come up empty-handed.

"I'll be back later," I told Bur seconds before he slammed the door in my face. I climbed in my car just as the sun flashed over the treetops. I yawned so hard I came close to dislocating my jaw and drove back to the high school.

Harve was standing in the parking lot, looking as gray and tired as I'm sure I did. I pulled up beside him and said, "Her husband didn't burst into tears, but he was never in danger of winning any awards for sensitivity. For all I know, he may have been puking out his guts by the time I reached the county road."

"You know him?" asked Harve as he fished a cigar stub and a book of matches out of his shirt pocket.

"He was the head coach when I was in high school, and a real bastard. He screamed obscenities at his players, bawled out their parents if they interfered, insulted the school board, and went out of his way to be rude to the students. He was not your basic beloved father figure."

Harve struck several matches until he got the stub smoldering to his satisfaction (and my dismay). "If he was so gawdawful, why didn't they fire him?"

"His teams always made it to at least the quarter finals of the state tournament and won more often than not. I wasn't around when he finally retired, but Ruby Bee wrote me a letter about how he socked a referee or something along those lines. I gathered his retirement wasn't altogether voluntary."

"What about his wife? Was she sleeping around?"

"I don't know, Harve," I said as I fought back another yawn. "I'll see what I can find out. As Malachi Hope implied, it shouldn't be all that challenging to find out if she was having an affair. There's not a nook or cranny through which the grapevine fails to curl." The yawn came despite my efforts. Once I'd recovered, I said, "McBeen say anything else before he left?"

Harve ground out the cigar stub. "He said there was a bruise on her cheek that she'd tried to cover with makeup. There wasn't any makeup in her purse or in a desk drawer, so we can assume it happened earlier."

"Yesterday?"

"McBeen will let us know when he sees fit. In the meantime, keep nosing around and see what you can dig up about this so-called affair. I let the Hope fellow go home a few minutes ago. Give him a little time to get hisself cleaned up, then drop by to run through his story several more times. Also, see if anyone can confirm his coming, leaving, and then coming back. Something about it smells fishier than a johnboat."

Rather than launch into an argument about who was better equipped to head the investigation (I have one gun, three bullets, and a radio that works only during lunar eclipses), I drove home to shower, brush my teeth, and tap into the grapevine over biscuits and grits.

"Dahlia, my love bunny," gasped Kevin as he read over the shopping list she'd thrust at him. "Cookies? Orange soda pop? Three pounds of pork chops? Ten pounds of potatoes? This ain't on your diet. You know what the doctor told you."

"I don't have diabetes anymore," she countered with a blissful smile. "You heard what Malachi Hope said last night, dint you? I'm cured, so there's no reason to keep nibbling carrots when I can eat real food. Why don't you sneak away later this morning and bring home the groceries? I was thinking I'd make a chocolate cake with fudge icing while I listen to my soaps. We kin have some after supper."

Kevin winced as she continued to gaze at him like a cow in a field of lush clover. "I heard what Malachi Hope said," he began timidly, "but you still got to ask the doctor before you commence to eating pork chops and chocolate cake."

"Malachi Hope put his hands on my shoulders and prayed to Jesus to make my diabetes go away; then he told me loud and clear that I was cured." She lumbered into the kitchen and opened the refrigerator. "You believe in Jesus, doncha?" she continued. "He's not going to lie. As soon as Malachi said I was cured, the diabetes disappeared just like drops of water in a hot skillet. I could feel the tingle, and that's good enough for me. Why doncha get some bacon, too? I think I'll fry up some for lunch."

He crumpled onto the couch and tried not to groan as he looked down the list that covered one whole page. There wasn't so much as a leaf of lettuce or a single radish anywhere on it.

Kevin believed in Jesus, having been baptized in Boone Creek on his fourteenth birthday, but he had some doubts about Malachi Hope.

Eula Lemoy lifted her feet to inspect her ankle. It was definitely less swollen, she decided as she took a sip of tea and a nibble of toast. Here she'd been spending forty dollars every month for two years on pink pills to keep her blood thin, not to mention the ordeal of blood tests and having to sit in the waiting room half the day just so the mealymouthed doctor could tell her to keep taking the pills.

Now that she was cured, she could put that money to better use. She put down the teacup and picked up a mail-order catalog. It must have been divine intervention that the first thing she looked at was a real pretty comforter that cost exactly forty dollars.

"Where is your walker?" Mrs. Twayblade asked Petrol Buchanon, who was shuffling down the hall. "We don't want to have another nasty fall, do we? Medicaid isn't going to keep paying for hip operations forever. We have to take precautions."

"Don't reckon I need it," he said, cackling. "This time next week I'll be kicking up my heels with Miz Teasel down in room twenty-two."

Mrs. Twayblade was not amused. "I want you to wait right here while I fetch your walker—and I don't want to hear any more of this gibberish. This preacher may have told you that you could walk like you used to, but that's no excuse to risk a broken hip. Do you know what's involved with the necessary Medicaid and Medicare forms? I am already drowning in paperwork."

"When Jesus eased my arthritis, I felt it from my toes to the tip of my nose. Iff'n I ain't crippled no more, I ain't gonna use the walker."

"I hope that when the time comes, Jesus is going to fill out the Medicaid forms," she said with a sniff.

As she went past him, he pinched her buttocks. The subsequent dialogue was so spirited that heads popped out of doorways all the way to the end of the hall.

Lottie Estes squinted at the recipe in the newspaper, but the tiny print was too blurry for her to make out. Last night when Malachi had squeezed her shoulders and prayed that her vision be restored, she'd felt an odd sensation all over her body. Otherwise, she wouldn't have pulled off her glasses and given them to Seraphina, who was standing right there in a sparkly white dress, smiling and telling her how it was a blessing direct from Jesus. The way everybody in the audience cheered and hollered when she read the Twenty-third Psalm made her feel like when she'd won a blue ribbon for her strawberry preserves.

She finally put down the newspaper and tried to see what time it was, but the numbers on her watch were no larger than the print. It had to be going on eight, she told herself as she made sure she had a clean hankie in her purse, picked up her lesson plan book, and went out to her car. As she backed the car out of the driveway, she wondered if asking Seraphina Hope to give back her glasses would constitute blasphemy. Jesus had cured her, after all. Implying that he hadn't was likely to be a sin of some sort or other.

"What's this I heard about you waltzing out of the store yesterday afternoon with a Mr. Coffee?" Jim Bob asked as he stuffed a forkful of pancakes into his mouth.

"I don't care to discuss it," Mrs. Jim Bob said from in front of the sink, where she was scrubbing the skillet.

"I gave you a Mr. Coffee for your birthday last year,

and it's been gurgling just fine ever since. Why'd you want a new one?"

"You heard me the first time." She left the skillet to soak and busied herself fixing a cup of tea. "Wipe that dribble of syrup off your chin. Sometimes I wonder if you were under the porch when the good Lord was passing out the manners."

On that note, she sailed into the sunroom, leaving him to speculate on why she was so hoppin' mad when he hadn't done a blessed thing except eat his breakfast. The previous night he'd come home as soon as the SuperSaver closed, and he'd kept the television real low so's not to disturb her. He'd even remembered to put the beer cans in the garbage can out by the garage instead of in the wastebasket under the sink, where she claimed they made the kitchen reek.

"Did you go to the revival last night?" he called, feigning interest in an effort to mollify her.

"I did not."

He put his plate next to the sink, made sure his chin was no longer glistening, and went to the doorway. "I'm surprised you didn't. I thought you and Brother Verber would go together."

She looked at him. "What's that supposed to mean?"

Damned if he knew. "Well, I just thought . . . you being so devout and all, that you'd want to be sitting in the first pew with your Bible in your lap."

"Why would I want to do that?"

His jaw waggled like a mule's tail as he tried to come up with an answer. "You haven't missed a Sunday night service since I met you. Why, even when we were on our honeymoon over at Eureka Springs, you—"

"I said I don't care to discuss it!"

The conversation was getting murkier than the stock pond behind Raz Buchanon's shack—and somehow or other, the Mr. Coffee was at the bottom of it (the murkiness, not the stock pond). Scratching his head, he went back into the kitchen and wasted a few minutes stealthily opening cabinets to see if he could find the Mr. Coffee. When he was satisfied it wasn't there, he took a quick peek at his wife (she hadn't moved a muscle, as far as he could tell), took his truck key from the bowl on the counter, and let himself out the front door.

Maybe it was his fault he came within inches of smashing into Lottie Estes's ancient Edsel up at the intersection. He assured her he'd been distracted, and he went so far as to offer her his handkerchief when she started blubbering apologies. Only afterward did he realize it had been a miracle neither of them had been killed.

8

"I t's about time you showed up," Ruby Bee said as I came across the barroom, my hair still damp from the shower and my eyeballs aching as if they'd been skinned. "I suppose you'll be wantin' breakfast, even though it's as plain as the nose on your face you've got more important things to do."

Avoiding eye contact (a technique espoused at the police academy for dealing with the deranged), I went to the end of the bar to fill a mug with coffee, then sat down. "I can't think of anything more important than warding off starvation with the best cooking west of the Mississippi."

"How about solving a murder, Miss National Geographic? Or is police work just a hobby?"

I choked on a mouthful of coffee. Once I'd wiped my face and caught my breath, I opted for full frontal eye contact. "What murder do you have in mind?"

"Norma Kay Grapper's, of course. I never cared for Bur—and still don't—but she was always mannersome when I saw her at the SuperSaver. The girls on the basketball team are going to be mighty upset when they hear the news. Maybe you should talk to them after you finish getting a statement from Malachi Hope. Do you want I should call Darla Jean McIlhaney and have her set up a meeting?"

"She's not home," said Estelle as she came up behind me. "I saw her and Heather Reilly driving toward Farberville not five minutes ago. They were in a big hurry, but most likely on account of having to be back at eleven for practice." She gave Ruby Bee the same worldly half smile that Gloria Swanson had given William Holden just the night before in *Sunset Boulevard*. "Imagine the girls with their little gym bags, gathered in the parking lot, waiting for Norma Kay to unlock the door for them."

Ruby Bee wiped her cheeks on the hem of her apron. "I was just telling Arly that she should be the one to break the news to the team."

"Hold your horses," I said before they sank into such maudlin sentimentality that it would take a dredger to pull them to the surface. "How do you two know about Norma Kay's death last night?"

"Ruby Bee called me," Estelle said hastily. "That's how I know."

I glared at the accused, who had the grace to pretend to be abashed. As she noticed how tightly I was gripping the mug, she prudently moved out of range and said, "When I opened up this morning, the telephone was ringing. It proved to be LaBelle over at the sheriff's office. She was trying to find you on account of the sheriff wanting to tell you something real important. LaBelle said she'd called your office *and* your apartment, but you hadn't answered. All she could think to do was leave a message with me for you to call Harvey Dorfer when you turned up."

"And she told you all the details?"

"She may have felt the need to explain why it was so urgent you call back. I was so distressed over the news that I had to talk to someone . . ."

Someone nodded but kept her mouth shut.

My face was hotter than the coffee in the mug. I gave myself a moment to cool off and then said, "LaBelle had no business telling you what happened last night. And you have no business embellishing it and then spreading it all over town."

"Embellishing it? I beg your pardon, missy—I didn't say one syllable that's not the gospel truth."

"You said it was murder," I countered sternly, "and we don't have the results of the autopsy yet. It very well may turn out to be suicide."

Ruby Bee gave Estelle a look that presumably was fraught with significance, then said, "Norma Kay would rather die than commit suicide. She used to be a Catholic before she married Bur Grapper and moved here."

"How do you know that?" I asked.

Estelle must have decided that it was safe to butt back in. "I was the one who found that out. It happens that Edwina Spitz's niece married a boy from Topeka. I disremember her name, but she used to visit Edwina in the summer with a whole suitcase full of Barbie dolls and accessories. One morning Edwina tripped over a little pink convertible and came within inches of falling off her back porch into the azaleas."

"Could we stick to the story?" I said.

"Her name was Justine," Ruby Bee said, then caught my glare and retreated to the far end of the bar.

"That's it," said Estelle. "Justine married a real nice boy whose daddy owned a clothing store on the main street in Topeka. They had twins right off the bat, but then Justine started dwindling away till she was nothing but skin and bones. She upped and died before the twins reached kindergarten."

I wished I had a clicker so I could fast-forward the narrative. "Does this have anything to do with Norma Kay Grapper? Anything whatsoever?"

She gave me a haughty look. "If you'll stop interrupting after every other word, I'll get to the point. Edwina went all the way to Topeka on a Greyhound bus to attend the funeral. To her surprise, it was held in a Catholic church because Justine's husband and his family were all Catholics. In her Christmas letters to Edwina, Justine made out like she was still a Baptist."

"She was never one to spit in the very devil's teeth," murmured Ruby Bee.

"Edwina would have been heartsick," Estelle said, bobbling her head in agreement. "She's real worried that papists are scheming to take over the country. So there's Edwina, sitting in a Catholic church not knowing what she's gonna do if folks take to kneeling, and down sits a woman who introduces herself as Justine's neighbor. They get to talking afterward, and Edwina says she's come all the way from Maggody. This neighbor asks if she knows Norma Kay Hunniman. Edwina can't outsmart a whiffle-bird, but she figures out it's Norma Kay Grapper. That's when the girl says Norma Kay used to attend the very church where the funeral was held. Ain't that something?"

Although I was aware more was expected of me, all I could manage was a mildly interested expression. "So Norma Kay was a Catholic at one time. Is that it?"

Ruby Bee put her hands on her hips. "Everybody knows Catholics aren't allowed to commit suicide. They'll get kicked out of the church by the pope hisself."

"I'll make a note of that," I said. "What have you heard about any extramarital activities involving Norma Kay?"

"I'm not one to speak ill of the dead!" Estelle gasped, so offended that she snatched up a menu to fan herself.

I watched her for a moment to see if she was going to enliven the scene by toppling off the stool, then turned to Ruby Bee. "Was Norma Kay having an affair?"

"There's been talk. Do you want some breakfast?"

"I want to know the man's name."

"Bear in mind that Norma Kay never lingered in the teachers' lounge to discuss her personal affairs. When she first moved here, she joined the County Extension Homemakers and the Missionary Society, but the story is that Bur didn't like for her to go out in the evenings unless it was related to her job. I'd say Cory Jenks is a possibility, what with them working together and riding to games on the same bus."

Estelle recovered from her conveniently brief bout of the vapors. "Then again, Millicent saw John Robert Scurfpea's delivery truck parked in the side yard one Saturday when Bur was visiting Amos at the nursing home in Farberville."

"Jim Bob prefers them younger," added Ruby Bee, "but I saw him carrying Norma Kay's groceries out to her car not that long ago. He was flashing his teeth like a TV weatherman."

"What about Eddie Joe Whitbread?" Estelle said, pensively sucking on a pretzel. "I heard he changed a flat tire for Norma Kay on the road to Emmet. She'd gone to the flea market out that way and ran over a nail. She was sitting on the side of the road when Eddie Joe drove up, and she told him he'd saved her life."

Ruby Bee frowned at her. "Where'd you hear that?"

"From Eddie Joe's sister. She used to get her hair done at the Casa de Coiffure over in Hasty, but they botched her perm something awful. She used to have hair thick as a dog's back, but when she came slinking in, I could see right off the bat where great big clumps had come out."

I slid off the stool, wondering why we paid good money to the CIA when we had such talented operatives in our own backyard. "I'd better go call Harve," I said as I headed for the door. Neither one responded, being too occupied with analyzing Eddie Joe Whitbread's sister's cataclysmic experience at the Casa de Coiffure.

"I'm not in the mood to play hide-and-seek," Mrs. Twayblade said from the doorway, her foot tapping so loudly the aides in the kitchen were convinced there was a woodpecker on the roof. "I want you to tell me where

Mrs. Teasel is. According to the schedule, it's time for her crafts class. I believe they're decorating little mint cups for our Labor Day festivities."

Mrs. Teasel's roommate pulled up the covers until only the upper half of her face was visible. "Don't know where she is."

"Was she in her bed when you woke up this morning?"

"I seem to recollect she was."

Mrs. Twayblade clutched her clipboard more tightly to her chest as she struggled to maintain her professional aplomb. "No one saw her at breakfast or at any time this morning. Did she say anything to indicate she might leave the grounds?"

Mrs. Teasel's roommate pondered this for a long while, mostly to annoy Mrs. Twayblade. "She said that Malachi Hope had cured her, and since she was as good as new, there was no reason to stay here anymore. She had her purse with her when she left, but she didn't say where she was going."

"She has Alzheimer's," Mrs. Twayblade said as her stomach began to churn.

"Not anymore she doesn't. Last night that preacher told her she was cured. Tonight I'm gonna ask him do something about this dadburned gallbladder infection of mine. I wouldn't mind getting away from this place, neither. Labor Day festivities!"

Mrs. Twayblade went back to her office, locked the door, and sank down on the settee, usually reserved for bureaucrats from the state licensing office. If they found out she'd allowed a patient with Alzheimer's to wander away, they'd revoke her license in a Little Rock minute.

She began to moan in a very unprofessional fashion.

I detoured by the SuperSaver to buy a box of animal crackers for breakfast and then went to the PD. Once I'd started the coffee, I called the sheriff's office.

"Why, Arly," simpered LaBelle, "I was trying to find you all over the place earlier. I called every place I could think."

"Including Ruby Bee's Bar and Grill."

"I believe I did," she said, switching to a more cautious voice.

"And told the proprietress about the body in the gym."

"I had to explain why I was calling there. If Ruby Bee thought I was calling about something insignificant like raffle tickets to benefit the summer youth program, it might have slipped her mind."

There wasn't much point in berating LaBelle, who was notoriously loquacious when it came to potentially juicy cases. She'd been an employee since long before Hiram's barn burned, and she never complained about cigar smoke. She was also married to Harve's first cousin. "Let me speak to Harve," I said.

"He went over to the morgue to have a word with McBeen."

"What word would that be?"

She took her sweet time before she said, "Well, McBeen called over here to say there were some real suspicious marks on that poor woman's neck—and most likely not from the cord. McBeen practically came out and said it was murder!"

I told her to have Harve call me. Then I transferred my notes from the scrap of paper to a more appropriate form with spaces for names and dates and top-secret stuff like that. The chronology didn't run off the bottom of the page as yet. Malachi had received the note from Norma Kay before the revival revved up. She'd gone home at 10:00 and to the gym at 11:00. At 12:10, Malachi had arrived and found her distraught. At 12:30, he left her (presumably alive and kicking), and returned at 1:30 or so to find her in a remarkably less animated condition. If LaBelle had been accurate in her information, someone had arrived in the significant hour and murdered Norma Kay.

There were some conspicuous gaps in my scenario. Estelle had said basketball practice was at 11:00; I could talk to the girls then to find out which one had delivered Norma Kay's note to Malachi. He was the one who could tell me who, if anyone else, might have seen the note or learned of its contents. It seemed like a good place to start.

I nibbled enough animal crackers to appease the beast in my belly, found a gnawed pencil and a notebook with a few clean pages, and was halfway out the door when the telephone rang. I retraced my steps and picked up the receiver, hoping it was Harve with a more complete report from McBeen—as opposed to Ruby Bee with an update on Edwina's niece's defection to the Vatican camp.

"Chief Hanks? This is Mrs. Twayblade at the county home. How are you today?"

Our last encounter having been less than congenial, I was somewhat startled. "Fine, I suppose. Is there something I can do for you?"

She made an odd noise that might have been a laugh (on another planet, anyway). "It's a minor matter, and I'm quite sure I'm overreacting. One of our patients, a woman named Lucille Teasel, took it upon herself to go for a little stroll this morning. She has real thin white hair, a prominent overbite, and a sharp chin. I'm a teensy bit worried she might miss lunch. When you're driving around town, would you keep an eye out for her?"

"Sure. Is that all?"

The dial tone implied it was. I went outside and started to open the car door, then veered across the road, where Roy Stiver was sitting in a rocking chair in front of his antiques store, waiting like a turkey buzzard for some hapless tourist to pull up. I gave him the description of the patient and he agreed to watch for her.

Having done my duty in that regard, I drove out County 102 and up the hill to the pasture. A few men were picking up paper cups and crumpled popcorn sacks, but that was the only indication that anything had taken place there the previous night. Six more nights, I told myself as I knocked on the door of the RV.

Malachi had showered and shaved, but he still looked like something the cat wouldn't have bothered to drag in. "Have you found out anything more?" he asked me as he held open the door.

"Maybe." I went inside and sat down on a leather sofa. As Thomas Fratelleon had said, the interior was fairly spacious. He had failed to mention that it was expensively furnished—but, hey, we'd only just met. "I need to ask you some more questions about last night. What exactly did the note from Norma Kay say?"

"That she wanted me to come to the gym at midnight. It was pretty vague."

"Do you still have it?"

He considered this for a moment, then said, "After I read it, I put it in my coat pocket. Let me go in the bedroom and see if it's there."

He came back with a folded piece of paper and handed it to me. The typed message read: "Malachi, you must meet me at the gym tonight at midnight!!! He won't leave me alone—and I don't know what to do!!!" She must have been too exhausted from pounding out all the exclamation points to sign it.

I tucked it in my notebook. "One of the ushers delivered this to you before the service. Could anyone else have read it between then and midnight?"

"I don't see how," he said as he sat down at the far end of the sofa and shook his head. "I went on stage less than five minutes later. I didn't take off my coat until I got back here at eleven. Thomas came by, but he didn't go into the bedroom to rummage through my pockets."

"No one else was here? What about Seraphina and Chastity?"

"After the revival, Chastity went off with some of the local girls to get a soda, even though she wasn't supposed to go anywhere without my permission. Seraphina went to find her and bring her back."

"Did she?" I asked.

"Chastity was here when I got back a little after 12:30.

I made it clear she was in trouble and told her I'd decide on her punishment in the morning. She's been a problem since the day she came to live with us. No matter how strict I am with her, she continues to lie, steal money, and use foul language. The only thing I can see to control the girl is to arrange for her to do her schoolwork at home. That will also allow me to make sure her curriculum stresses Christian principles."

"So Seraphina and Chastity were here when you got back from the gym. I guess I'd better have a word with them."

Malachi tried to smile, but it wouldn't have fooled the most backwoods Buchanon. "According to Chastity, she and Seraphina had an argument in the car. Seraphina ordered her out of the car and said she was going for a drive to cool down. She hasn't come back. Chastity was asleep when I returned an hour ago, but she left while I was in the shower. I'm alone at the moment."

"Where do you think Seraphina might have gone? Maggody's not the sort of place where one can fade into the teeming masses or hide out under an assumed name in some fleabag hotel."

"Most likely she went into Farberville to find a hotel," he said. "She's done that sort of thing in the past when she needed to put some distance between herself and Chastity—or when she's feeling claustrophobic. Quite often after the final night of a revival, she'll check into a suite and treat herself to a leisurely soak in a Jacuzzi and room service."

I wasn't as nonchalant as he appeared to be, but it would have been premature to bring in the bloodhounds. "Let's talk some more about last night, Mr.

Hope. Did Norma Kay say anything that might have hinted at her lover's identity? Any reference to his occupation or marital status?"

"Not really. I can give you her file if you want to read her letters. She might have let something slip."

"I'll return them as soon as possible," I said without enthusiasm. If she'd really written every month for the last ten years, I was going to spend a fun-filled evening immersing myself in more than a hundred accounts of her misery. I made a mental note to buy a roll of antacids before I went home. "You drove to the gym twice last night. Did you see anyone along the way either time?"

"Do I need an alibi?"

"It wouldn't hurt," I said evenly.

He went across the room to a small table and picked up a dishearteningly thick folder. After he'd given it to me, he said, "There's a house down the road from the Grappers'. The first time I went by, a man was getting out of a blue or maybe black pickup. He jerked around when I went by. When I came back twenty minutes later, I noticed the truck was gone."

"Was it there the second time you drove to the high school?"

"I'd just seen that Norma Kay's car was not in her driveway. I was too worried about her to pay any attention."

"I'll return the folder," I said as I started for the door. "I need to talk to Seraphina—and Chastity—when they show up. If I'm not in my office, tell them to call the sheriff's department and leave a message for me."

He caught my arm. "Norma Kay committed suicide, didn't she?"

"The state lab will conduct an autopsy within a few days. In the interim, I'm just tying up some loose ends, Mr. Hope." I removed his hand from my arm and reached for the doorknob.

"I shouldn't have left her alone," he said as if I were a member of the jury. "Even though she'd calmed down, I should have realized she was still deeply troubled. Perhaps the idea of breaking off the affair was too much for her to bear—or begging her husband's forgiveness. She'd been smacked in the face recently. She gave me some transparently false story about running into a door, but I've done enough counseling to know the earmarks of physical abuse."

"We're aware of the bruise. Now, if you don't mind, I have other potential witnesses to interview. Don't forget to have Seraphina and Chastity call me."

I made it outside without any more angst-ridden outbursts. If he was telling the truth, he didn't have a motive to murder Norma Kay Grapper. Of course, I had no way of knowing if he was or not. His livelihood required the ability to convince others of his sincerity in order to divest them of their hard-earned money. The Oriental rug and brass lamps in the RV indicated he was talented.

Thomas Fratelleon was waiting beside my car. "Malachi told me about that woman's suicide," he said. "I feel partially responsible. She was desperate to talk to him, but I refused and hung up abruptly. I wish I'd listened more carefully to her."

"Did she say anything about why she wanted to have a session with Malachi?"

He gestured at the folder. "No, but I glanced at some

of her most recent letters. The fact that she was unable to put a stop to her infidelity had become an obsession, as you'll see. Norma Kay Grapper was a tortured soul; if Malachi had suggested that she flagellate herself until she passed out from the pain, she would have asked where to buy the leather strap."

"On a less theatrical note, did Malachi suggest she see a psychiatrist?"

Fratelleon hesitated. "I'm sure he would have if he'd suspected how mentally disturbed she was, Miss Hanks. He must have felt that her problems were spiritual in nature and could be cured through prayer. Malachi has helped many people over the years; we have boxes and boxes of letters thanking him. From First Corinthians: 'For to one is given by the Spirit the word of wisdom; to another the word of knowledge by the same Spirit; to another faith by the same Spirit; to another the working of miracles.' Malachi has been blessed with all four."

"He said you came by the RV after the revival," I said, changing the subject before I bashed him with the folder.

"I dropped off the cash and checks, then went to bed."

"Did you hear Seraphina drive up shortly thereafter?"

He regarded me soberly. "I was listening to classical music on my transistor radio, but I thought I heard a car door slam perhaps five minutes after Malachi left. Assuming Seraphina had been successful in her mission to fetch Chastity, I did not put on a robe and go outside to investigate."

"Did Malachi tell you that Seraphina spent the night elsewhere?"

"She did the same thing three nights last month when

we were in Texas and Oklahoma. There are times when she finds the RV too confining, and at Malachi's insistence, goes off to find a lavish suite."

"She won't find one in Farberville," I said. "Do you have any idea where Chastity went this morning?"

"I was unaware she left until Malachi told me a few minutes ago. I was supervising the cleanup crew and deliveries. Our turnout last night was unexpectedly—" He broke off as Joey Lerner came out of the tent, a backpack slung across his shoulder and a duffel bag in his hand. "Excuse me, Miss Hanks," he said, his forehead wrinkling. "I need to have a word with my young friend."

So did I, so I tagged along. Joey had climbed onto his motorcycle by the time we reached him. He held up his hand and said, "Don't bother, Thomas. I'm out of here."

"Out of here?" Thomas echoed, stopping so abruptly I stepped on his heel. "Whatever do you mean?"

"I'm leaving—okay? When I have an address, I'll let you know so you can send a check. I'm not in the mood to hang around while you figure out what you owe me."

He looked more in the mood to start throwing punches. I gave Fratelleon a chance to do something other than stare at Joey, then said, "I have some questions for you before you go. Would you please come sit in the car with me?"

"Go ahead and ask them right here."

"Okay," I said, doubting I could drag him off the motorcycle without unduly endangering myself. "Why are you leaving so hastily?"

"Seraphina fired me last night."

Fratelleon was still in his echo mode. "Fired you?"

"That's right. Five minutes after the show was over,

she came out to the van and told me I was fired. Good-bye, Thomas. I hope you end up on that Caribbean island you keep talking about in your sleep."

"You can't leave like this. What about the show? You're the only one who can handle all the special effects. You're vital to the operation, Joey; we can't continue without you. Please don't do this."

"Tell it to Seraphina."

Fratelleon put his hand on Joey's back. "Please wait here until I speak with Malachi. I'm quite certain he can persuade Seraphina to forget whatever it was that upset her and ask you to stay. Perhaps I can arrange for an increase in your salary and a paid vacation next week while we're finalizing the property sale."

"You can go talk to him," Joey said, dropping the duffel bag and rocking back on the seat of the motorcycle. He watched Thomas scurry across the trampled grass to the RV, then lit a cigarette and looked at me. "Any more questions?"

"Why did she fire you?"

"Hell, I don't know."

"You don't know?" I said, allowing derision to taint my voice like a strep infection. "Didn't you bother to ask her?"

"I asked her, sure, but she was so mad I thought she was going to assault me. I got my ass out of there and went into Farberville. Everything there was closed, so I just cruised around the county until I cooled off. She and Malachi both have weird ideas about their positions in the heavenly hierarchy. Maybe she decided she no longer needs any mortal assistance to float down from the rafters in a pink cloud. She'll have a tough time finding someone else to run the show, though. Even Jesus might have trouble with the synthesizer."

"Do you handle all the special effects by yourself?" I asked.

"Everything's linked to a computer in a van behind the tent. All I do is run the programs and listen for indications something's not working properly."

Malachi came out of the RV. "Joey!" he called. "I beg you come talk this over. It doesn't matter why Seraphina said whatever she did—and I'll make sure that she apologizes later today. You're absolutely vital to the operation. There's no way we can go on tonight without you!"

Joey climbed off the motorcycle and gave me a sly smile. "Guess I'll see what they're offering in terms of a raise."

I had more questions, but he swaggered away before I could blurt them out. At this point, there was no particular reason to link him with what had taken place in the gym or doubt his account of where he'd been after the revival. It sounded as though he'd be around later, I decided as I went to my car, and I'd never been much help in delicate labor negotiations.

Besides, I had other fish to fry. The very thought reminded me of the inadequacy of my breakfast, so I headed for the Dairee Dee-Lishus.

9

Estelle chewed on a pencil as she read the list in front of her. "How about Fergie Bidens? He ain't much to look at, but he's been known to sniff around divorcées and widows."

"Norma Kay was married," Ruby Bee said, "and Fergie's too much of a yellowbelly to risk messing with Bur Grapper. He's not a likely candidate, but I suppose you can add his name to the list."

"That's makes six, and we have no way of knowing if she was carrying on with someone from another town."

"We have to start somewhere."

Frowning, Estelle put down the pencil and took a sip of sherry. "How do you plan to go about this? None of these fellows is gonna cotton to being asked if he was having an affair with a married woman—much less with a murder victim. That John Robert Scurfpea is meaner than a coyote in a steel trap, and Lewis Ferncliff spends more time in the county jail than he does at home. I hear they reserve a cell for him every Saturday night—and he ends up checking in more often than not."

"I'm aware of their reputations," said Ruby Bee. "I never said we ought to flat-out ask them. I just thought we could help Arly by giving her a list of suspects."

"Just because one of these fellows was having an affair with Norma Kay doesn't make him a murderer."

Ruby Bee went into the kitchen to stir the turnip greens while she mulled this over. "The way I see it," she said as she came back into the barroom, flushed with triumph, "is that Malachi Hope convinced Norma Kay to break off the affair. He left her sitting right there by the telephone. She called the man and told him how the cow ate the cabbage. He was so upset that he went to the gym, strangled her, and left her dangling from the backboard so everybody'd think it was suicide."

"Or," Estelle said slowly, "she called Bur Grapper and confessed to him."

Ruby Bee preferred her own theory, but she pretended to weigh this alternative before shaking her head. "You can add him if you want, but I still think it was her lover. Most likely he's married and got all worried about Norma Kay confessing her sin in front of everybody at the revival, including his wife."

"It sure wouldn't sit well with Bur Grapper if Norma Kay made a fool of him in front of his neighbors and former players. His family has lived in these parts since God made little green apples. Do you recall how his sister wrote that pamphlet about their family history and had copies printed up? Why on earth she thought any of the rest of us cared about her dead kinfolk was a mystery to me."

Ruby Bee grinned. "I heard she did it to prove there weren't any Buchanons in the family tree."

"Bur Grapper might have killed his wife to protect the family's reputation." Estelle printed his name in large letters at the bottom of the page. "I don't guess we have any proof, though. If he'd been someplace where Norma Kay had to call him long-distance, the telephone company would have a record."

"Let me look at the list, Estelle. Maybe there's a way we could eliminate some of these suspects so Arly doesn't have to waste time barking at the moon. When she starts investigating a crime, I always worry she'll get so frustrated that she'll quit her job and move away to some sorry excuse for a place like Manhattan—or Washington, D.C. It's been a long while since she had herself a beau. As her mother, I can tell she's harboring some feelings for that IRS fellow. She may not know it, but I sure do."

"How do you aim to eliminate some of the suspects?" asked Estelle, politely ignoring the catch in Ruby Bee's voice.

Ruby Bee made herself quit thinking about painful prospects. "For starters, Fergie's married, so his wife might be able to give him an alibi for the time of the murder. Same with Eddie Joe and Lewis. No woman in her right mind would have John Robert, but he might have had company."

"Are you crossing out Jim Bob?"

"No, but I can't see us asking Mrs. Jim Bob if she and her husband were sharing a bed last night. I wouldn't be surprised if she makes him sleep in the laundry room or the garage."

"You heard any more about the bingo games at the Assembly Hall?"

"Only that she's going ahead with them even though not one soul showed up yesterday evening, leaving her and Brother Verber by themselves. I wonder which of them won the Mr. Coffee?"

"Why don't you ask her after you finish asking her for the details of her sex life?"

Ruby Bee snatched up the list. "I reckon I'll close up for an hour this afternoon and drop by Fergie's house to visit with Leslie. If I have time, I can do the same with Lewis's wife. Eddie Joe's sister lives with them. You can run by to see if she's having more problems with her hair. She might have heard the phone ring or know if Eddie Joe left the house around midnight."

"Licensed cosmetologists don't make house calls."

"Then take her some strawberry jam, for pity's sake."

Estelle plucked the list out of Ruby Bee's hand and tapped it with the pencil. "What about Cory Jenks, John Robert Scurfpea, and Bur Grapper?"

"I'll think of something," Ruby Bee said, sighing as she imagined Arly packing her bags and arranging for a ride to the bus station in Farberville to purchase a one-way ticket.

A dozen girls were standing beside the gym, their bleak expressions indicating that they knew about their coach's death. I parked in a patch of shade and walked across the gravel to join them.

"How did you all hear about it?" I asked.

Heather Reilly cleared her throat. "I was just now telling them. My sister's boyfriend called this morning. He works at the hospital, and he was mopping the floor in the basement when they—" She covered her face with her hands and began to whimper. The other girls circled her, patting her back and murmuring inanities.

I realized I needed to distract them before they all burst into tears. I didn't believe for an instant that they had been overly fond of Norma Kay, but they were young enough to be frightened by the sudden proximity of violence and death. "I have some questions for you," I said loudly and with enough authority to get their teary-eyed attention. "Last night right before the revival began, one of you delivered a note to Malachi Hope. Who was it?"

Darla Jean McIlhaney emerged from the circle. "I did. Coach Grapper pressed an envelope in my hand and told me to go give it to him. She said it in a low voice so Mr. Grapper couldn't hear her, but he stared real hard at me."

"Did you read what was in it?"

She gave me an offended look. "That'd be like reading someone's letters or diary."

"Did you tell anyone else?"

"I didn't know how to go about finding him, so I asked Heather what she thought," Darla Jean said, squirming as if admitting to some petty crime.

"That's right," said Heather. "I said I supposed he'd be in the back of the tent where they have all the sound equipment and stuff. I offered to go with her, but then one of the old folks started screeching at me to move her wheelchair closer to the stage."

I turned back to Darla Jean. "So what happened?"

"I went down the side aisle and behind the curtain. Mr. Hope was talking to an old guy with glasses. I was kinda nervous about interrupting, so I just stood there waiting for them to notice me. After a minute, Chastity appeared from the back and came over to where I was. She was wearing a long white gown, droopy wings made out of fabric, and a lopsided halo. She looked pissed, but she usually does. We whispered for a minute, and then Mr. Hope finished talking to the man. I gave him the envelope and went back to being an usher."

"What about Chastity?" I asked.

"He told her to go out to the van and get Seraphina to adjust her halo. I had to bite my lip to keep from giggling."

None of the other girls had any reservations about giggling. I gave them a moment and then asked Darla Jean if she'd seen Malachi open the note.

"Yeah," she said, "he read it, put it in his pocket, and went out the way Chastity had gone."

"How did he seem when he read the note?"

She squeezed her eyes closed for a moment, then blinked at me. "I don't know how to describe it exactly. I guess I'd say he looked thoughtful and a little annoyed like my ma does when she's making a new recipe."

I'd been hoping for something along the lines of a fiendish sneer or an outburst of profanity. "Did any of the rest of you speak to Mrs. Grapper?"

They pretty much agreed she'd nodded or spoken curtly to all of them before the overhead lights had dimmed and all kinds of strange and amazing things started happening onstage. I couldn't make much sense out of what they were saying, but I nodded until they ran out of hyperbole.

"I understand Chastity left with some of you," I said. "Who, what time, and where did you go?"

Darla Jean waggled her fingers. "She was out in the parking lot at about ten, dressed in regular clothes. She went with me, Heather, and Traci to the Dairee Dee-Lishus. Not long after that, the guys showed up, and we were just hanging out talking about the miracles when Seraphina drove up and told Chastity to get her ass in the car."

"She was madder than a stuck pig," said one of the Dahlton twins, "and drops of spit was flying out of her mouth. Chastity got up off the picnic table and climbed into the car without saying a word."

"It was a little after eleven," volunteered the other twin. "I happened to notice 'cause we were supposed to be home by then. We got in all kinds of trouble, even though it wasn't a school night."

"We got grounded," said the first.

I gave Darla Jean a hard look. "Have you seen Chastity since then?"

"No, ma'am," she said so quickly that I suspected she'd been anticipating the question.

"Are you positive?" I persisted in my best cop voice (which, to be honest, isn't very good).

Heather stepped in front of her. "This morning me and Darla Jean went into Farberville to shop, and we didn't get back here until half an hour ago. Chastity must have heard about Coach Grapper and figured there wouldn't be practice. Do you know when the funeral's gonna be?"

"Not for a few days," I said. "You all had better go home now." I waited until they'd drifted away into various vehicles and then tried the gym door. It was locked, so I walked around to the main entrance. A sign taped to the door announced that all meetings and planning sessions were canceled for the day out of respect for Norma Kay. I peered through the glass door, but the hallways were dark and uninhabited.

I was walking back to my car and grumbling about the necessity of driving to the sheriff's office to get a key to the gym when a dark blue pickup parked near my car. Cory Jenks glanced incuriously at me as he got out, then took out a key and moved toward the door.

"Wait a second!" I called. "You can't go in there."

"Why not?"

"Haven't you heard what happened?"

He gave me an embarrassed smile, but it did little to brighten his distinctly wan pallor. "I drank so much beer last night that I forgot to set my alarm. When I finally woke up, I took a shower, got dressed, and came straight up here on the double to meet with the principal so he can approve the budget." For the first time he seemed to notice there were no other vehicles in the lot. "Norma Kay's supposed to be having practice now. Where is everybody?"

"Norma Kay's body was found in the gym last night," I said.

His jaw sank until it bumped his chest. "Norma Kay? Are you sure . . . ?"

"I'm sure," I said, then described the scene, carefully omitting any references to Malachi.

He clamped a hand over his mouth and staggered

around the corner of the gym. Retching noises persuaded me to wait where I was rather than go charging after him to make sure he didn't escape into the brush. The noises eventually subsided and he returned, his eyes wet and his skin as green as a dollar bill.

"Did I mention I have a hangover?" he said weakly. "I guess I just wasn't prepared for—for what you said. Gawd, I saw her last night at the revival. Bur was with her, but if she was that upset, she could have found a way to say something to me. What was she doing up here that late? Who found her?"

"I think we'd better discuss all this in your office," I said. "Go ahead and unlock the door."

He recoiled as if I'd told him to yank open a drawer at the morgue. "I don't think it'd be fitting for us to talk about Norma Kay in the next room when she hasn't even been buried."

"I'm in charge of the investigation, so I get to say where we talk. It's hot out here, and it's possible sightseers will drive by. Just unlock the door—okay?"

Cory did as ordered, although he kept his head down as we walked across the gym, our shoes squeaking like frightened mice. I told him to wait in his office and went into Norma Kay's office. As I'd recalled, there was a typewriter on a table off to one side of the room. I sorted through the clutter on her desk until I found a typed team roster. Wishing I had a magnifying glass, I compared it with the note she'd sent to Malachi, and concluded that the letters were as identical as the Dahlton twins. I put both in my notebook, switched off the light, and went into Cory Jenks's office.

He dropped something into a desk drawer and gazed

up at me with an innocent expression. It might have been more convincing if a trickle of whiskey had not been visible at the corner of his mouth. "I don't know how I can be of any help," he said, drying his lip with the cuff of his gray sweatshirt. "Like I said, I saw her last night but she didn't say anything to indicate she was planning to take her life. She's been acting kind of weird ever since Malachi Hope arrived in town, but it never occurred to me she was . . ."

I opened the notebook and wrote his name at the top of a nice, clean page. "You attended the revival with her and Bur. Is that correct?"

"Yeah, and afterward we walked down the hill and said good night at the end of their yard. I went on home, but then I started getting thirsty, so I drove over to Emmet to see if I could scrounge up some beer on a Sunday. I was way too successful, I'm afraid."

"What time did you get back from Emmet?"

"A little bit after midnight."

That coincided with Malachi's remark about seeing a figure next to a dark pickup. I made a note of the time, then said, "Did you go out again last night or early this morning?"

"No, I just watched old movies and drank beer."

"Alone, I suppose." I waited until he nodded. "So if a witness claimed your truck wasn't in your driveway half an hour later, that witness would be lying—right?"

He shrugged. "I was home, watching television."

"You can see the Grappers' yard from your porch. When you got back from Emmet, did you happen to notice that Norma Kay's car was gone?"

"I was thinking about other things."

"Like where Malachi Hope was going at such a late hour."

"I saw the Cadillac, if that's what you're talking about, but I didn't know who was driving it and I sure as hell didn't care where it was going." He uncurled his fingers and rocked back in the chair, his arms crossed and his face stony. He would have made a dandy school-yard bully—or Mafia enforcer. "Is that all?"

"Oh, I have a few more questions. Were you aware Norma Kay often came here late at night to work?"

"Yeah, but she was always real careful. A couple of years back some jerks got into the gym and spray painted obscenities on the walls of the locker room. She made sure she locked the door whenever she was here by herself."

"You have a key," I said.

"Yeah, I have a key, but I already told you that I didn't go out again after I got back from Emmet."

"One more question," I said. "How long have you been sleeping with Norma Kay?"

He came close to tipping over backward but caught himself at the fateful second and regained his balance. He did not regain his composure, alas. "What's that sup-posed to mean? I know there's been some gossip, but that doesn't give you any call to accuse me of that! We worked together. That's all we did, and anyone who can prove otherwise is a damned liar!"

"Were you here Friday morning?"

"I got here at eight and spent the morning on the phone, trying to cut a better deal on warm-up jackets. The vice-principal came by with my class schedule, and the boys that were doing inventory in the equipment room interrupted me every ten minutes with stupid questions. Were you planning to accuse me of holding up a liquor store or something?"

I stood up. "Give me the key to the gym, then gather up what you need to work elsewhere. This building is off-limits until we complete the investigation."

He stomped around the room, cursing under his breath as he grabbed notebooks and folders, then followed me outside and glared at me while I locked the door. I doubted I would receive a complimentary season pass to root for the Marauders.

"Don't leave town," I said as I pocketed the key. The shade had shifted, and my car was hotter than a kiln. However, being a stoic, I did not wince as I slid into the driver's side.

Jim Bob was fantasizing about a white beach and skimpy bikinis when the office door opened. "What do you want?" he said without looking up.

Kevin shuffled into the office. "I got to take the afternoon off, Jim Bob. It's real important."

"So's the presidential election, but you don't see me making a sign to stick in my front yard. You know damn well we're shorthanded today. Get back to work."

"But I have to take Dahlia to the clinic," Kevin said, bug-eyed with desperation. "Otherwise, she's gonna start eating pork chops and chocolate cake."

Jim Bob reluctantly let the last bikini fade away. "Dahlia's been eating pork chops and chocolate cake since she was three days old. She probably hasn't missed a day of eating pork chops and chocolate cake since then—and I don't know why today should be any different. Now how many times do I have to tell you to get back to work before it sinks into your pimple of a brain?"

"I cain't." Kevin collapsed into a chair and tried to keep hisself from bawling like a calf. "I got to take Dahlia to the clinic so the doctor can see if she still has diabetes. She swears she tingled—"

"I don't want to hear how she tingled," Jim Bob said, "any more than I want to listen to your pitiful whining. Take the goddamn day off and get your sorry ass out of my sight."

"Gee, thanks," Kevin said, leaping up so quickly he came near tumping the wastebasket. "I promise I won't ask for another day off ever again. I'll come in early and work late. You won't be sorry, Jim Bob."

Jim Bob was sorry he'd ever hired Kevin in the first place, but familial pressure had been applied. "Now what?" he growled as Kevin hovered in the doorway.

"Mrs. Jim Bob came into the store earlier while you was out on the loading dock. She was carrying on something fierce. I jest thought you'd want to know." Having done his duty, he started to close the door.

"Wait a minute, asshole! Why was she carrying on?"

"I don't rightly know. It might have been because she couldn't find any extension cords and was gonna have to drive to Farberville to get some."

Jim Bob was relieved she hadn't appropriated the remaining Mr. Coffees, but he was also perplexed. "Did she say why she needs extension cords?"

Kevin sucked on his lip as he did his best to recollect

what all she'd said. "Nope," he said at last. "She just said she couldn't believe there weren't any extension cords anywhere in the store, then told me to stop staring at her like she was a two-headed chicken. I ain't never seen a two-headed chicken, but I guess if I chanced across one, I'd be right bumfuzzled. Wouldn't you, Jim Bob? I'd call one of those tabloids so they could—"

"Get out of here," Jim Bob said, although without the exasperation that usually entered his voice when speaking to Kevin. Extension cords?

"I think I can make a case," I said to Harve, who'd called with the results of the preliminary report. Any lingering hopes that Norma Kay had committed suicide had been vanquished; the contusions and abrasions on her neck indicated she'd been manually strangled. The bruise from the slipknot was slight, indicating she'd been dead before the cord was put around her neck. The image was ghoulish, to put it mildly.

"Against who?"

"Cory Jenks," I said, looking down at the chronology I'd written earlier and appended when I arrived at the PD. "He's the most likely choice for her lover. He denied it, but I'll bet the basketball players were aware of the affair. They must have felt it was to their advantage not to spread it around and find themselves on separate buses."

"Teenagers keeping their traps shut?" Harve said doubtfully. "I ain't run across one of those in a long time. There was a kid over in Bugscuffle who busted into a car to steal the stereo system, then bragged about it in his homeroom the next day. We picked him up while he was eating tacos in the cafeteria."

"I'll talk to some of the players," I said, writing down Darla Jean's name and drawing a circle around it. "Cory admits he was in his office Friday morning when Malachi showed up. He could have overheard Norma Kay begging Malachi to give her the courage to end the affair and publicly confess."

"That's not much of a motive."

"I didn't say I *had* a case, Harve—I said I thought I could make one. The body was discovered less than twelve hours ago, and this is not an episode from a TV detective show. Give me a break, okay?" I took a deep breath, then continued. "Cory may have seen Norma Kay hand the note to the usher and guessed what was going on, or she may have warned him in advance of her intentions to ask Malachi to meet her later. In either case, he saw the Cadillac come down the hill and head toward town. He could have followed it to the gym, waited across the road until Malachi left, and gone inside to try to reason with Norma Kay. When he realized she was too determined to listen to him, he strangled her. He's already admitted he was drinking; that may have been a factor. What's more, both he and Bur were adamant that Norma Kay would have locked the gym door for security reasons. Cory has a key."

"Can you place his truck anywhere in the vicinity of the high school after midnight?"

"Not yet, but I will," I said with more conviction than I felt. Harve might have reservations about Cory's guilt, but I was proud of my theory. "I'm going to talk to the players, and then I'll start questioning people who live near the high school. Why don't you send a deputy to the Dew Drop Inn in Emmet to find out what time Cory left there?"

"You reckon that's where he bought beer?"

"Come on, Harve, you raid the joint every election year, close it down, and get your photograph on the front page of the newspaper. Where else do you think he could buy beer on Sunday?"

"Okay, I'll send Les over there this afternoon. If nothing else, it'll scare the piss out of the owner. What you've got is circumstantial at best and flimsy at worst."

I was about to protest, when the front door flew open and Ruby Bee skittered into the room.

"Call an ambulance!" she shrieked.

"Hang on," I said into the receiver, then frowned at Ruby Bee. "What's going on?"

"There's been an accident right in front of the bar and grill. I could have called the ambulance from there, but I thought I'd kill two birds with one stone by coming here to tell you. Don't just sit there like you're glued to the chair—call an ambulance!"

10

HARVE agreed to make the call. I grabbed Ruby Bee's arm and propelled her outside, where pedestrians were gathering in the middle of the road. Traffic was already snarled up in both directions. "Who's involved?" I said as we hurried toward the scene.

"Lottie Estes," Ruby Bee panted. "She ran over some little old lady. I think she lives out at the county home. The old lady, I mean. Lottie lives on Coot Road."

"I know where Lottie lives." I pushed through the crowd and saw Estelle kneeling next to a supine figure partially covered by a jacket. "How badly is she hurt?" I demanded.

"She's mostly shook up and bruised. I'm just trying to keep her quiet until the ambulance gets here. If she's not in shock, she should be."

"I'm so sorry," wailed Lottie Estes, stumbling forward. She put her fist to her mouth and stared down with wide, horrified eyes.

Ruby Bee put her arm around Lottie's shoulders and

eased her out of the crowd. I looked down at the victim, who was conscious if somewhat confused. White hair and an overbite, I noted as I gave her an encouraging smile, then found Lottie and Ruby Bee next to a beige Edsel.

"What happened, Lottie?" I asked.

"I don't know. I went out to the high school earlier, but it was locked and nobody was there. I sat in the parking lot for the longest time, waiting for everybody to arrive for the teachers' meeting. Finally, I gave up and left, although I couldn't for the life of me imagine why no one was there."

"You didn't see the sign on the door?"

"I can't say that I did. I decided to stop by the Super-Saver and pick up a few things. All of a sudden that poor woman was right there in the middle of the street. I swerved, but I'm afraid I knocked her down. She's going to be all right, isn't she?"

"Of course, she is," Ruby Bee said soothingly. "It was an accident that could have happened to any of us."

"I disagree," I said, earning a sharp look from Ruby Bee and a startled one from Lottie. "If you'd been wearing your glasses, you would have seen the sign at the school—and Mrs. Teasel when she started across the street. Why aren't you wearing them?"

Instead of answering, she leaned against her car and began to sob. Ruby Bee patted her on the back, then turned to me and in a low voice, said, "She isn't wearing her glasses because Malachi Hope cured her astigmatism last night. He told her to come up on the stage, put his hands on her shoulders, and prayed that Jesus should restore her vision. He carried on until I thought he was going to blow her off the stage. Then he announced that she was cured, and she fell backward into Seraphina's arms."

"That's it?" I said. "Somebody ought to give him a shot at the federal deficit."

"This is not the time for wisecracks, Miss Glib Lips. After Seraphina got Lottie steadied on her feet, she told Lottie to throw away her glasses and prove she was cured by reading the Twenty-third Psalm. Lottie took a card and read it, although she was so choked up that it was hard to hear her."

"Lottie Estes could recite the Twenty-third Psalm while undergoing a triple bypass. For that matter, so could you." I looked up as I heard a siren. "I don't want Lottie to drive until she either replaces her glasses or has her eyes tested by a professional. Can you take her home and fix her some tea?"

"I'll see to her. You might drop by the bar later and find out what else went on last night at the revival. Malachi Hope performed more than one so-called miracle."

"Hallelujah," I said as I went to speak to the paramedics, get traffic rolling, and call the county home.

"That comes to two hundred and eighty-six dollars and seventeen cents," the clerk said, wishing her manager would come back from lunch and deal with this unbalanced woman who'd just about cleared three shelves—and here it was only August.

Mrs. Jim Bob slapped down a credit card.

Joey came out of the tent in time to see Chastity get out of a battered car with fins high enough to scrape an underpass. The car itself dishonored the entire automotive industry.

"Thanks for the lift, Arnie," she said to the unseen driver and waved as the car careened back toward the road. Then she came across the pasture. "Where's Malachi?"

"He and Thomas went into Farberville to look for Seraphina. They're worried about her, so they decided to cruise by some motels and restaurant parking lots in hopes of spotting her car. Where have you been?"

"Around."

Joey grimaced. "You'd better come up with a more plausible explanation by the time Malachi gets back. He raised all kinds of hell about you taking off this morning while he was in the shower. If I were you, I'd think twice before I did something calculated to infuriate him."

"I don't give a shit about him," Chastity said, pushing back her bangs and staring angrily at the road that led down the hill. "And I don't give a shit about Seraphina, either."

"What happened between you and her last night?"

She went past him into the tent and sat down on the end of a metal bench. "She yelled at me, so I yelled back at her. When we got here, she practically shoved me out of her car and told me she was going for a drive to cool off."

"She was in a real bad mood," Joey said, sitting

across from her. "Right after the show, she stormed into the van and fired me, but I had enough sense to wait until this morning to make my dramatic exit. Malachi ended up having to double my salary." He took a pack of cigarettes out of his pocket and lit one, wondering what Chastity was up to.

Instead of asking the obvious question, she extended her hand. "Gimme one, Joey."

"Get rid of it damn fast if you hear a car coming," he said as he handed her the pack and a lighter. "Did you hear about the basketball coach killing herself last night?"

"I heard about it." She lit a cigarette, dropped the pack and lighter, and walked out of the tent.

Joey watched her until she'd disappeared down the hill. Agreeing to stay might have been a bad decision, he thought as he finished his cigarette. When he took a vacation next week, he might take off for Mexico and points south. The five-thousand-dollar bonus he'd demanded to stay through the weekend could buy a lot of enchiladas.

Darla Jean was staring at the dashboard, her expression reminiscent of a possum paralyzed by headlights. I got back in the car, handed her a cherry limeade, and said, "Do you want to stay here and talk, or go for a drive?"

"Not here," she whispered. "Somebody'll see us."

I pulled away from the Dairee Dee-Lishus and turned north. If Darla Jean was responsive, we might not make it all the way to the Missouri line, but I had a full tank of gas and as much time as it took.

As we passed the remains of Purtle's Esso, I said, "Where would you like to begin, Darla Jean?"

"I'd like to begin by asking you to turn around and take me back to my car, but I don't guess that's going to happen anytime soon."

"How about Chastity's current whereabouts?"

"She called me this morning, all upset, and begged me to give her a ride to Farberville. Heather and I picked her up by the low-water bridge around nine."

"Did you bring her back?"

"No, she insisted that we let her out on Thurber Street, down at the railroad tracks. She said she'd hitch a ride back when she was ready. The last I saw of her, she was walking up the hill in the direction of the college campus."

"Did she say where she was going or what she was going to do?"

Darla Jean slurped the last of her drink before she answered. "We asked her, of course, but she told us to shut up. She can be pretty hateful when she's a mind to."

"And after you were nice enough to give her a ride," I said. "I don't know why you put up with her."

"Well, we're just about her only friends, and I feel sorry for her having to live in that RV and sleep on a sofa and be bossed around all the time like she's a little kid. She's nearly sixteen, but Malachi won't let her learn to drive or date or do anything except stand up on the stage in an angel costume and make a fool of herself. She tried to run away once, but he sent a private detective after her. I'd have been so humiliated I would have died."

"Is that what she's doing today?" I asked, watching Darla Jean as best I could while navigating the narrow road. It occurred to me that it might be wise to find a wide shoulder and pull over before I plowed into a chicken truck. "Did she take a suitcase with her?"

"She's not running away."

"What *is* she doing?"

"I told you that she wouldn't say," Darla Jean muttered as she crumpled the cup and dropped it onto the floorboard of the car. It fit in nicely with the existing decor (twentieth-century landfill). "I don't understand why you're so concerned about Chastity. Going into Farberville isn't against the law, is it?"

"Not that I know of," I said mildly. "Nor is having an affair when you're married, but I wouldn't recommend it. It can lead to divorce—or even murder."

"Murder?"

"Coach Grapper didn't hang herself. Someone strangled her and hung her body on the steel supports that hold up the backboard." I took a breath and went in for the kill, metaphorically speaking. I wasn't especially proud of myself, but I needed to jolt Darla Jean into a more forthright disposition. "Her face was beet red, and her eyes were bulged out. Her feet were dangling about three inches off the floor."

"Stop the car! I'm gonna be sick!"

It probably wouldn't have been a catastrophe, considering the debris on the floorboard, but I pulled over. Before I'd come to a full stop, Darla Jean scrambled out of the car and fell to her knees in the yellowed weeds. I waited for a moment, then grabbed a handful of napkins from the glove compartment and took them to her.

"Better?" I said.

"Yeah," she said as she cleaned her face and stood up. "How could somebody do something awful like that? Coach Grapper could be mean sometimes, but she was just doing her job. We were third in the conference last year, and we won the tournament down in Pine Bluff."

"Her credentials weren't the cause of death. She was having an affair with Cory Jenks, and you and your teammates knew it." So I was bluffing. I'm a firm believer in the "the end justifies the means" school of thought, and I was after a murderer, not a bowling trophy.

Darla Jean looked as if she might repeat her performance of a few minutes earlier. "Did Coach Jenks kill her?"

I crossed my fingers and said, "I doubt it. All I'm trying to do is get an idea of what was happening in Coach Grapper's life. But it's really important that you stay quiet until I've finished my investigation, so please don't repeat what I said about her being murdered. You know how garbled gossip can become, especially when it's gruesome like this. Now tell me what you know about Coach Jenks and Coach Grapper."

Ten minutes later, I had the story—or at least what Darla Jean suspected had taken place between Norma Kay and Cory in motel rooms and cabins during the previous basketball season. The county prosecutor wouldn't be eager to file charges based on what amounted to adolescent speculation, however, and it sounded as if the two had been discreet enough to avoid being seen slipping in and out of each other's rooms in the wee hours.

She looked so dejected that I didn't ask any more questions as we returned to Maggody. I made her promise not to say anything about the murder, dropped her off near her station wagon, and went to the PD to call Harve with an update. I was opening the door when Kevin Buchanon drove up and almost fell on his face in his haste to get out of the car. (Buchanons are mechanically challenged.)

"Arly! You got to do something!" he gasped, his arms waving like branches in a windstorm. "You got to come with me!"

"I do?" I continued inside, ascertained that the air conditioner was producing a cool if placid breeze, and sat behind my desk, where I was in less danger of being knocked over by his frenzied outburst.

"It's all that Malachi Hope feller's fault! Now she's bakin' a cake and eatin' cookies and drinkin' orange soda pop. I been on my knees in the kitchen for over an hour, but I cain't make her stop, and when I told her I was gonna make her go to the clinic iff'n I had to drag her like a skinned mule carcass, she liked to—"

"Stop," I said as the telephone rang, "but hold that thought." I picked up the receiver. "Arly Hanks."

"I was beginning to wonder if I'd ever track you down," LaBelle said accusingly. "You really should stay in your office more, Arly. It's bad enough around here without me having to call you back over and over—"

"Hold that thought," I said to her, put my hand over the mouthpiece, and looked at Kevin. "You have five seconds to tell me what's wrong. Go."

"Dahlia sez Malachi Hope cured her of diabetes and she don't have to stay on her diet. I made an appointment at the clinic, but—"

I pointed a finger at the door. "Time's up. If you want, you can wait outside for me and we'll discuss this further." I removed my hand and said, "Why have you been calling me over and over, LaBelle?"

"Harve wants you to meet him out on County 102, about a quarter mile past the low-water bridge."

"Should I bring a fishing pole and a bucket of bait?"

"You shouldn't joke about these things," she said in a hushed voice. "Some kids playing in the woods found a car, and there's a dead body in it."

"Did you and Fergie happen to be watching television last night at 12:30?" Ruby Bee asked as she took a swallow of iced tea and smiled brightly.

Leslie Bidens wasn't sure what all to make of her unexpected visitor, who'd never before stopped by in the middle of the afternoon—or any other time, for that matter. At best they had a nodding acquaintance. "No, Fergie has to be at work at seven o'clock, so we always turn in early. Why?"

It was a poser. Ruby Bee hastily finished her tea and picked up her handbag. "There was a real amusing commercial, that's all. I happened to see it and was just wondering if you and Fergie did, too."

"What kind of commercial?"

"A real amusing commercial. I suppose I'd better be running along, Leslie. Thank you kindly for the tea."

Once she was safely outside, Ruby Bee paused to think about the exchange. Leslie had said they *always* turned in early, but she hadn't specifically said they'd done so last night. And she'd looked suspicious, even worried, as if she had an inkling of the significance of the time.

She made a cryptic note (in case her copy of the list fell into the wrong hands) next to Fergie's name, checked the time, and drove out Finger Lane to find out if Lewis Ferncliff's wife, Besseya, was home.

Across town, Estelle was faring better. As she sat in Eddie Joe Whitbread's driveway, she drew a heavy line, and then another for good measure, right through his name. Once Kirsten had stopped blubbering about her hair and thanking Estelle for doing everything humanly possible short of shaving her head, she'd admitted that she was up until well after two, talking to her boyfriend who lived in Starley City and was in the process of divorcing his third wife. There was no way Eddie Joe could have gotten a phone call from the president of the United States, much less from Norma Kay.

Estelle considered her next move. Ruby Bee had said she'd think of a way to question Mrs. Jim Bob, and she was welcome to try. John Robert Scurfpea could wait until she and Ruby Bee could go together. The only other name on the list was Cory Jenks. The high school was closed and the gym locked, so it was possible she might catch him at home. There was a small problem of what

to say to him if she did, but she figured she'd think of
something by the time she got there.

"The total's three hundred and sixteen dollars," the
clerk said, warily keeping an eye on his customer. The
last time someone like this had come into the store, a
weapon had been brandished and the cash register
drawer cleaned out. "And fifty-five cents," he added.

Mrs. Jim Bob slapped down a credit card.

"What do you have, Harve?" I asked as I walked
down the edge of the road.

Sweat had spread across his shirt like an oil slick,
turning the khaki fabric dark. He pulled off his hat,
wiped his forehead with a handkerchief, and sighed. "We
ran the plate first thing. The car's registered to Malachi Hope. I was kinda surprised that's his real name; it
sounds fake to me."

"Maybe he petitioned the court to change it. Where's
the car?"

"About two hundred feet down a logging road in a
clump of scrub pines. You have to get right up to it before you can see it. It's a good thing those youngsters
happened to take that way to the creek." He took out a
cigar and spent forever fiddling with it; I could have
blurted out a bunch of questions, but I waited silently.
"There's a blond woman in the car," he said at last. "We
didn't find a driver's license in her purse, but there were

all sorts of credit cards and a photograph of her and the preacher on a stage in a football stadium. We're damn near certain it's Seraphina Hope."

"Natural causes?"

"What do you think?" growled Harve, then set off down the weedy road, obliging me to choke on his smoke as I followed him. One of these days I was going to report him to the EPA.

"McBeen's on his way," he went on as we arrived in a clearing crowded with deputies and the crime squad, "but we don't need him to tell us she was strangled. For starters, there's a leather thong cutting into her neck." He took the cigar stub out of his mouth and studied it as if it were a significant clue in a dog theft. "There's a whistle on the thong. The only folks I've met that wear them are coaches. You may be on to something with this Cory Jenks."

I took a quick look through the passenger's window, then backed away as the photographer moved in. "I was told that she was last seen at a quarter after twelve. The story is that she delivered Chastity to the RV and drove away to be alone for a while. Earlier today both Malachi and Thomas mentioned that she did that kind of thing fairly often, and I can't say I blame her. I'd get tired of breathing secondhand air and bumping into a wall every time I turned around."

"It beats getting murdered," Harve said. "Could there be a connection between her and either of the coaches?"

"Not that I know of," I admitted. "There was definitely something between the coaches, and they were both at the revival. I don't see where Seraphina Hope fits into any of this, though. Cory could have seen her drive by on her way to the RV or on her way to wherever she was going afterward. He claims he arrived home a little after twelve, but he also claims he didn't leave his house. As soon as we have an approximate time of death, I'll talk to him, maybe bring him in to your office for questioning."

"It was cool last night, but it's been hot as blazes all day. McBeen's not gonna be happy about this particular corpse. He gets all riled up when he has to count maggots."

A young deputy covered his mouth and darted into the thicket. There was a lot of that going on, it seemed. And I was tempted to join him.

"We don't take credit cards," the assistant manager repeated, but with hesitation. The customer had already reduced one clerk to tears, and she was showing no signs of remorse. "We can take a check now, or put aside the merchandise if you'd like to come back later. Your total is twenty-three hundred and eleven dollars and forty-seven cents. We won't charge you for delivery."

Mrs. Jim Bob slapped down a checkbook.

Ruby Bee glanced up from her magazine as Estelle came clattering across the dance floor like a flamenco dancer. "I thought you were gonna be back here at four," she said, letting her eyes fall back on an advertisement for a state-of-the-art food processor that came with so many attachments it could chop, mince, shred, slice, dice, and do everything short of wrapping a birthday present.

"Just get me a glass of sherry," Estelle said as she sat on her stool and took a napkin from the dispenser to dab her forehead. "You will not believe what just happened. I swear, it was like an X-rated movie. It was all I could do not to faint right there on the porch."

"Whose porch?" asked Ruby Bee, setting down the glass of sherry.

Estelle took a gulp and shuddered. "Cory Jenks's porch. You'd think in the middle of the afternoon folks would know better than to engage in that kind of tom-foolery, but I saw what I saw with my own two eyes!" She made sure Ruby Bee was appropriately attentive, then continued. "I went to Eddie Joe's house and found out that Kirsten was on the telephone at the time we figured Norma Kay called her boyfriend."

"I thought you said you were on Cory Jenks's porch?"

"Do you mind letting me tell this my own way? I'm the one who had the misfortune to be at the wrong place at the wrong time, while all you were doing was reading a magazine."

Ruby Bee sniffed. "I was reading this magazine because I was back here at three-forty-five. Fergie's still a suspect, but Lewis Ferncliff is in the clear on account of him and Besseya having left Saturday morning to visit their son in Muskogee. Eula watched them load their car, and she said they were arguing so loudly she could hear every word from her kitchen window. I thought we'd said that it might not be smart to have a word with the two bachelors until we came up with a plan."

"Maybe so," Estelle said, taking dainty sips of sherry like she was perched on a bar stool in Buckingham Palace exchanging recipes with the queen—or at least the head chef. "If you must know, I came up with a plan all by myself and decided to carry it out without asking for your permission. It's not gonna do Arly much good if we're still working on the list of suspects when Dahlia goes into labor, is it?"

"Would you get on with your story? Folks will start showing up for happy hour any minute."

"Well, I drove to the house where Cory lives and knocked on his door. When he didn't open it, I kept right on knocking because his truck was parked in the yard. I was feeling like a redheaded woodpecker by the time he came to the door. He had jeans on, but his shirt was unbuttoned and his feet were bare. He pretended to be pleased to see me, but I could tell right off the bat he was real pissed about being interrupted. I jumped in with my story, and he was just standing there scratching his butt and staring at me when a door behind him opened and out waltzed Chastity Hope."

"Could be she went by to borrow a cup of sugar," Ruby Bee said, "or to find out what's gonna happen to the girls' basketball team."

Estelle gave her a pitying look. "I don't think they were discussing basketball. She was naked as a picked chicken except for a shirt that looked like it came off his floor. Her makeup was smeared and her hair was all tousled, too."

Ruby Bee was so stunned that she poured herself

a glass of sherry and drank half of it without realizing what she was doing. "Why, she can't be half as old as he is."

"You could have knocked me over with a feather. Cory snapped at her to get back in the other room, but she sauntered right over and gave me a smirky smile. My plan went clean out of my mind, and I sputtered something and made a beeline for my car. My hands were shaking so hard I could hardly get the key in the ignition."

"And her being a preacher's adopted daughter. After seeing her last night in that white gown, I'd have thought she would behave better than a common strumpet."

"You didn't think that when Sagina Buchanon played the angel in the Sunday-school Christmas pageant three years back," Estelle pointed out. "You were muttering so loudly I was embarrassed to be in the same pew with you. Anybody can get dressed up like an angel. Or undressed, as the case may be."

Ruby Bee put her glass in the sink while she tried to decide what this meant in terms of the murder in the gym. "If Cory was having an affair with Norma Kay, he didn't take her death real hard. He was a conceited sort back when he was in high school, always strutting around like he was being recruited left and right to play for one of those professional teams. His mother and I used to be in the same county extension club, and she told me he was so grateful he liked to have cried when some little college finally offered him a scholarship. I heard he had to beg Bur Grapper for three days straight to get a job at the high school and get paid less than seventeen thousand dollars, and I don't recollect him in any television commercials for overpriced athletic shoes."

Estelle reached for a basket of pretzels and carefully selected one that wasn't broken. "If he was having an affair with Norma Kay, maybe the only reason he was doing it was so she'd help him get the head coach's job. Once she was dead, he wouldn't have any call to keep pretending he was smitten with her. He was free to take up with the first strumpet that came along, and it happened to be Chastity Hope."

"That could be," Ruby Bee said, wishing she could make better sense of everything that had happened in the last two days—or the last seven days. She had a feeling that no matter how long and hard Malachi prayed, he wouldn't be able to coax Jesus into curing her of her confusion.

And it might take a miracle to keep Arly in Maggody.

11

I PARKED by the tent in what was becoming a familiar spot and went over to the RV to deliver the deplorable news. Chastity came to the door and gave me a sullen stare, clearly more than willing to kill the messenger (meaning me).

"What do you want?" she demanded.

"I need to speak to Malachi."

"He's not here. He and Thomas went to Farberville. I'll tell him you were here."

She tried to close the door, but I caught the knob and kept it open. "Then I need to speak to you," I said as I forced my way into the RV. "You'd better sit down." Once she'd done so, I told her about Seraphina, but without the storm trooper kind of description I'd used to jar Darla Jean.

"Murdered?" she said as her eyes filled with tears. "But who . . . ?"

"I don't know." I went into the bathroom to get a box of tissues, then sat down and waited until she'd finished crying and blowing her nose. I was a little bit surprised at her display of what appeared to be genuine distress; our previous encounter had not suggested she was devoted to her sister. "I know this is a bad time," I said, "but I need to ask you a few questions about last night."

"Oh, God," she said, her face wrinkling with a second bout of distress, this time approaching anguish, "the last thing I said to her was that I hated her. I didn't hate her, though—I was just mad at her. I slammed the car door and went inside without so much as looking back at her."

"I'm sure she knew you didn't mean it."

"All I ever did was gripe at her about how she took me away from my friends and dragged me all over the country. I stole money from her purse every time I got a chance. Last month someone gave her a kitten, and one night when she and Malachi were gone, I took it out in the desert and dumped it. She suspected what I'd done, but I swore I'd left the door open by accident. I tore up the only photograph she had of our mother and flushed the pieces down the toilet." She doubled over as if she'd been punched in the gut and began to moan. "How could I have been so goddamn awful?"

By this time, I had no doubt her reaction was genuine, but nothing in my training had covered handling a spontaneous effusion of guilt and I was relieved to hear a car drive up and stop. I watched out the window as Thomas went into the tent; seconds later, Malachi halted in the doorway of the RV, staring first at Chastity and then at me. "What's going on?" he said. "Is she in trouble with the law?"

"We found Seraphina's body near Boone Creek. There's evidence of foul play," I said.

Malachi's knees buckled, and he barely made it to a chair. He bent his head, clasped his hands together, and began to mumble under his breath. I couldn't see his face, but his shoulders were twitching and his breathing was labored and erratic. Chastity stared at him, then rose unsteadily and went into the bathroom.

Some days it's mildly entertaining to be a cop. This was not one of them. "I have to ask some questions," I said apologetically. When he looked up at me, pale but composed, I added, "We need to move quickly to catch this person."

"The same one who killed Norma Kay Grapper?"

"It's possible. I'm trying to find a link between the two victims. Did Seraphina ever meet Norma Kay or talk to her on the telephone?"

Malachi thought for a moment, then frowned. "If she did, she didn't mention it to me. I told her about what happened in Norma Kay's office last week, of course, and we discussed how to handle the situation. It would not have been wise to alienate the property owner's wife. On the other hand, previous scandals involving evangelists have made it clear that there should be no hint of impropriety, which is why I initially decided not to meet her at the gym."

"Did Seraphina know you changed your mind?"

"She knew nothing about it. I didn't have a chance to tell her about the note before the revival, and once the revival began, I completely forgot about it. The spirit of the Lord is a powerful and mysterious force that prevails over earthly concerns. Only after Seraphina had left to find Chastity and I was changing clothes did I rediscover Norma Kay's note in my pocket. I couldn't leave her sitting alone in her office, waiting for me."

Despite the gravity of the moment, I allowed myself the petty indulgence of a digression. "The spirit of the Lord didn't do much for Lottie Estes's driving skills. It seems you cured her last night and told her she wouldn't need her glasses anymore. Today she ran down an old woman in the road."

"How unfortunate," he murmured. "Her faith must not have been as strong as she professed it to be. Tell her to come tonight and I'll pray again for her."

"Tonight?"

"I can't ignore the Lord's work because of a personal tragedy. I have a calling to bring lost souls back from the brink of the abyss and provide them with the opportunity to experience prosperity and inner peace."

"Your wife was murdered early this morning, Mr. Hope. Surely the Lord will give you the night off."

"I am in great pain, Miss Hanks, but I cannot turn people away or ignore their needs. The Lord allowed Job to lose his property and his children and be afflicted with boils in order to test his faith. Perhaps this is my test—to continue the Lord's work while struggling to understand why this dreadful thing happened."

It was impassioned, but I suspected it was motivated by the less lofty goal of raising cash for the corporation. "At the moment, I don't have a reason to close you down, but rest assured that I will the first chance I get. Please tell me everything you did after I left you this morning."

"I made a few phone calls to motels, hoping I'd get

lucky and find out where Seraphina was. At noon, I asked Thomas to go with me to Farberville to look for her car. You saw us arrive back here."

"You weren't worried about her earlier," I pointed out. "You said she did this all the time. Why was this time different?"

"She'd had an argument with Chastity."

"So I've been told," I said, glancing at the closed bathroom door. "What was the argument about?"

"Chastity went off with some teenagers. Seraphina was quite angry when she found her almost an hour later. I can't tell you the exact conversation, but Chastity was nearly hysterical when I arrived back from the gym. In fact, she used such profanity that I was forced to threaten her with my belt. She locked herself in the bathroom, and she was still there when I decided to make sure Norma Kay was safely at home."

"All that seems excessive for a minor lapse," I said. "From what I heard, the teenagers were doing nothing more heinous than drinking sodas on the picnic table in the Dairee Dee-Lishus parking lot. If that's all they ever did, their parents would sleep better at night and I might be out of a job."

Malachi Hope gave me a condescending smile. "Your local teenagers will earn high school diplomas, marry each other, and settle down to a life of unpaid bills, alcoholism, adultery, ailing parents, rebellious children, and eventually an unappetizing demise in a cheap nursing home. I know these people, Miss Hanks. They write me letters, they clutch at my hands when I walk down the aisle, they come crawling to me to tell them how to help themselves rise out of their pathos. Chastity is different.

She's unpolished now, even crude at times, but I will take her and shape her until she is touched by the glory of God and can take a significant role on the stage. To achieve this, I must protect her from not only the common people but also from her own primitive instincts. A child is born with a pure soul; only when she is indoctrinated into the ways of the world does she become contaminated with sin."

Thomas had told me Malachi was not an Old Testament prophet. If this was the contemporary yuppie version, I sure as hell didn't want to run into an older model in a dark alley. "I'd like to speak to Chastity," I said stiffly as I stood up. "Out in my car, I think."

"She's a minor. I will not allow you to question her unless it's in the presence of an attorney."

"No one's accusing her of anything. All I want to do is find out if she might have any idea where Seraphina might have gone last night."

"Either get a warrant citing probable cause to arrest her or wait for me to arrange for a time when an attorney can be present," Malachi said. He opened the door and watched me as I went past him and down the concrete block steps.

I should have said something to wipe the self-righteous smirk off his face, but I'd been trying to do the same with Mrs. Jim Bob for ages. I might as well have been filling in the Grand Canyon with a teaspoon.

"We are not going to drive to Topeka!" Estelle said so loudly the truckers in the back booths liked to have spilled their beers. "Topeka is all the way in Kansas. Do you know how long that would take?"

Refusing to look at Estelle, Ruby Bee refilled a pitcher and set it down in front of Earl Buchanon, who should have been home instead of getting drunk. She went into the kitchen to check the mashed potatoes while she futilely tried to remember where Topeka was. Kansas was nothing but a big, flat, boring expanse of wheat fields and highways; even if Topeka was tucked up in a corner, how long could it take to get there?

She came out of the kitchen, made sure nobody was wanting anything, and went down to the end of the bar. "I just have a feeling that Norma Kay's past has something to do with all this," she said in a low voice so Earl couldn't overhear. "We might ought to ask Edwina Spitz about this neighbor of her niece's that she met at the funeral. Norma Kay wasn't your run-of-the-mill girls' basketball coach. I could tell there was something gnawing at her."

Estelle had to pause while she pondered what exactly constituted a run-of-the-mill girls' basketball coach. She finally realized Norma Kay was the only girls' basketball coach she'd ever met, but she wasn't about to admit it. "I ain't sure Edwina Spitz can pull out the name after all these years," she said, hoping she sounded meditative instead of bewildered. "Just last week, I saw her talking to the rutabagas in the produce department."

"We're doing this for Arly."

"To keep her in Maggody?"

"Why else, Estelle?" Ruby Bee went back into the kitchen before allowing herself to wipe her eyes with the hem of her apron. To think she herself had kinda liked the fellow from Washington, D.C. If he'd materialized at that moment, she'd have grabbed a rolling pin and chased him clean out of the county.

"We can get this to you tomorrow afternoon," the owner said after consulting the delivery schedule. "With the deposit, the first payment comes to fourteen hundred sixty-two dollars and nine cents."

Mrs. Jim Bob slapped down a fresh credit card.

Going door to door in search of witnesses is not nearly as effortless as movies and television shows would have you believe. No one was home at half the houses; I kept a list of them as I worked my way down the road toward the high school. In two instances, I'd barely escaped being dragged inside for refreshments. In another, I'd been regaled with a long-winded account of the perils of allowing Communists to infiltrate the town council. (I wasn't sure which members were the guilty parties, but it was hard to picture Jim Bob, Larry Joe Lambertino, and Roy Stiver consulting *Das Kapital* before voting not to put in a second stoplight.) Virella Buchanon wanted me to arrest her next-door neighbor for impersonation. Her next-door neighbor wanted me to haul Virella off to a psychiatric facility.

I was almost directly across from the gym when I finally got a break. Edwina Spitz listened to my question, smiled brightly, and said, "I reckon I did. Why don't you come inside out of the heat while I tell you?"

"Yes, ma'am," I said, resisting the urge to throw my arms around her.

Once I was settled in a rocking chair with a glass of lemonade, she said, "I've been having trouble with my lower back lately. There are nights I can't hardly sleep, so I get out of bed and watch those infomercials on cable. Only last night this scientist was saying how dangerous it is to drink water straight from the tap on account of all the poisons that seep into the ground and—"

"You saw cars at the gym?" I inserted hastily.

Edwina gave me a disapproving look that rivaled Ruby Bee's best efforts. "As I was saying, Arly, after I finished watching this scientist, I went into the kitchen and filled a glass with water to see if there was anything drifting in it. I happened to hear a car door slam across the road, so I looked out the window just as a big, gold car drove away."

"Did you notice the time?"

"It would have been just after twelve-thirty. I could see Norma Kay's car parked next to the door in her usual spot. I thought it was kinda curious, but I told myself it was none of my business and put on the kettle to make a cup of tea. Sometimes it helps me sleep."

The earth was not trembling beneath my feet. I set down the glass and stood up. "Thanks, Edwina. I guess I'd better get back to work."

"You don't want to hear the rest?" she said, the corners of her mouth drooping. They perked up when I nodded. "While I was spooning sugar into the tea, I heard another car door. I figured Norma Kay was going home, but to my surprise, her car was still there and a truck was parked next to it."

"What color?"

"My eyesight's not as good as it used to be. You'll have to ask Cory Jenks if it's black or real dark blue."

I sat back down and stared at her. "You recognized it? Are you positive it was Cory's truck?"

"He's been parking it by the gym almost every day for two years now. There was enough light from the utility pole for me to make out the gun rack on the back window and the bumper stickers on the tailgate."

"Oh, Edwina," I said, "I think your eyesight's just fine."

Brother Verber poured the last drops of sacramental wine into a tumbler and jammed the empty bottle into a grocery bag under the sink with the others. It was getting time to put the bag in his trunk and find a Dumpster in another town, he thought as he drank the wine. As a servant of the Lord, it wouldn't be fitting for him to have bottles in the garbage can behind the Assembly Hall, where mischievous little tykes might find them and get the wrong impression about him.

Then again, it might not matter what anybody thought if Malachi Hope stole the whole darn congregation. He'd be preaching to empty pews—except for Sister Barbara, who was too faithful to be blinded by slick promises. Preaching to her would be like preaching to the choir, though. There wasn't any need to warn such a saintly woman about eternal damnation. Why, she was the guardian angel of his flock and an inspiration to everyone she met.

The flock, on the other hand, had some explainin' to do. Not one of them had showed up for the evening service and the opportunity for a fun-filled session of popcorn, soda pop, and bingo. He didn't need a stool pigeon to tell him where they'd been. No, the traitors had trooped right up to the pasture behind Bur Grapper's house and sold their souls to Satan himself. Judas held out for thirty pieces of silver, but Lottie Estes and Eula Lemoy and the lot of them had been seduced by cotton candy—and whatever else was going on up there.

From what he'd overheard at the SuperSaver, it sounded like a rock concert combined with a carnival. Spotlights going every which way, peppy hymns, clouds of pink and white smoke, an angel descending from the top of the tent, and dozens of aluminum buckets going up and down the rows and filling up with dollar bills. Brother Verber figured any one of those buckets was likely to have more in it than he collected from his entire congregation at any given service. Ex-congregation, he corrected hisself with a sigh. This time next year he might be in some godforsaken mission in the middle of the jungle. There he'd be, shivering with fever, battling mosquitoes and snakes, eventually succumbing to malaria and dying in a bleak room with heathens hovering over him to steal the gold fillings right out of his teeth.

The scenario was so painful that he opened another bottle of sacramental wine, filled his glass, and tried to think of a plan. Part of the problem was he didn't know exactly what all Malachi Hope and his hussy were doing that impressed folks. As a child, little Willard Verber had

Joan Hess

been hauled to camp meetings and tent revivals with homespun preachers, hell-and-damnation sermons, gospel music that rocked the rafters, and folks writhing on the floor when they were possessed by the Holy Spirit. Between services, there'd be picnic suppers and relay races, and an occasional walk in the woods with a pretty girl.

But Malachi Hope was too sophisticated for that.

Brother Verber was halfway through the bottle when the Lord blessed him with an idea. It wasn't a complicated plan, mind you, but it was better than dying in the jungle. What he needed to do was go to one of the services and see for hisself exactly what the enemy was up to. Only then could he prepare a plan to win back the loyalty of his congregation and continue to live in his cozy rectory under the sycamore trees.

There was one small problem with the idea: If he went to the service, there was no way on God's earth that Sister Barbara wouldn't hear about it by noon the following day. Her heart would break right on the spot and she'd wither away and die on account of his treachery, while other folks would snicker and make impudent comments about how he was doing the very thing he'd bawled them out for even considering.

What he needed was a disguise so that no one would know what he was up to. Sunglasses and a fake beard wouldn't fool anybody. A trench coat would only call attention to him. The good Lord got busy and made a suggestion that sounded promising, if a bit outlandish.

Brother Verber was well past being able to make sober judgments. He took the keys to the Assembly Hall, weaved across the lawn, and went in through the back door. In the storeroom were boxes and boxes of items collected years ago to be sent to the heathens as soon as he got their address in Africa. He thudded to his knees and pawed through a box of clothes until he found what he wanted. A second box was equally fruitful. Others were less so, but he finally assembled his disguise and weaved back to the rectory in a haze of gratitude to the Lord, who could always be counted on to come through in a pinch.

"The witness recognized Cory's truck," I said to Harve, my feet propped on his desk for a change. I could barely see him over the heap of cigar stubs and burnt matches in the ashtray, but I had no problem hearing him harrumphing and wheezing. "I asked him point-blank if he'd left his house after he got home from Emmet shortly after twelve, and he said he hadn't. He also denied that he was having an affair with Norma Kay. It may be time to see if he wants to change his story."

Harve regarded me with the impassivity of a backwoods Buddha. "I don't know if you've got enough of a case against him to go to the county prosecutor as yet. Even if Cory was sleeping with Norma Kay, that don't mean he killed her. He ain't much more than thirty years old, and he's not married. The worst thing that could happen if Norma Kay went public was that he'd lose his job and slink out of town with his tail between his legs. I can't see why he'd risk life imprisonment—or worse, if the jury was in a bad mood—just to save his job."

"People who are obsessed with a goal can commit irrational acts to achieve it," I said, thinking of Dahlia's most recent misdemeanor. It occurred to me that I'd not yet allowed Kevin to explain the crisis on the home front; when I had a free moment, I'd have to hear him out. "We need to bring Cory in, let him repeat his lies, and then confront him with what witnesses have said. He might fall apart."

"It might be better to let him stew for a day or two," Harve said. He stuck a cigar in his mouth, got it lit, and assessed my reaction through a cloud of smoke. "Besides, you still need to find a link between him and Seraphina Hope—unless you're going to convince the prosecutor there are two murderers out in Maggody, both using the same method."

I grabbed a folder and fanned the air in an unsuccessful effort to keep the smoke out of my face. "Malachi Hope won't let me question Chastity without an attorney. She must know something important, but damned if I can even guess what it is."

Harve and I were looking at each other when the door opened and LaBelle stuck her head into the office. "Arly, honey, your mother's on the phone. She says it's real urgent."

"Tell her I already left," I said.

"But I told her you were in here talking to Harve."

"Tell her I left through the back door."

"We don't have a back door."

"Don't tell her that," I said, then waited until LaBelle retreated before I told Harve about Lottie Estes's driving mishap. "Is there a chance I can nail Malachi Hope with practicing medicine without a license?"

Harve shrugged his beefy shoulders. "Call the prosecutor if you've a mind, but I don't know if calling on Jesus to heal folks is in the same league with peddling pills and home-brewed tonics."

"I suppose I'd better find out what he *is* doing," I said as I started for the door.

"Who knows—maybe you'll get yourself some religion."

"If I do," I said with a grimace, "I'll find myself a nice, quiet convent where nothing ever happens." I could hear Harve's chuckles as I left (through the front door).

Kevin was on his knees in the middle of the kitchen, battling back tears as he watched his love goddess shovel down forkfuls of chocolate cake. He waited until she paused to wipe crumbs off her chins, and said, "If you won't go to the clinic, at least say you'll go talk to Malachi Hope and make sure he understands how delicate your condition is. Considering how you've kept your figure so far, he might not have suspected you're pregnant."

Dahlia flung her napkin on the table and glared down at him. "Are you saying Jesus doesn't know I'm pregnant? He sits right there on the throne next to God, and God knows everything. Don't you think God might have told Jesus if there was a reason not to cure my diabetes? What would your pa do if he heard how you were spouting off this kind of blasphemy?" Having settled that, she resumed eating. "The cake's real tasty, Kevvie. Are you sure you don't want some?"

"Please let me take you to the revival tonight," he

said with such intensity that Dahlia came close to jabbing herself in the lip. "Malachi Hope was the one who said you were cured. Maybe he was confused about what Jesus was doing. Jesus could have cured someone else's diabetes."

"Are you planning to stop at the Dairee Dee-Lishus afterward?" she asked slyly.

"Oh, yes, my beloved wife!"

He looked so pitiful that she took mercy on him and said, "I don't reckon it can hurt to go to the revival. It was kinda fun watching those crippled people staggering all over the stage. Do you recollect that man with the snake tattoo that was so blind he had to be led onstage? I know for dead certain he was cured, because I saw him driving down the road this morning in one of those Hope Is Here trucks. If he was still blind, do you think they'd let him drive?"

Kevin was forced to agree.

Eula Lemoy was limping as she made her way to Elsie McMay's car. "I appreciate you giving me a ride to the revival," she said as she got in the front seat. "How's Lottie doing?"

"She said she was feeling poorly and was going to go to bed early, but I think she's embarrassed about running over that old woman from the county home. I know my face would be as red as a tomato."

"I heard tell that Arly won't allow Lottie to drive until she gets new glasses," said Eula.

Elsie turned down County 102. "That borders on sacrilege, her doubting that Jesus cured Lottie of the astigmatism. Then again, Arly doesn't attend church or even come to the Christmas pageant. She very well may be an atheist."

Eula looked at her ankle. Surely it was less swollen than it had been earlier in the day. She of all people was not an atheist.

"I'll bet there'll be a bigger crowd tonight," Earl Buchanon said as he turned down County 102. "Maybe that murder at the high school gym got folks to worrying about getting into heaven without having made a reservation."

Eilene took a tissue from her purse and surreptitiously wiped the corner of her eye. "I'm so upset about Dahlia that all I did today was pace around the house, hoping Kevin would call to say she was willing to go to the clinic. He never did. I called over there while you were in the tub, but nobody answered."

"She'll come to her senses once the sugar wears off."

"I'm not so sure. Maybe Brother Verber was right about Malachi Hope coming here to con us out of our money. Don't you go putting another ten-dollar bill in the bucket, Earl Buchanon—not unless you fancy fixing your own meals and ironing your own shirts while I spend the next three months with my sister in Arkadelphia."

Earl opened his mouth, then closed it before he said something stupid.

Ruby Bee sighed as she turned down County 102. "I didn't see Arly's car at the PD. I suppose she could have parked behind the antiques store, but her apartment was dark. I left a passel of messages on her answering machine to call me. I feel awful that we haven't told her about Chastity and Cory Jenks."

"It's her own fault," Estelle said promptly. "If she can't bother to return her own mother's calls, she'll have to get along without a vital clue."

"Why's it vital?"

"How should I know? Arly's the one always carryin' on how she's a trained professional. Do you think Malachi Hope is gonna bring his wife back from the dead?"

"That is the most awful thing I've ever heard you say, Estelle!" Ruby Bee said, punctuating her sentence with a snort.

"Wasn't there some fellow down by Van Buren who put his wife's body in a glass coffin and made his cult followers pray over it all the time?"

"There was something in the newspapers along those lines, but I can't seem to remember what happened."

Estelle waved at a customer, then dropped her hand and said, "They lost both her and the coffin."

"How can you lose a coffin?" countered Ruby Bee.

They continued discussing the possibilities all the way to the turnoff.

12

I PARKED my car at the bottom of the hill (position has its privileges, and I wasn't going to give myself a ticket) and trudged up the road, noticing as I passed Bur Grapper's house that the curtains were drawn. At the top of the hill, there was an impressive crowd, some in their Sunday best and others in clean work shirts and neatly patched jeans. Everyone seemed to be in a lighthearted mood as they called to one another and munched popcorn. Souvenir tables were doing a brisk business; I might have been the only one there not excited about the chance to buy an autographed copy of *Invest In Jesus!*, by none other than Malachi Hope.

Nodding and acknowledging greetings, I made my way to the tent. Darla Jean, Heather, and a few other girls from the basketball team were milling near the entrance, each wearing a large, round badge that identified her as an usher. One of the Dahlton twins grabbed an elderly lady and guided her down the center aisle. Seconds later, the other twin grabbed Eula Lemoy's elbow and took off with her.

Darla Jean gave me a perplexed look as I arrived beside her. "Evening, Arly," she said. "I'm kinda surprised to see you here. My ma says she heard you're an atheist."

No suitable retort came to mind, so I settled for a vague smile and said, "I thought I'd see what's going on. Did you hear about Seraphina Hope?"

"It's awful, isn't it? I met her only last night, but we all feel real bad for Chastity. Now she's practically an orphan. Do you think Malachi will send her off to a boarding school?"

"I have no idea." I watched Heather capture a stout woman in a plaid housedress, excessive makeup, thick glasses, and a floppy straw hat adorned with plastic flowers. "Have you spoken to Chastity since she got back from Farberville?"

"I'm not supposed to stand here and talk. Let me take you to your seat."

"On the last row, by an exit," I said as we went into the tent. A Broadway theater it was not, but the deli at the SuperSaver did not compete with Zabar's, and the view from my apartment window was hardly a spectacular skyline. The odds on receiving a copy of *Playbill* were slim. Then again, the price of admission was nowhere near sixty or seventy-five dollars. We don't fall for that kind of crap in Maggody.

The benches down front were packed, and there were at least a dozen people in wheelchairs directly in front of the stage. Conversations competed with music from speakers on scaffolds at both sides of the stage. High school boys with badges identical to Darla Jean's moved up and down the aisles, selling Bibles and cassettes. Traci nearly ran over my toes as she maneuvered a wheelchair around us and rolled it toward the stage.

"Are you okay, Arly?" Darla Jean asked in a concerned voice. "You look a little pale."

I brushed her hand off my arm. "I'll find my own seat, Darla Jean."

"Oh, no, we're supposed to escort folks to a seat to make sure they feel welcome and then ask them if they want a prayer card." She handed me a card that had blanks for a name, mailing address, and specific request. "If you fill it out and say how you're still brooding about your divorce or despairing of ever gettin' married again, then Malachi Hope will pray for you."

"I think I'll pass." I gave her back the card and moved a chair to within a few feet of an illuminated exit sign above an opening in the tent. The benches filled up steadily, until latecomers were obliged to accept folding chairs in the back. I recognized some of them, but others must have come from all over Stump County. Ruby Bee and Estelle failed to spot me in my shadowy corner, and were chatting with Heather as she settled them on the far side and gave them cards. Elsie McMay stared at me as she was hustled down the aisle; Earl and Eilene Buchanon waved. I thought I glimpsed Diesel Buchanon, but I quickly closed my eyes. When I opened them, he was gone.

The noise was growing unbearable. I was considering a discreet (okay, cowardly) withdrawal, when the music swept to a deafening crescendo, the overheard lights dimmed, and Thomas Fratelleon bounded onto the stage as if he were an emcee. He was wearing a pastel blue tuxedo and carrying a microphone. Could the Chippendale strippers be far behind?

"Thank you for coming!" he boomed. "It's so heartwarming to see all you good Christians out there, eager to be blessed by Malachi Hope and help him bring the healing spirit of Jesus into our very midst!"

This elicited a round of applause and pious cheers, but it faded as Thomas assumed a mournful expression. "As many of you know, our beloved angel of love, Seraphina Hope, was taken from us in the early hours of the morning. Malachi and Chastity prayed all day and have found the strength to come out tonight and share with you not only their grief but their belief that Seraphina is watching us from a special place alongside Jesus. She doesn't want us to weep and wail for her, brothers and sisters. She wants us to celebrate her grand entrance through the Pearly Gates!"

As Thomas left the stage, music began to blare and spotlights splashed onto the stage and curtain. Glitter drifted down from the ceiling like fine snow. The crowd reacted with enthusiasm, clapping and stomping and bellowing out the words to a brisk version of "Shall We Gather by the River." When Malachi stepped out from the center of the curtain, the decibel level rose so much that I caught myself speculating about the sturdiness of the cables holding up the tent.

I folded my arms and leaned back as Malachi dashed from one end of the stage to the other, always in a puddle of light, exhorting the audience to praise Jesus and open their hearts to the Holy Spirit. He was also exhorting them to open their wallets; buckets were passed down the benches every ten minutes while Malachi raved about "the seeds of prosperity" and the opportunity to "make a touchdown for Jesus" by jumping on "the elevator to heaven." No one else seemed to object to this peculiar mixture of metaphors or wonder why Jesus needed bribes to bestow blessings.

Malachi finally calmed down and came to the edge of the stage. "I can sense," he said in the hushed voice of a funeral director, "that someone out there is troubled. That same someone went to the doctor last week and heard bad news, and now is worried that she'll end up in a hospital. But you know what?"

The crowd dutifully roared, "What?"

"I feel a miracle coming on! You heard me—a miracle is coming on!" He put his fingertips on his temples, closed his eyes, and then threw up his hands. "I want Leslie Biden to come up here and join me as I pray to Jesus to perform a miracle."

Amidst squeals and shouts of encouragement, Leslie timidly climbed the steps at one end of the stage and allowed Thomas to lead her to Malachi. The latter clutched her shoulders and said, "Leslie, the doctor said you might have an ulcer, didn't he? He said he could give you some medicine, but this ulcer could get so bad he might need to operate on it."

Leslie came close to crumpling but managed a faint nod as Thomas stuck a microphone in her face. "That's right," she said, looking out at the crowd. "But I haven't told Fergie yet, on account of him bein' worried about gettin' laid off at the poultry plant in Starley City. I haven't told a single soul except my ma, and she lives in Mississippi."

"And you didn't tell me," Malachi cut in. "Jesus told me. He wants to heal you, Leslie, if you'll let him. He doesn't want you to worry about your ulcer anymore. He wants you to be happy, to enjoy wealth and prosperity. Is that what you want, Leslie?"

When she nodded, he launched into a prayer of at least three minutes' duration, begging Jesus to heal her and encouraging Leslie to affirm her belief that it could happen. Just as it was beginning to look as if Jesus was occupied elsewhere, Malachi shrieked, "Thank you, Jesus!" and Leslie fell backward into Thomas's arms.

The crowd went wild—for the most part, that is. I kept my arms folded and my lips tight as I pondered what I'd seen. Ruby Bee and Estelle were whispering to each other. Darla Jean had a puzzled expression on her face.

Things quieted down only when Chastity came onstage, dressed in a white gown, wings, and a halo that was definitely lopsided. "I'd like to dedicate this to my sister," she said, "because now she's with Jesus." She sang a fairly acceptable rendition of "Amazing Grace," curtsied, and fled behind the curtain. I may have had the only dry eyes in the tent, but we atheists are notoriously cynical.

Malachi let the applause die down. "I am so touched by little Chastity's song that I feel another miracle coming on. This time Jesus tells me there's someone out in the audience who's enduring the agony of arthritis. Someone's fingers are stiff and sore."

An unfamiliar woman from the front bench stood up. "I have arthritis!" she yelled, clearly proud to be the next afflicted party. Several minutes later, Thomas was dragging her limp body offstage. A burly man in tattered overalls and dark glasses was brought onstage and "healed" of his blindness as well as the brain tumor that had caused it. Malachi went into the audience and persuaded a gaunt woman in a wheelchair to stand up and take a few steps. A young woman with a baby was assured her husband would stop drinking and stay home with her. Another woman was assured her daughter would stop sleeping with every trucker she met. (Knowing the girl, I wouldn't have put money on it.)

It was interesting—from a voyeuristic standpoint. Malachi was dynamic, his voice rising to an ecstatic frenzy, then dropping to a hoarse, theatrical whisper. His candidates had no reluctance about spilling their family secrets, although there might be regrets in the morning when reality replaced religious fervor. I had no doubt Ruby Bee was taking notes for the grapevine.

"I feel a miracle coming on!" Malachi said for the umpteenth time. "Wilma, I know you're afraid you're going to lose your job. Jesus knows it, too. Where are you, Wilma? Come up here with me, and we can pray together that Jesus will make sure you don't find yourself out on the cold, hard streets, scavenging for food from garbage cans."

An expectant buzz filled the tent as people craned their heads to locate the hapless soul, but no one stood up. As Malachi came down the steps to the aisle, he said, "You don't have to be afraid of Jesus, Wilma. He wants me to find you and pray with you." He pressed his fingers to his temple for a moment. "I can see you in my mind, Wilma. You're wearing a dress, glasses, and a big ol' hat with pretty pink and yellow flowers."

"Here she is!" shouted a woman in the last row, waving her arms over her head as if directing an airplane to a gate. "I reckon this here's Wilma!"

Malachi approached his next candidate, who was slumped down in her seat with her face hidden beneath the wide brim of the hat. "Wilma," he said gently, "don't be ashamed to let Jesus help you. When I asked all these generous, loving Christians to help Jesus, they dug in their pockets and purses and their very hearts. Now Jesus is helping us. Can you feel it?" He put his hand on her back. "Can you feel Jesus, Wilma?"

Wilma bobbled her head, which was good enough for Malachi and the audience. The music came back up, the buckets appeared, and the show went on.

At the end of three hours, Malachi had discarded his coat and his sleeves were rolled up "to work hard for Jesus." Several people in the audience had fainted and been revived with cups of water provided by the ushers. Chastity had appeared in a pink haze to sing another hymn. Malachi had described his proposed City of Hope, with its crystal cathedral, hundred-foot-tall cross illuminated by five thousand lightbulbs, audio and video recording studios, and the vast expanse set aside for carnival rides, condos, a two-acre artificial lake designed for baptisms (as well as paddleboats), and meeting rooms that could be rented for weddings and family reunions.

None of this would be cheap, he'd warned them as ushers passed out brochures, but he'd prayed long and hard and felt sure it could happen—if the folks in the tent would help Jesus. After another round of the buckets, everyone had been blessed and promised a featured role in Malachi's prayers. The curtain closed, the music faded, and overhead lights came back up. Ushers began to push wheelchairs toward the door, although I noticed that several occupants preferred to walk.

Mrs. Twayblade waylaid me outside the tent. "Mrs. Teasel is spending a few days at the hospital, but the doctor said she didn't suffer any serious injuries. It wasn't my fault that she wandered off, you know. I try as hard as I can to take care of my patients. I not only see to their health but also provide crafts projects and a variety of seasonal activities. I can't lock the exits or chain folks to their beds. There's a door at the end of every corridor, and—"

"I didn't say anything was your fault," I said as she glared at me like a protective hen, "but you're going to have to find a way to keep Mrs. Teasel from doing this again. Lottie Estes has never driven over twenty miles per hour in her life. Truckers and tourists are another matter. We don't want Mrs. Teasel to share the same fate as Raz Buchanon's dog."

"Which was?"

"Roadkill," I said glumly, then watched her scuttle away to gather up her gray-haired chicks and hustle them into a large van. I started once again toward my car at the bottom of the hill, but before I could make my escape, Ruby Bee appeared on one side of me and Estelle on the other.

"I told you to come by the barroom," Ruby Bee said, "and I left half a dozen messages on that answering machine of yours. It seems to me with two murders in the last twenty-four hours, with Lottie running over that old lady, and who knows what else going on in Maggody, you might be more concerned with doing your job than gallivanting all over the place."

Estelle poked my arm. "Your mother and I sacrificed half the day trying to assist you, and then you don't have the common courtesy to—"

I held up my hands. "I can assure you that I have not been neglecting my duty. What's got the two of you stirred up like hornets?"

"Estelle learned something important," Ruby Bee said with a sniff. "Because of its nature, I didn't want to say anything about it on the answering machine. You never lock the door at the PD, so anyone could waltz right in and listen to your messages."

"And what a thrill that would be," I said. "It's late and I had all of two hours of sleep last night. Tell me whatever it is that's so important and let me go home."

Estelle looked at Ruby Bee. "Maybe we should put it off until Arly here has a good night's sleep. We don't have any call to burden her when she's tired."

"Just tell me," I said.

Ruby Bee opened her mouth, but Estelle leapt in first. "I happened to be at Cory Jenks's house earlier today. I wanted to ask him something, but before I could get out more than a word or two, Chastity came out of the bedroom—practically buck naked. I knew right away that they'd been fornicating, and in the middle of the afternoon, too."

This stopped me cold. "Chastity and Cory Jenks?" I said.

"He was embarrassed, but she was as proud as a homecoming queen in a taffeta dress. Watching her tonight on the stage, all simpery and innocent—it was enough to gag a goat!"

"I'll say it was," Ruby Bee added.

That pretty much summed it up for me, too.

Mrs. Twayblade sat at the table in the foyer, where she could monitor all four corridors and thus prevent any attempts at licentious activity. It was outrageous how some of her charges behaved when they got the chance; Petrol Buchanon in particular imagined himself to be quite the satyr, despite the fact he was hairless, toothless, and witless.

With a pinched frown, she looked down at the medication schedule to make sure everybody had received whatever he or she was supposed to take at bedtime. The new aide was grossly incompetent, always fussing with her hair in the lounge instead of following orders, but it was nigh onto impossible to find reliable girls willing to work for minimum wage.

The new aide's writing was so cramped and smudged that Mrs. Twayblade had to take the clipboard into the office, where the light was better. It seemed no one was being taught penmanship these days, much less meticulous attention to detail. Or spelling, unless some higher authority had decreed that *nite* and *capsool* were now acceptable.

They were not, in Mrs. Twayblade's opinion.

She returned to the table and sat down, planning to read a journal geared toward nursing-home management. Something was not right, however, and she could find no distraction in an article discussing ways to integrate the four food groups into each meal in exciting and innovative ways.

Armed with a small flashlight, she prowled down the corridors, occasionally shining the light into rooms to assure herself that the residents were peaceful. The snores and gurgles were as pleasing to her as a pastoral, yet she remained uneasy as she sat back down.

It had to do with this latest evening at the revival, she decided as the recipe for sweet potato puff pancakes blurred before her eyes. Mr. Buckhorn had been taken onstage to be cured of his rheumatism, but he'd griped afterward about how much his knees still ached that there had been an attempt to shove him out a window in the van. Mrs. Teasel's roommate had not been given a chance to be cured of her gallbladder infection, nor had Petrol . . .

Mrs. Twayblade put her hand to her mouth to muffle a gasp. After she had supervised the loading of the van, she'd counted heads as best she could in the dark. She'd asked very clearly if everyone was there and been assured they were. The subsequent altercation had given her a dreadful headache; back at the county home, she'd ordered the new aide to help everyone out of the van, then gone into her office for a well-deserved swallow of the brandy she kept hidden for such moments.

But she hadn't heard Petrol's voice as they had come into the foyer, and he was by far the loudest of her charges. His choice of words was often enough to merit a scolding or a withholding of dessert.

She hurried down the hall, counting doors under her

breath, and went into the pertinent room. In one bed, Mr. Linum snored like an outboard motor. In the other bed, the blankets were bunched enough to allow a casual observer to see a human form, but the mound on the pillow was a bathrobe.

"I am going to throttle that aide," Mrs. Twayblade said, but softly, so as not to disturb Mr. Linum. The only time he wasn't a pain in the ass was when he was asleep. The last thing she needed was to deal with his puerile complaints.

Eula Lemoy sat on her sofa and stared at her ankle, which was propped on a stack of pillows. The skin seemed unnaturally white, almost opaque, and her whole leg felt like it had been squeezed into a support stocking. Jesus most likely wouldn't mind if she finished what pills she had left, but she wasn't sure. There wasn't any way she could sneak into the bathroom and take one, on account of Jesus always knows what you're doing. Brother Verber was real fond of that theme and only last month had delivered a stirring sermon about folks that thought they could keep their perversities a secret. He'd practically begged the sinners in the congregation to come to him and confess all the sordid details—because they couldn't fool Jesus. Brother Verber had made Jesus sound like J. Edgar Hoover.

Eula was afraid to risk doing something that might get her labeled as an atheist, so she took the pillows into her bedroom and arranged them so she could keep her leg elevated while she tried to sleep.

Guilt had sent Lottie Estes into her kitchen to bake cookies, even though it was nearly midnight. She didn't know how she was going to get them to the hospital in Farberville, since she wasn't supposed to drive without her glasses. She wouldn't drive if she had them, either, because that would tell folks that her faith was flawed so badly that Jesus hadn't cured her astigmatism.

She opened her file box and hunted for her sister's recipe for lemon snaps. She found it but then realized there was no way she could decipher her sister's spindly handwriting. Having taught home economics all these years, Lottie knew what could happen if you used a tablespoon when a teaspoon was called for or put in a third of a cup of something when you needed a fourth of a cup.

She put the card back into the box. Hadn't she made enough sugar cookies in her lifetime to pave the road all the way to the Missouri line? She set out the canisters of flour and sugar, took eggs and butter from the refrigerator, and preset the oven. Only when she opened the cabinet to get out the bottle of vanilla extract did she hesitate. There was a whole line of little brown bottles of extract, all with small print on the labels.

She opened the first and took a whiff of almonds. It was going to be a long night, she thought as she reached for the next bottle.

"Doncha want to come to bed?" Kevin said, watching Dahlia from the doorway to the bedroom.

"Later." She belched delicately and put another cookie into her mouth. "I'm watching this movie about this rancher's daughter and an outlaw. You kin watch it with me if you want."

"I got to be at work at five. Jim Bob wants the floors waxed, so I got to start early so they'll be dry when the store opens. They always look real pretty afore folks track mud on 'em."

"That's nice," Dahlia said as she chewed thoughtfully and tried to decide if the rancher's daughter was falling in love with the outlaw. It looked like it, but movies could fool you sometimes.

Kevin held in a groan as her hand slid into the box and emerged with another cookie. "Honey bunch, doncha think you should stay on your diet until the doctor at the clinic does a test and makes sure you're cured? I ain't saying you're not, mind you, but it can't hurt to make sure."

"Are you sayin' Jesus needs a second opinion? If that don't smack of blasphemy, I don't know what does," she said, albeit distractedly on account of the rancher's daughter riding out by her lonesome to save a heifer in a blizzard. Dahlia could tell from the way the horse was floundering in the snowdrifts that the rancher's daughter was in for a hard night.

I turned off the overhead light, thus granting kitchen and bathroom privileges to the cockroaches with which I cohabited, and crawled into bed with the thick folder of letters that Norma Kay had written to Malachi over the last decade. I doubted they could compete with the lurid potboilers I'd read on the beach; Norma Kay had not been a member of the jet set or waged any battles for control of an international diamond cartel.

I debated whether to start with the most recent letter and work my way back, or tackle them in chronological order.

Choices, choices.

13

"You aim to question Cory Jenks?" Ruby Bee asked me as she set down a plate of buttermilk pancakes and sausage.

According to my calculations, I was still short on sleep by about eight hours. Norma Kay had kept me up until two with her steady litany of complaints of injustices, sacrifices, and pathetic entreaties for Malachi's prayers. If she'd been at Ruby Bee's drinking coffee (instead of at the state lab on a stainless-steel table), I would have lectured her up one wall and down the other about personal responsibility. All of which was why I was feeling surly.

"When I get around to it," I said.

Ruby Bee was equally chipper. "And that'll be when you've finished stuffing your face, I suppose. I don't recollect Perry Mason asking the judge for a recess so he could go have a pizza."

"Sure he did," I said between bites. "I think his favorite was pepperoni—or was it Italian sausage?"

This sent Ruby Bee into the kitchen, which was what it was intended to do. I was not left to eat in peace, of course. Cabinet doors were slammed and pots and pans banged about so I would appreciate exactly how irritated she was. Ruby Bee is many things, but never subtle.

"I want to ask you something," I said when she came out of the kitchen. "Did you notice any differences between the first night of the revival and last night's performance?"

Momentarily defused, she thought for a moment. "On the first night, Seraphina came floating down in a big billow of pink smoke. You could see the wires, but it was still enough to take your breath away. She sang a real sweet song about the angel of love coming into folks' heart and helping them to find Jesus. Last night Chastity just came out and sang a second hymn. I guess she couldn't bring herself to do what her sister used to do. I wonder why they didn't just skip that part?"

"All the lights and music are run by computer. It may require major programming to make any changes," I said, trying to remember what Joey had said about controlling the special effects from a van.

"The ushers were subdued last night," Ruby Bee continued, oblivious to my faint frown. "That's understandable, what with their coach being murdered. On the first night, they were as friendly as puppies. Darla Jean took my arm and escorted me right down to the front row, all the while asking how I was doing and if I had any health problems that Malachi should pray about. I considered mentioning my ingrown toenail, but decided not to."

"Did you fill out one of the cards?"

"Darla Jean made me take one, but I didn't have a pencil handy and Estelle's pen was leaking all over her fingers, so I put the card in my purse." She paused, her eyes flickering as she thought. "Do you reckon Malachi knew about folks' problems from reading their cards before he came out onstage? He'd sure have to have some memory to keep all the names and details straight. What's more, on the first night I was sitting so close to Petrol Buchanon that I couldn't help but be aware of his body odor—and I happened to notice he stuck his card in his pocket instead of writing anything on it. Just the same, Malachi Hope called Petrol by name, prayed over him, and told him to stand up out of his wheelchair and walk. Estelle and I weren't all that impressed, since we'd seen him walking under his own steam toward the tent before the revival started. He had a walker, but he was moving right sprightly for an old geezer."

I finished my coffee and slid off the stool. "Thanks for breakfast."

"Are you going to Cory's house now? The fact that he and Chastity were carrying on like that gives him a motive to kill Seraphina, assuming she found out about it. Maybe she went to Norma Kay to get Cory fired. That's why Cory killed her, too."

"He killed two women in order to continue coaching the Maggody Marauders?"

"Well, maybe he was afraid he'd go to jail on account of Chastity's age."

"Even if he were convicted of statutory rape or contributing to the delinquency of a minor, he'd end up on probation. The state prisons are packed to overflowing with violent criminals; having consensual sex with a fifteen-year-old wouldn't earn him a cell."

"I'm just trying to help," she said, sighing.

She looked so dejected that I went behind the bar to give her a hug. "I know you are, but I wish you wouldn't," I said. I also wished that Third World nations would quit having civil wars, Mexican food would be determined to be fat-free, people would stop talking about cyberspace until I figured out what it meant, and a publisher would show up at my front door with a million-dollar contract for my memoirs.

Ruby Bee arched her eyebrows. "What about John Robert Scurfpea? He might—"

"Do I smell something burning in the kitchen?"

As she bustled away, I headed across the dance floor. Cory Jenks would have to wait while I made a small detour by the PD to call Harve and hash over the significance of the thread linking Norma Kay and Seraphina.

The door of the PD was ajar, which meant what precious little cold air the air conditioner produced was escaping. It also meant I'd had a visitor. Or still had one. I eased open the door and looked around, but the stacks of notebooks and folders on the desk appeared to be undisturbed. The pile of catalogs and magazines in the corner had shifted, but that could have happened during the Mesozoic period when a brontosaurus thudded by. (Did I mention I'm not much on housekeeping?) The answering machine, bless its fiendish red flasher, was still on the desk. I continued inside and was reaching for the telephone when I heard a noise in the back room.

It was not the snarl of a homicidal maniac, but I rather wished I had a weapon more lethal than a rolled-up copy (complimentary) of *Field & Stream*. Reminding myself that I'd once been trained in self-defense, I tiptoed across the room, mentally composed a sentence along the lines of "Come out with your hands up or I'll shoot," and stepped into the doorway.

And promptly crashed into Kevin Buchanon.

Both of us were too alarmed to do more than stagger backward, gasping and gaping. Kevin looked as if he might pass out; I myself was having trouble keeping my balance as I banged into the desk.

"What the hell do you think you're doing?" I demanded when I found my voice. "Get your sorry ass out here and explain before"—I struggled to find a suitable threat—"I get out my gun and shoot you between the eyes! I mean it, Kevin."

He came to the doorway. "Golly, Arly, I din't mean to scare you. I came by to ask you something, but you weren't in here so I went in the back room to see if you were there. Then all of a sudden, I heard somebody sneaking into the PD, so I thought I'd better make sure who it was in case it was a criminal that was going to steal your gun."

"And you were going to render him unconscious with that?" I asked, pointing at the flyswatter in his hand.

He blushed, but it was not becoming. "I 'spose I'm acting doddly on account of being about as worried as my skin will hold."

Accepting the inevitability of the situation, I sat down behind my desk and said, "About Dahlia, right?"

"Yeah, like I tried to tell you yesterday, Malachi Hope called her up on stage and told her that if she trusted Jesus, she was cured of diabetes. She swears she felt a tingle when it happened, so it had to be true. Now she's back to eating cookies and pork chops, even more than she used to in order to make up for when she was on the diet. I tried to talk to her, but she just keeps saying that I'm blasphemin' if I don't believe Jesus cured her."

"Oh, shit," I said under my breath.

"Please, can't you make her go to the clinic?" Kevin said, leaning so far forward I had a distasteful view of his latest outbreak of pimples. "She finally agreed to go to the revival last night and make sure Malachi Hope knew she was pregnant when he cured her, but her name din't get called and she says she won't go tonight because she's gonna fry up some chickens."

I leaned back and gazed at the ceiling. Taking a drumstick out of Dahlia's fist would be more dangerous than snatching a piece of raw flesh out of a pit bull's mouth. The so-called miracles from the previous evening had struck me as nothing more than subterfuges to fill the aluminum buckets; now they took on a more sinister air.

"Would you like to come to supper?" Kevin said eagerly. "Mebbe you can reason with her after we eat and she's in a good mood."

The thought of watching Dahlia devour an entire chicken and everything else she could reach was enough to make me queasy. "I don't think I'll have time," I managed to say with a measure of regret, all of it feigned. "I'm going to interview Malachi Hope later today. Perhaps I can persuade him to call Dahlia and order her back on the diet until she sees her doctor."

"Will he do it?"

"He may, if I threaten to file charges for practicing

medicine without a license. That's the kind of publicity he might prefer to avoid. In the meantime, don't worry too much about Dahlia. She's been off her diet only two days."

"Thanks, Arly," he said. "You know, when I was in the back room I got to remembering how I used to clean the PD for you and be your unofficial deputy. Jim Bob keeps saying how he's gonna fire me, so I was wondering if—"

"No!" I gestured at the door. "Now, if you don't mind, I have work to do."

He stood up and made it to the door without tripping over his feet. "If you change your mind, just lemme know."

"May I have my flyswatter?"

He stared at it as if it were an alien life-form that had wormed its way into his hand during the conversation. "Do you want I should put it back where I found it?"

"On my desk will be fine, Kevin."

Once he was gone, I decided to put off calling Harve and made a list of the so-called miracles Malachi Hope had performed for the gullible crowd. Some of the specifics, such as Leslie Biden's ulcer and Dahlia's diabetes, could have been gleaned from prayer cards—but Ruby Bee had said that Petrol Buchanon had not filled one out and Malachi had used his name. The mysterious Wilma had been reluctant to be singled out; even if she'd filled out a card, she would not have described her clothing. Malachi had, though, right down to the color of the flowers on her hat. If Jesus hadn't told him, someone else had. I sat back and tried again to recall what Joey had told me about the special effects.

Ten minutes later I parked in front of the McIlhaney house. Before I could get out of the car, Darla Jean came out the front door and flew across the yard as if the prison guards and bloodhounds were not far behind.

"You looking for me?" she said.

"You and Heather," I said, nodding. "Let's go find her, and then the three of us are going to have a talk."

Darla Jean looked back at her house as she got into the car. "I already told you what I know."

"Now you're going to tell me some things you didn't know you knew. Where's Heather likely to be?"

"She's at home. I just got finished talking to her on the telephone five minutes ago. I don't understand how I can tell you things I don't know."

But I did.

I drove to Heather's house, and shortly thereafter the two girls and I sat down at the picnic table next to the Dairee Dee-Lishus. They were not pleased that they might be spotted in close proximity to the enemy, but I was hoping some of their teammates might show up and contribute to the subject.

"Okay," I began, "what instructions did Seraphina give you before the opening night of the revival?"

From her expression, it was obvious Darla Jean had been expecting a different question. She had been holding her cup so tightly that limeade had trickled down her fingers, but now she released her grip and said, "She told us to put on the badges and make sure we greeted everybody by name and talked with them so they would feel comfortable."

"In a loud voice," Heather added. "She said most of the folks that come to the revival are older, so their hearing might not be real good. She said old folks get cranky if they can't make out what you're saying."

"Were you supposed to ask questions?" I said.

Darla Jean shrugged. "Yeah, if we didn't know 'em, we asked their names and where they lived. If this was the first time they'd been to a Hope Is Here revival. If they were wanting Malachi to say a special prayer. I smiled so much my cheeks were aching by the end of the first hour."

I turned to Heather. "Last night I saw you escort the woman named Wilma to her seat. What happened with her?"

"I guess she's shy. I had to ask her three times what her name was before she mumbled that it was Wilma. When I asked her about the special prayer, she finally said she was worried about losing her job. I couldn't get another word out of her, even after I lied and said I liked her hat. It looked to be right out of a thrift shop."

"What did Leslie Bidens say to you, Darla Jean? Did she mention her ulcer?"

"Yeah, and she made me swear not to say anything until she finds out for sure how serious it is. I suggested she write it down on the prayer card, but she just took the card from me and stuffed it in her purse."

This pretty much fit my theory concerning Malachi's inside knowledge. I moved on to the next issue. "I want you to tell me every last word you said to Heather after Norma Kay told you to deliver her note."

"I can't tell you," she said, staring down at the table. "I promised that I wouldn't."

"Two women have been murdered," I persisted. "I can't stop this madness unless I know what's been going on. A half-truth's no better than a lie. If you don't tell the whole truth right now, I'm going to take you and Heather to the sheriff's office and keep you in separate interrogation rooms until you change your minds. Some real unsanitary suspects have sat in those rooms, spitting and scratching. The sheriff has been trying for years to convince the mayor to supplement the budget so the rooms can be fumigated, but he hasn't had any luck."

Heather's imagination was working well. Gulping, she said, "Go ahead and tell her, Darla Jean. If you won't, I will."

"Okay," Darla Jean said unhappily. "I pulled Heather over to one side and asked her if she thought Coach Grapper had found out somehow that Chastity's pregnant and if the coach was going to tell Malachi. Heather said she didn't see how Coach Grapper could have, so I went behind the curtain and delivered the note like I told you earlier."

I nodded as if I'd known this all along. "What did you say to Chastity while you waited for Malachi to finish his conversation with the other man?"

"Pretty much what I said to Heather. Chastity tried to convince me not to give it to him, but I was afraid Coach Grapper would find out and kick me off the team. Then my parents would get all fired up and go ask her why, and she'd tell 'em, and I'd be up to my neck in bull hockey. I said all that to Chastity. She was pissed, but after I wouldn't back down, she made me promise to wait for her after the revival."

"Who's the father?" I asked.

Darla Jean hesitated for a moment, working the straw up and down in her cup. "I promised I wouldn't tell anyone. Besides, all I know is what Chastity said in the locker room after the first practice. She could have been lying, and it's a sin to bear false witness."

"You already told Heather," I said. "Now tell me."

"Joey," she whispered.

"What else did Chastity say in the locker room?"

When Darla Jean mutely shook her head, Heather said, "I don't see what difference it makes now. Chastity wanted to know where she could get an abortion without her sister or Malachi finding out. Or Joey, for that matter."

"That's why you took her to Farberville," I said, trying to sound matter-of-fact, if not downright omniscient. "Which clinic did you take her to?"

Darla Jean looked up with a trace of defiance. "I told Chastity I didn't know of any place in Farberville where a minor could get an abortion without parental consent. All she said when she called yesterday morning was that she was desperate for a ride into town. We dropped her off where I told you; she didn't say where she was going and I didn't ask her. For all I know, she was planning to panhandle on the street to get enough money to run away."

I watched a yellow jacket wallowing in a puddle of limeade as I struggled to assimilate all this. It was obvious that Seraphina knew about the pregnancy; she'd fired Joey, then tracked Chastity down at the table where I was currently sitting. They'd argued for more than an hour before Seraphina had left Chastity at the RV and driven away. Or had she?

I thanked the girls for their candor and drove back to the PD. As soon as Harve came on the line, I said, "You

mentioned there was no driver's license in Seraphina
Hope's purse. Was there any money?"

"Just some loose change. You think she might have
picked up a hitchhiker that robbed and killed her? I
s'pose I can call down at the FBI office in Little Rock and
see if they know of a serial killer that might have come
this way. I don't much like talking to those shiny-shoed
sumbitches, but I will."

"Why would he take her driver's license instead of
her credit cards? If he was on foot, why didn't he dump
the body in some isolated spot and take the car?"

Harve rumbled, no doubt belching smoke like an
awakening volcano. "I ain't got time for guessing games,
Arly. The county prosecutor's on my ass like a spotted
tick, wanting to know when we'll have something.
McBeen is convinced you strangled the victims just to
screw up his vacation plans. I've got a damn bevy of reporters outside my office—you can expect 'em out your
way within hours as soon as the autopsy reports are released. Malachi Hope may not be as famous as some of
those ol' boys, but Elvis hasn't been seen since his
granddaughter married that stringy-haired fellow with
the glove, and this story's gonna make good copy."

I related what I'd learned from Darla Jean and
Heather, then said, "Chastity may have stolen the driver's license to use as proof of age at an abortion clinic.
There's some family resemblance. I didn't think to ask
what Chastity was wearing or if her hair was fluffed out
like Seraphina's, but I wouldn't be surprised to find out
that it was. She probably took money, too, so she could
pay cash. Can you have somebody check with all the

clinics and family planning centers and find out if she
was there?"

"I don't know if they'll tell us without a warrant."

"This is a murder investigation, dammit, and all
we're asking is if someone calling herself Seraphina
Hope came into the office yesterday morning. It doesn't
matter whether they performed a procedure, made an
appointment, or even booted her out on her butt for using a phony ID. What matters, Harve, is how Chastity
ended up with the license."

"Are you saying she might have strangled her sister?" asked Harve. "How old is she—fifteen, maybe sixteen? Doesn't that sound a little cold-blooded?"

"It sounds real cold-blooded," I said. "She was upset
yesterday when I informed her of her sister's death, but
maybe what I saw was guilt. It's possible that during the
argument Seraphina threatened to send Chastity to some
sort of fundamentalist boot camp for unwed mothers.
Chastity flipped out and strangled her, then drove the
car to the creek, stole what she could use from Seraphina's purse, and was back at the RV when Malachi
arrived."

"How did Seraphina know Chastity was pregnant?"

I permitted myself a smug smile. "I haven't confirmed this yet, but I think the badges the ushers wear
have concealed microphones. The girls had no idea that
everything they said was being monitored in the van.
Joey mentioned that once the show starts, he *listens* for
indications of trouble. My guess is that Seraphina takes
the first shift, choosing potential patsies and making
notes based on what they let slip to the ushers. Later,
when she's onstage, Joey or perhaps Thomas Fratelleon

communicates with Malachi through a hearing aid. When Malachi presses his temple in order to hear Jesus better, he may be listening to a less divine source."

"Did he know about the pregnancy?"

"I don't know. Seraphina might have told him, or Chastity, or he might have been hiding in a dirty towel hamper in the girls' locker room when Chastity told Darla Jean."

Harve chuckled at the frustration in my voice. "Guess you'd better get in gear and solve this before you find yourself featured on one of those unsolved-crime shows."

I replaced the receiver. After some more thought, I drove to the high school gym to see for myself how big the dirty towel hampers were.

What I ended up staring at was the intercom speaker above the door.

Brother Verber was on his knees in the sanctuary, his elbows propped on the back of the next pew, his fingers entwined, his eyes squeezed closed, and his face awash with sweat.

"How much trouble could it be to let me heal folks, Jesus? It's not like I'd tackle things like cancer or heart disease or kidney stones. I'd be pleased as punch to go after bunions, rashes, minor problems like that. Why, for the first year, I won't try poison ivy. It doesn't seem fair to let Malachi Hope be the only preacher in Stump County blessed with the ability to heal folks and fill those buckets with dollar bills."

He took a short recess to pull out a handkerchief and

wipe his face, all the while searching his mind for the most eloquent way to phrase his petition. "Jesus," he began again, "I don't have to have a cotton-candy machine or a fancy crystal cathedral. That's not to say a radio show wouldn't be right nice. It wouldn't have to be more than once a week for an hour. We might ought to find someone who can play the piano better than Lottie Estes, but she'll do at first. With all the offerings folks mail in, we can do wonderful things for the heathens in Africa. We can send them shoes and Bibles every month."

He waited to see if he felt a tingle that would let him know Jesus was mulling over the proposition. The only thing he felt was a dull ache in his knees.

"We can call it 'Brother Verber's Hour of . . .' " He stopped and scratched his chin. Nothing seemed to rhyme with Verber, except *Gerber*, which was baby food, and *Thurber*, which was a street in Farberville. Maybe they could fudge on the rhyme. " 'Brother Verber's Hour of Fervor'?" he suggested tentatively. "Just give me one little ol' tingle if I come across one you like, okay? I don't need a bolt of lightning or anything wasteful—just a tingle."

Ruby Bee knocked on Bur Grapper's door, and when he opened it, said real smoothly, "Estelle and I thought we'd drop by and see how you're doing, Bur. We brought casseroles for when all of Norma Kay's kinfolk arrive for the funeral. Why don't I just put 'em in the refrigerator for you?" She pushed past him and into the living room, dearly hoping Estelle wasn't dashing for the station wagon.

"That's right nice of you, Ruby Bee," Bur said as he shuffled back to let them come inside. "I just this morning got hold of Norma Kay's sister, but I couldn't tell her when the funeral will be."

He was wearing a bathrobe and slippers, even though it was the middle of the afternoon. It wasn't hard to see that he hadn't shaved in two days. His eyelids were puffy, his nose red, his skin slack and sallow. The floor was strewn with beer cans, but there were no dirty dishes to indicate he'd had a meal.

Ruby Bee had anticipated resistance, even anger, but he looked so pathetic that she said, "You sit down and let me fix you something to eat, Bur. Estelle, why don't you come into the kitchen with me and start a pot of coffee while I make some sandwiches?"

Bur sat down on a tattered recliner and picked up a remote control. His thumb moved across the buttons, but the television screen remained as blank as his expression.

"What's wrong with him?" Estelle demanded in a low voice as she filled a glass pot with water.

"We might have been mistaken," Ruby Bee said, peering at the skimpy contents of the refrigerator. "His heart may be broken on account of Norma Kay."

"The only thing about him that's broken is his nose," Estelle countered.

Ruby Bee found that on the uncharitable side, but she didn't say so as she took out eggs and butter. After all, they'd agreed on the purpose of their mission, and squabbling wouldn't help. "How 'bout an omelet and toast?" she called to Bur. She took silence for agreement and got busy hunting for a spatula and a skillet. "He barely knows we're here," she whispered. "This is a golden opportunity for you to search the other rooms."

"Me? I wouldn't know where to start, and besides, what if he catches me red-handed?"

"He ain't gonna do anything but sit out there and stare at the wall like he's been hit up the side of the head with a two-by-four." Ruby Bee raised her voice. "Bur, would you happen to know where Norma Kay keeps her spatula?" When there was no reply, she said more softly, "See? He's too depressed to catch a cold, much less catch you snooping around in the bedroom. Look for a bundle of letters tied with a ribbon, or a heart-shaped box."

Estelle took a quick peek into the living room. "He hasn't twitched," she said, "but what if he starts roaming around?"

"I'll keep him occupied," Ruby Bee said firmly. She put on the apron she'd found, turned on a burner on the stove, and took a bowl from a cabinet. "We don't have all day, Estelle. As soon as this is ready, I'll sit with him while he eats. If he acts like he's gonna get up, I'll say something real loud about how we have to go. You can come out and say you were washing your hands in the bathroom."

"This stinks worse than a buzzard's roost."

Ruby Bee would have put her hands on her hips if she hadn't been whisking the eggs. "You saw him, for pity's sake. He's nothing but an old man that lost his wife two days ago."

"I lost her a long time ago," Bur said from the doorway. He spoke in a monotone, but his eyes were no longer flat and lifeless. "She made me the laughingstock of the town, what with her wanton ways. Now I aim to kill myself. It remains to be seen if I kill you two first."

Neither Ruby Bee nor Estelle said anything to contradict him. They didn't say anything at all—not with a shotgun pointing at them.

14

CORY JENKS did not offer me a glass of iced tea, much
less a peck on the cheek. He'd tried to keep me standing
on his porch, but I'd given him a choice: his living room
or the sheriff's department. The whimsical description of
the interrogation room that had worked so well with
Heather and Darla Jean had not been necessary.

"What do you want now?" he said as we stood in the
middle of the room. "How many times do I have to tell
you that after I got back from Emmet I didn't go anywhere or see anyone? Do you want to count the beer
cans in the trash?"

I moved some papers and soiled shirts off a chair and
sat down. "I know you were sleeping with Norma Kay.
I don't have adequate evidence to convince a jury,
but—"

"Jury?" he said, so startled he dropped his jock posture and sank down on the edge of his couch. "I didn't
hurt Norma Kay. We may have spent some time together
at tournaments, but I didn't pressure her into anything.

Hell, it was her idea from the start. Her marriage was dead; she could hardly stand to be in the same room with her husband. She wanted sex and affection—and I couldn't afford to rebuff her overtures."

"Because she might screw up your likelihood of getting the head coach position?" I asked. "Are you implying that she coerced you into the affair?"

Cory studied my overtly hostile expression, assessing his chances of conning me with some crock-of-shit story of sexual harassment. "Not really, but there were things she could tell Bur that would hurt my chances."

"For instance?"

"For some stupid reason, she thought I might have had something to do with Amos Dooley's accident. I was at a bar in Starley City that night, with plenty of witnesses, but she saw a truck parked down the road from Amos's house. How many blue trucks with gun racks are there in Stump County, fer crissake?"

"Let's talk about your truck," I said. "Yesterday I had a witness who said your truck was not in your driveway at the time Norma Kay was killed. Now I have another witness who puts your truck outside the gym at that very time."

"That's crazy," he growled.

"She saw not only the gun rack but also the bumper stickers on the tailgate."

"I was here, dammit!"

"Alone?"

Cory slumped back and began to play with a torn throw pillow. "Yeah, alone."

"It's too bad Chastity wasn't here to give you an alibi," I said, clucking sympathetically. "I haven't taken her statement yet, but several people have agreed she was in the RV by 12:30 at the latest." I paused while I ran through the chronology. "Were you still out in your front yard when a white Mercedes drove up the road?"

"After the Cadillac went by, I took the case of beer inside, locked the door, and closed the curtains. I warmed up some pizza, opened a beer, and flipped through the channels until I found a John Wayne war movie with lots of bazookas and hand grenades. When it was over, I found something else along the same lines. I didn't set foot outside this house until I drove over to the gym a little after eleven yesterday morning. Give me a lie detector test if you want." He gulped as what I'd said sank through his thick skull, then tried to cover his reaction with unconvincing belligerence. "What's that smart-ass crack about Chastity supposed to mean? Why the hell would she have been here to give me an alibi?"

"Oh, Cory, I'm disappointed in you. Estelle Oppers saw her in this very room yesterday afternoon, reportedly in provocative attire. Do you truly believe Estelle decided to take it with her to the grave rather than risk tarnishing your reputation? Did you just get off the turnip truck?"

Cory looked as though he wished he could get on the turnip truck and disappear in a cloud of dust. "The one and only time anything happened was yesterday. Chastity showed up at maybe 1:30 or 2:00, asking if she could use the telephone because the one in the RV wasn't working. I said okay and went back to working on the playbook. Before I knew what was going on, she came out in nothing but her underwear. I told her to get dressed and leave, but she started crawling all over me like a kudzu vine, and we ended up ... well, you know."

"All I know is Chastity is a minor and you just confessed to a felony. Jesus, Cory—did you ever consider saying no to this veritable queue of seductresses outside your front door? Is your brain in your jockstrap?"

"Are you gonna arrest me?"

"When I have time, I'll discuss it with the county prosecutor. I'm not sure what he'll do, but if I were you, I wouldn't be trying on Amos's whistle. Where's yours, by the way?"

He gave me a befuddled look. "I dunno. The last time I saw it was on my desk in my office. I haven't been there since Friday. I guess it's still there."

I was beginning to think he might be telling the truth, at least about the night Norma Kay and Seraphina were killed. I repeated my previous order that he not leave town, slammed the door on my way out, and started across the cluttered yard. Cory's truck was in the driveway, complete with stocked gun rack. The NRA bumper stickers were on the tailgate for the simple reason there was no bumper.

I stuck my head through the open window. The upholstery was cracked and crisscrossed with silver tape, tins of chewing tobacco were scattered on the floorboard, and several magazines indicated Cory's taste ran in directions other than scientific inquiry or quaint literary journals. The swimsuit issue of *Sports Illustrated* was so smeared with greasy fingerprints that the cover model looked as if she'd been paddling in the wake of the

Exxon Valdez. A plastic nude posed on the dashboard. From the key chain dangled another plastic nude.

I got in my car and drove up the hill, wryly noting Estelle's station wagon parked in front of Bur Grapper's house. Ruby Bee could have taken my request to heart and was doing nothing more devious than making a condolence call with a green bean casserole and a compassionate smile.

And I could anticipate a dinner invitation from the White House in the morning mail.

I told myself she and Estelle couldn't get themselves into too much trouble, then resumed thinking about microphones, intercoms, pregnancies, and motives for murder.

Thomas Fratelleon came out of the tent and waited in the shade as I parked and got out of the car. He still resembled a headmaster, but this time he wasn't playing the gracious host. "Is there something I can do for you, Miss Hanks?"

"You can persuade Malachi to allow me to question Chastity without a lawyer or anyone else present. Otherwise, when I arrange for a formal interview, I'll request that it be held at the sheriff's office in Farberville. This isn't an election year, but the sheriff is as hungry for media coverage as he is for black-eyed peas on New Year's Day. He usually holds his press conferences on the courthouse steps for the convenience of the television cameras. The angles are flattering."

"Is that to be construed as a threat?"

"It's not a dinner invitation from the White House, Mr. Fratelleon. Before we explore it any further, I'd like to see the van."

"The van?" he said, frowning at me as if I'd asked him to drop his trousers so I could see his boxer shorts. "That is Joey's realm of expertise, and I don't think I could explain the equipment with any lucidity. Perhaps you might come back later when he's here?"

"There's his bike."

Fratelleon tugged at his knotted necktie. "Well, it's possible he's around here somewhere. I'm so distressed by Seraphina's death that I hardly know what I'm doing. We worked very closely for the last two years, choosing sites for revivals, dealing with financial aspects, finding reliable employees, even keeping track of other evangelists to make sure we didn't overlap territories. Malachi can be moody at times, but Seraphina was always congenial and pleasant to be around. She and I were the ones who saw the potential of the City of Hope. I may have been more concerned than she with the financial prospects; she thought about nothing but the sinners who could be saved and the blessings—"

"The van," I said to disrupt the eulogy.

"As you wish."

I followed him into the tent, where a few workmen were sweeping up debris and straightening benches. The stillness was a contrast to the previous evening's electrified atmosphere.

"How much did you rake in last night?" I asked.

"Close to twenty thousand dollars," Fratelleon said as he held back the curtain and gestured for me to proceed him. "That's the gross amount. We have expenses such as salaries, housing, restaurant tabs, publicity, and utilities. The contributions usually taper off during the week, then shoot up on the final night. The trend may be different this week. When Seraphina's death is more widely publicized, people will come out of curiosity as well as spiritual concerns."

"To take a stroll through the valley of the shadow of death," I said, glumly acknowledging the accuracy of his observation.

"Very good, Miss Hanks. I understand you attended the revival last night. Did it stir up some deeply buried memories from your religious training as a child?"

I didn't bother to answer him. The equipment behind the curtain was impressive, although I wasn't sure of each component's purpose. Multicolored cables and wires curled across the floor like motionless snakes; some disappeared beneath the curtain, while others went under the back wall of the tent. Cardboard cartons were set along one side; the nearest one was filled with cellophane-wrapped packages of blank prayer cards. Two cots were stacked in a corner, and at least three dozen buckets made a precarious pyramid. The fuse box could have hung on a wall in a modern art gallery.

"Making miracles requires an investment in technology," Fratelleon murmured. "We were exceedingly lucky to find Joey."

"Then why don't we find him now?"

He led the way out of the tent and rapped on the windshield of a large van. "Joey's redoing the portion of the programming that involved Seraphina's dramatic descent. Eventually we'll put it back in, when Chastity feels able to assume more responsibility."

Joey slid open a door on the side of the van. "Can it wait, Thomas? I'm right in the middle of making the changes, and I don't want to . . ." He looked at me. "Is this official business?"

"I'd like to see the interior," I said.

He stepped back to allow me to climb inside. It was cool, almost chilly, and very crowded with panels, monitors, a control board, and headphones. Two folding chairs had been fitted in, but there was scarcely room for two people.

I told Joey to close the door. Once he'd complied, leaving Fratelleon outside, I said, "Let's not waste any time. The badges the ushers wear have concealed microphones. Someone can sit in here and listen to what's said in the tent." I picked up a file card from a stack on the narrow table and scanned it. At the top was an unfamiliar name and beneath it: "Sprained left ankle while gardening."

"I guess sprained ankles are too tough to tackle," I said to Joey, who was watching me with a wary expression. "The person might still be limping at the end of the show. Something with no overt symptoms, like an ulcer or diabetes, would be a better prospect. By the time the victim is doubled over with pain, Hope Is Here is long gone." I sorted through more cards until I found one with my name on it and a notation that read: "Divorcée, not adjusting well." I managed not to wad it up and hurl it at him.

He nodded. "Yeah, Seraphina was always real careful to choose people in wheelchairs who'd made it to the tent under their own power. The ushers are supposed to coerce the elderly into agreeing to the wheelchairs in order to have the best seats. Most of them get so caught up in the enthusiasm that they don't want to spoil the moment. Warhol's fifteen minutes of fame, I guess."

I tapped the microphone. "And this is how the information is sent to Malachi. He wears some sort of device in his ear, doesn't he? Which of you tells him about his next quarry?"

"Me, since Thomas and Seraphina are onstage a lot of the time."

"Was Seraphina here Sunday night during the hour before the revival started?"

"More than likely. I was doing a last-minute tour to make sure everything was set. When I got back here, she was gone but the cards were arranged in the order she'd decided on. All I did after that was listen to what was happening and feed Malachi bits when he cued me. The music, smoke, and lights run themselves. Every now and then a problem arises when Malachi screws up the timing, but it all went smoothly Sunday night."

"Until Seraphina fired you," I said. "I know why, Joey. She heard two of the ushers talking about Chastity's pregnancy. Your name was mentioned. She waited until the show was over, hunted you down, and let you have it, didn't she?"

"She was furious," he admitted. "I just let her scream at me until she ran out of steam. Then told her I'd be gone first thing in the morning. That's when she got in her car and went to find Chastity. I'm glad I wasn't there when she did. Seraphina believed in the old-fashioned version of morality—all the 'thou shalt not' stuff. She truly wanted to save Chastity from doing things that might ruin her chances of a normal, happy life."

"By dressing her in a halo and shoving her out in front of a thousand religious zealots?"

"Bringing Chastity on these tours was the only way Seraphina could keep an eye on her night and day."

I gave him a wry smile. "But they slipped up at least one time, didn't they? Chastity didn't get pregnant up onstage while everybody was occupied passing buckets."

"Chastity is her stage name," Joey said, rolling his eyes. "Seraphina and Malachi must have chosen it in hopes that hearing it all the time might influence her behavior. 'Lolita' would have been more accurate."

"So she seduced you, huh?"

"You could say that."

"I just did, Joey." I gave him a moment to embellish his response, then said, "I'm a little surprised Malachi asked you to stay. He's not what I'd call a liberal thinker in matters of parenting."

"He's as determined as Thomas to build the City of Hope and make a friggin' fortune. He eventually could find someone to replace me, but right now he needs the razzle-dazzle to keep his audience entertained enough to shell out big bucks. He can't risk not having someone who can handle the glitches that inevitably happen."

"What about Chastity?" I said, trying (but not very hard) to keep the disgust out of my voice. "Is he going to drag her onstage as a reminder of the consequences of lust? Public degradation was big in the seventeenth century, but I'm not sure it's all that popular these days."

"I dunno what he'll do. I'm probably not going to stick around much longer, even for seventy-five hundred a month. I think I'll get a job with a Southern California outfit so in my free time I can do something more stimulating than count cows."

In that he earned roughly ten times what I did, I

didn't offer any financial advice. I stood up, banging my head on the roof of the van in the process. "Don't leave town until I give you permission."

"Hey, I didn't murder Seraphina," he said quickly. "Malachi was certain he could convince her to keep me on until he had the funding for the project lined up. If not, I just told you I'm not worried about finding another job. These guys spy on one another all the time, and they care about results, not references."

My head was spinning as I stepped back out into the sweltering sunshine. Evangelical espionage? Maybe I'd have to recruit Ruby Bee and Estelle to investigate. One of them could slap on an usher's badge and artfully grill suspects while the other one eavesdropped from the station wagon.

Thomas Fratelleon had vanished. Wondering if he'd gone to the RV to relay my message to Malachi, I went back into the tent and lay down on a bench by the stage. The cleaning crew had departed. A faint breeze made the heat tolerable. The only sound was that of the distant generator.

It was time to do some serious thinking.

"Honey," Jim Bob began tentatively, "I had a funny phone call at the store this morning."

Mrs. Jim Bob did not look up from the notebook in her lap. "Take your feet off the coffee table. This is not a pool hall, despite the stench of beer that seems to surround you all the time. Furthermore, I distinctly smelled cigar smoke when I came home last night. I thought we'd agreed that you would go outside when indulging in that filthy habit."

She'd done the agreeing for the both of them, but he wasn't about to point that out. "About this phone call," he tried again.

"Were you smoking a cigar in this room yesterday?"

"I smoked one out in the hammock. Maybe there was smoke in my clothes when I came back inside. Now, this woman called from—"

"I have no desire to hear about your womanizing, Jim Bob. You may think I was unaware of your late-night visits to that harlot's apartment last spring, but I can always tell when you're bending the truth. I cannot begin to count the hours I've spent in the Voice of the Almighty Lord Assembly Hall on my knees to pray for your soul. I have beseeched the Lord to forgive your lascivious ways and put you back on the path of righteousness. If Malachi Hope wasn't a charlatan, I'd ask him to cure you. It's going to take a miracle."

Jim Bob sat back, resigned to waiting until the bill came and he could find out where she'd spent the two thousand dollars that had caught the notice of the credit card company. He had a pretty good guess what was likely to be involved; whenever she got a bug up her ass, new upholstery was in the foreseeable future.

Brother Verber applied lipstick, then stepped back to admire the overall effect in the bathroom mirror. He wasn't any Marilyn Monroe or Dorothy Lamour, but no one would accuse him of being as ugly as a mud fence stuck with tadpoles. He adjusted the wig so the one side partially covered his eye à la Veronica Lake, pursed his lips, and gave hisself a sultry look.

Even though he'd drawn the blinds, he stopped in the hallway and peered around the corner to make sure there was no way imaginable anyone could see into the living room. Folks wouldn't understand, he told hisself as he wobbled across the carpet. They'd go leaping to the wrong conclusion—that he, spiritual leader of the community and a card-carryin' Republican, was putting on women's clothes for a sinful reason. Before he could explain, he'd be hearing snide insinuations about how he'd become a homosexual. Why, didn't he know better than any of them what feisty ol' Paul had written to the Romans on account of their propensity for graven images?

Brother Verber clutched the back of a chair, pretending it was his pulpit, and held up a finger to hold the attention of his illusive congregation. " 'For this cause God gave them up into vile affections: for even their women did change the natural use into that which is against nature; and likewise also the men, leaving the natural use of the woman, burned in their lust one toward another.' "

After giving them a minute to think this over, he sat down and pulled off the high-heeled shoes to massage his feet. "I am dressed this way," he continued, "because Jesus may want me to go out again in a disguise. He may want me to spy on fornicating devil worshipers. To do that, I'm gonna have to be able to sneak up on them without letting them know who it is. I'm trying on different costumes for Jesus, brothers and sisters."

"Bur, you're acting crazy," Ruby Bee said, forcing herself not to stare openly at the shotgun in case he'd forgotten that it was right there in his lap. She and Estelle were on the sofa, and there wasn't much chance either of them could lunge across the room and grab the shotgun without getting plugged. "We all understand how upset you are about Norma Kay, but that doesn't give you the right to treat us like this."

He glanced at her, then resumed his study of the shotgun. "I already told you to shut up, Ruby Bee. I didn't take any sass from my players, and I ain't gonna take any from you, either."

"Now, Bur," Estelle said, "why don't you let Ruby Bee finish fixing you a nourishing omelet? You'll feel a lot better with something in your stomach."

"Good idea. Go get me a beer, and don't pull any tricks. If I hear the back door open, I'll splatter Ruby Bee across the wall. I never did care for the wallpaper, but Norma Kay picked it out after she moved here."

Estelle skittered into the kitchen. Ruby Bee sucked in a breath and let it out only when Estelle returned with a beer in her hand. "Didn't Norma Kay live in Topeka?" she asked to distract him.

"Yeah, she was the basketball coach."

"Isn't that an interesting coincidence?" said Estelle, smiling real nicely at him.

He opened the beer and took a swallow. "It wasn't much of a coincidence. I took the team to a tournament there. The girls' teams weren't playing, so Norma Kay was running the hospitality room for the coaches and referees."

Ruby Bee managed a smile. "Really?"

"Did you think we met while being abducted by aliens?" he said irritably. "After the game, I asked her if she wanted to go for coffee and we got to know each other. I saw her again at another tournament—it doesn't matter where—and we had dinner. Then all the trouble started. She used to call me and whimper like a baby, and I even drove up there twice to try to help out. When she got fired, I asked her if she wanted to get married."

"How romantic," Estelle gushed. "I'll bet she was swept off her feet when you came riding up like a knight in white armor." She was dying to ask for details, but it was too risky.

"It wasn't romantic," Bur said, giving her a sour look. "I was a widower. The house is plenty big for two people, and I don't like cleanin' or having to cook for myself. I'd already started thinking about retiring, but I wasn't sure I could get by on a pension and a check from the government. Norma Kay could have worked another twenty years."

Ruby Bee nodded. "Then it worked out for both of you. There you were, needing a wife, and there Norma Kay was, in all that trouble. I don't believe you told us what caused it."

He lifted the shotgun so it was pointing at her face. "I don't believe I did. Would you care to tell me why it's any of your damn business?" He ran his free hand through his hair. "I don't even know why you're here, unless you came to snoop around like you think you're amateur detectives. Were you going to search through Norma Kay's drawers while I sat here eating a goddamn omelet?"

The two Nancy Drews earnestly shook their heads.

"It's not as if he's totally without common sense," Mrs. Twayblade told the more reliable aide. "Mrs. Teasel's unauthorized stroll was one thing; she might have ended up out on some lonely road with no idea where she was. Petrol Buchanon knew exactly what he was doing last night when it was time to come back here in the van. He slipped away into the crowd and is most likely at some relative's house, chortling about how clever he is. You can't turn around in this county without bumping into a Buchanon."

"Is Diesel still up on Cotter's Ridge?" asked the aide.

"I do not keep track of their antics unless they are residents in this facility. The day Diesel moves in will coincide with the day I apply for a position elsewhere, preferably in another state. My point is that it would be premature to raise an alarm about Petrol. People will get the impression that security is lax."

The aide knew what was expected of her. "I, like, totally agree, Miz Twayblade. Petrol can take care of himself. It's not like it's cold outside, or even raining. He'll come crawling back real soon, all sorry for causing you to worry."

"I just finished explaining why there is no reason to worry," Mrs. Twayblade said, glaring at the aide.

"Gosh, no."

15

I was sitting on a bench when Chastity came from behind the curtain. She didn't seem all that excited to see me, but she boosted herself onto the edge of the stage, caught the tip of her ponytail and wound it around her finger, and offered me a patronizing smile. "Malachi says I have to talk to you to save him from being made an object of mockery on the local news. I guess the fact that my sister was murdered doesn't bother you. What do you want to know?"

"When you stole Seraphina's driver's license," I said.

"Who says I did?"

"I know you stole it to attempt to get an abortion without parental consent." Or at least I *thought* I knew, but this was not the time for irresolution.

She turned so pale that I was afraid she was going to pass out and do a Humpty-Dumpty number off the stage. All the king's horses and all the king's men being occupied elsewhere (meaning Jeeps and deputies), I stood up in case I needed to break her fall. She held up a hand. After a couple of deep breaths that were almost shudders, she said, "I'm just kinda surprised you know about that."

"Well, I do, but it's not a big-time felony and I won't follow up on it. There's no need to panic. Tell me the truth—okay?"

"While Seraphina was singing, I slipped into the RV and took the license and cash out of her purse. I didn't think she'd notice until—until it was too late. After a show, Malachi was always as randy as a tomcat, and they'd go into the bedroom and carry on for hours. There was no way I could keep from hearing them. God, it was so disgusting. All that piety in public and then acting like animals in private."

I did not want details. "But Seraphina did notice it was missing, didn't she?"

Chastity had overcome her initial shock and was back to being surly and resentful. "She didn't say anything about the license—just a piddly fifty dollars. It wasn't like it was the grocery money for the rest of the month. What set her off was that I was going to use it for an abortion. She was so mad she chewed me out for a solid hour, and she was still laying on a guilt trip when I jumped out of the car and ran into the RV. When I heard her car door slam, I locked myself in the bathroom. I was real relieved when I came out a few minutes later and saw her car was gone."

Some veiled emotion crossed her face, but she looked down before I could even speculate as to its meaning.

I offered an easy question to calm her down. "Where did the majority of this take place?"

"In the parking lot of that supermarket down the

road from the Dairee Dee-Lishus, but she didn't let up while she drove back here, either. I've never heard so much yammering in my life. 'Thou shalt not kill.' 'Be fruitful and multiply.' 'Though your sins be as scarlet, they shall be as white as snow.' Before Seraphina hooked up with Malachi, she sure as hell wasn't any naive virgin." Her eyes brimmed with tears, and her voice lost its belligerence. "Her name used to be Sandra. Mostly she worked as a waitress, but sometimes she got a job as an office temp or nursery school aide. She'd call me at the foster homes to see how I was doing, and once in a while I'd stay with her for a weekend. We'd eat pizza, do our hair funny, paint our nails, and talk all night. She wasn't so goody-goody then, but we always went to church Sunday mornings."

I let her sniffle while I thought over what she'd said. "She discovered the money was missing. If I had been in her position, I'd have assumed you were going to run away. Did you tell her you wanted to get an abortion?"

Chastity shook her head. "She knew about it when she made me get in the car. She was more upset about that than she was about me being pregnant, and she kept insisting Malachi would force Joey to marry me so the baby would be legitimate. Her brilliant idea was that Joey and I would live in some crummy apartment. He could get a glamorous job washing cars or working in a fast-food joint, and I'd stay in school until the baby came. She and Malachi would subsidize us to the overwhelmingly generous tune of five hundred a month. Heaven on earth, huh?"

"Did she tell you that she fired Joey?"

"Yeah, he wasn't going to be associated with Hope Is

Here ever again. She used to drive Thomas crazy by firing the dumb jerks who showed up for work with whiskey on their breath or bragged too loudly about picking up women in bars. Thomas would have to go rushing down to the employment office to replace them. The ones who kept their jobs were smart enough to pretend they were God-fearing Christians whenever she was around."

"But she knew about the abortion," I said, mostly to myself. "After basketball practice one day last week, you asked Darla Jean about clinics. Did you ask anyone else?"

"Nobody, and Darla Jean swore she didn't say anything to Coach Grapper."

I almost toppled off the bench. "Norma Kay Grapper knew about it, too? Did she tell you that?"

"It was in the note she sent to Malachi. Darla Jean showed it to me, then crossed her heart and swore she didn't tell her. That's when I decided I'd better get the driver's license right away and see if I could get a ride into Farberville after the show. I figured I could find a place to sleep and get an abortion first thing in the morning before they could stop me. I was trying to talk one of the boys into taking me when Seraphina drove up."

I had an idea, albeit a murky one. "You didn't have any luck yesterday morning, did you?"

"I tried four places, but none of them fell for it. The photograph was too distinctive, too beautiful. One of the nurses said she was gonna call Seraphina and tell her I had her ID. I was terrified the bitch recognized the name, but all she did was copy down the address in Little Rock."

"So you turned around and pulled that stunt with Cory Jenks so he might be led to believe he was the father. What about Joey? The last time I saw you and him together, you were acting as though you were infatuated."

Chastity hopped off the stage and brushed the seat of her shorts. "I don't think he's the type to live in an apartment and work at a gas station to support a baby and me."

"Once paternity's established, he has an obligation."

"It might be hard to collect child support from someone living on Venice Beach," she said. She flipped her ponytail over her shoulder and sauntered up the aisle.

I amended my list of things to do when I had time. Darla Jean McIlhaney was a contender for the number one spot. We needed a little work in the realm of telling "the truth, the whole truth, and nothing but the truth, so help me God."

Hey, I never said I was an atheist. That was Millicent McIlhaney.

Look how her daughter turned out.

"It's tied again," Bur said, "and there are seven seconds left on the clock when the referee calls an intentional foul. I yell at the kid to get his ass to the sideline, and I'm bawling him out for being so goddamn fuckin' obvious, when the referee orders me to shut up. What was I supposed to do—send the kid a picture postcard telling him that he'd blown the championship?"

Ruby Bee had dozed off during the lengthy and

mostly incomprehensible narrative, but she jerked up her head and said, "You're absolutely right, Bur." She poked Estelle, who was snoring next to her, but it would have taken a jackhammer to do much good.

Bur snorted. "So their guy makes the free throws, and we're down by two. I send in this kid that could make field goals from the middle of the court when his testosterone was up. They put on a full-court press. We can't get the ball in, so we call a time-out with the clock still at seven. The crowd's screaming so loud I can hardly make myself heard."

Ruby Bee drifted off, aware that Bur was rambling on but unable to keep her eyes open. He didn't seem to care that his captive audience was comatose, and she surely didn't care about the 1981 state basketball tournament.

When I emerged from the tent, I saw what appeared to be a small-scale press conference taking place. Malachi stood on the top step of the makeshift porch, his white suit reminiscent of the old-fashioned evangelists he seemed to scorn. Below him were a couple of reporters with notebooks and tape recorders, and the dreaded cameraman from one of the local television stations.

"Seraphina was an angel," Malachi was saying, his expression befitting a bereaved widower. "She was the light of my life, and I was proud to see her light shine on others as well. Her childhood was filled with hardship and misfortune. When I first met her, she was sitting alone in a bus station, with all her possessions in one small suitcase. But even though her clothes were dirty and her shoes were worn, I could see the purity in her heart. I sat beside her and pressed what money I had into her limp hand. She looked at me with a smile so radiant that it brought tears to my eyes. You remember what the apostle Paul wrote to the Hebrews, don't you? 'Be not forgetful to entertain strangers: for thereby some have entertained angels unawares.' "

"Are there any leads on her murder?" asked one of the reporters.

"I am here to bring redemption to skeptics and disbelievers, and prosperity to struggling Christians. So urgent is my mission that I cannot allow worldly matters to distract me. I know that Seraphina would want me to continue despite my heartache."

"So you don't know anything," the reporter said as he closed his notebook. His colleagues did the same, while the cameraman turned and panned the tent.

I ducked back inside and waited until they were gone. When I emerged, Malachi was still on the porch, watching them drive away and looking pleased with himself.

"That went well, didn't it?" he said. "If we make the six o'clock news, we'll have a full house again tonight."

"If I don't close you down, that is."

"Oh, dear, Miss Hanks, do you remain perturbed? I instructed Chastity to answer all your questions in a forthright manner. She has nothing to hide. We're here only to celebrate the glories of God by bringing wealth and happiness to the citizens of Stump County." Grinning, he rubbed his hands together. "This very night more than a thousand of them will lift up their eyes and thank Jesus for healing the lame and making the blind to see."

"Let's talk about that," I said. "These miracles of yours are beginning to border on quackery. Unless you've got a medical degree tucked away in your Bible, you'd better stick to selling seeds. I already told you about the woman who was convinced she could drive without her glasses and had an accident. You told a local girl that she no longer has diabetes. You'd better pray nothing bad happens to her, because if it does, I'm holding you responsible, Mr. Hope."

"The responsibility lies with a higher power, and you may have a hard time convicting Jesus of a felony. Now I think I'd better prepare for the service. Will we have the honor of your company again tonight?"

"I'm not finished yet. There's the small matter of the note you gave me yesterday. I guess someone must have performed a miracle on it, too. Jesus changed water into wine. Did he also change the wording on the note?"

I enjoyed watching his expression erode. "I don't know what you're talking about," he said. "I gave you the note that was delivered to me. Have you bothered to test the typewriter in Norma Kay's office to see if it was used?"

"It was typed on Norma Kay's typewriter, but it's not what she wrote. She overheard a conversation in the locker room during which Chastity asked one of the local girls about abortion possibilities. Norma Kay was real touchy about that, as you must have known from the letters she wrote about the unpleasantness in Topeka ten years ago. You remember, don't you?"

"I receive thousands of letters, and I don't read every one. I certainly don't commit them to memory."

"Let me refresh you," I said obligingly. "While she was the coach there, one of her best players came to her and admitted she was pregnant. The girl went on to say if she couldn't get an abortion, she'd be kicked out of school and packed away to an aunt in South Dakota. No more star center, no more conference championships. Norma Kay gave the girl the name of a back-alley butcher, who botched the job. Poor, ambitious Norma Kay came close to being arrested but was allowed to resign and leave town. From what I could gather from her letters, you told her to abandon the Catholic church because she would never be forgiven, and instead she could become a part of your cable congregation."

He crossed his arms and looked down at me. "Should I have told her to throw herself off a bridge? I welcome saints and sinners alike."

I decided it would be inappropriate to punch out his lights (blessed is the cop that endureth temptation—or something like that). "Norma Kay wasn't about to allow Chastity to get an abortion, legal or otherwise. The note she wrote demanded that you come to the gym to assure her that you would take steps to prevent it. You were too scared not to go, weren't you?"

"Scared?" he said with a caustic laugh.

"Norma Kay must have threatened to take the story to the media. The newspapers might not have carried anything, but the tabloids would have loved it—and trust me on this, those guys are ruthless. They'd gladly take the latest talking-potato story off the cover in order to have a doctored photo of you and Seraphina on either side of a fifteen-year-old fallen angel: 'Evangelist Dictates Abortion.' That'd put a dent in the ol' aluminum bucket, wouldn't it?"

Malachi came down the steps and turned on all the charm he could (it wasn't much). "Okay, Norma Kay and I discussed all this, and I swore Chastity would marry the culpable party and carry the baby to full term. After we prayed, she agreed not to tell anyone else. I had no reason to harm her. She was perfectly satisfied when I left."

"What about the note?"

"When I went back to the gym, I found her as I described earlier. I assumed all the old memories had returned with such painful clarity that she committed suicide. There was no reason to drag Chastity into it, so before I called you, I typed the second note. But as God is my witness, I did not strangle Norma Kay—and I would never even think of hurting Seraphina. She was my wife, my partner, my comfort in times of adversity. She believed in my miracles."

"Excuse me," I inserted. "She was the one monitoring the microphones and selecting the patsies each night. Are you saying she actually believed the workman from the crew was truly blind, or that the woman she saw walk into the tent was in need of a wheelchair until you begged Jesus for a cure?"

"She always said, 'What difference does it make if you're a fake—and still get the job done?' People *feel* better because they have something to cling to, if only the memory of a crowd screaming ecstatically as they walked across the stage. Jesus was there in their hearts. Some of them will experience some improvement because they believe they're better. A touch of my hand, a burst of faith, a surge of adrenaline, something. I cure people, Miss Hanks, and I bring them into the spiritual fold. I know you think it's callous of me not to cancel the revival, but you simply do not appreciate the enormity of my calling. I am God's chosen instrument to bring enlightenment to a world riddled with wickedness. I am here to save humanity."

I stepped back and eyed him with trepidation, not at all sure how sincere he was. Brother Verber was as transparent as a pane of glass, and Mrs. Jim Bob's motives weren't much more opaque. Hell, I wasn't even sure how sincere Burt Lancaster had been. Malachi Hope, however, seemed to have no problem characterizing himself as a modern-day Messiah.

Did he also consider himself above the law?

"The lucky shot made the score twenty-two to fifteen," Bur said as saliva bubbled out the corners of his mouth, mingling with the latest gulp of beer. "Amos wanted to run the two-one-two with the wing overload, but they came out of the quarter in a straight man-to-man. I yelled at the asshole playing point to run the one-three-one pass and cut, but the asshole thought he could take his man."

"Did he?" murmured Ruby Bee.

"How the hell could he! The point guard wasn't more than five-ten, and the guy guarding him was six-five if he was an inch."

"My goodness . . ."

Bur paused, stroking the shotgun as if it were a cat curled in his lap. Ruby Bee felt a flicker of optimism that he was going to doze off. Having owned a bar all these years, she knew about beer drinkers. Bur'd guzzled a half dozen, most likely on an empty stomach.

She was no longer interested in finding clues in dresser drawers and heart-shaped boxes, or in duping Bur into spilling secrets about Norma Kay's problems in Topeka. Getting out of there alive was all that mattered. She leaned forward, stealthily putting out her hand, and whispered, "Bur, are you awake?"

His head jerked upright. "The asshole fires a fifteen-footer, but the guy guarding him slaps the ball into the stands like he was swatting a fly."

Ruby Bee put her hand back on the arm of the sofa. "Then what happened, Bur?" She could only hope that Estelle's snores and her own question had prevented him from hearing the back door open.

"Where's Kevin?" Jim Bob asked a checker. "I need him to mop up a mess in the second aisle. Some shithead knocked over a bottle of ammonia, and the stench is driving away customers."

"He's not here. While you were gone, Mrs. Jim Bob came in and told Kevin to come with her. He tried to argue with her, but she was"—the checker searched for a tactful word—"persistent."

"Come with her where?"

"Gee, she didn't say. Kevin was real unhappy, but he

didn't have any choice but to leave his mop and follow her out to her car. That was an hour ago."

"I don't pay you to stand around staring at your wristwatch," Jim Bob said. "Go clean up the ammonia." He went into his office, shut the door, and sat down to scratch his head and try to figure out if Mrs. Jim Bob was plum off her rocker or up to something illegal. Either one might result in her being locked up, which was okay with him as long as the lawyer's bill wasn't sky-high. He damn well didn't want to waste his windfall from the land sale on some legal leech.

Not when he could lie on a beach, a drink in his hand, while some sweet young thing rubbed suntan oil on his back. Later, they'd watch the sunset from the balcony of his suite, and after that . . .

Jim Bob forced himself out of the reverie. With his luck, Mrs. Jim Bob would come storming into the office and catch him with a bulge in his britches. He didn't think he could blame it on the ammonia in the second aisle.

"That looks better," the clerk lied, smiling at the fat lady preening in front of the mirror. "It's not quite so snug around your hips. You know what would look real cute with that? A silk scarf, draped over your shoulder. Here, let me put it on for you, Wilma."

"Thank you, dear. I was thinking those earrings would go with the ensemble."

The clerk was thinking that the only thing that would save the ensemble was a paper bag with eyeholes, but she said, "Aren't these perfect!" As she put them on the customer, she couldn't help noticing the tufts of hair coming out of both ears and a few whiskers on the chin. As soon as she could, she took a break in the back room and made a few calls to see if she could find another job, preferably one in which she worked alone in a small, confined room. No windows, no doors—and no customers. Ever.

16

ESTELLE'S station wagon was still in Bur's driveway as I drove back down to County 102. She and Ruby Bee were making one heck of an extended condolence call, I thought with a resigned sigh. Instead of heading toward town, I turned right, splashed over the low-water bridge, and parked near the logging road that led to where Seraphina's Mercedes had been discovered.

I was not on a Sherlockian quest for clues. The car had been towed to Farberville to be examined for fingerprints, stray hairs, buttons, radioactive dust bunnies, blackmail notes, cryptic chemicals, and all those wonderfully exotic things that are found only in fiction. Seraphina's body was at the state lab in Little Rock. The official autopsy would not turn up a South American tree frog poison or a needle mark hidden in her scalp. She'd been strangled. In her case, there'd been no crude attempt to fake a suicide.

I went to the edge of Boone Creek and began to pitch

rocks into the water, causing blue jays in the trees to squawk and turtles on a sunlit log to plop into the water.

Cory Jenks's story could be true: He'd gone to Emmet, returned home at 12:05 with a case of bootlegged beer, and stayed inside the remainder of the night. Unbeknownst to him, his truck had been possessed by Satan and taken itself for a drive. Minor problem.

Malachi Hope's story could be true: He'd gone to the gym and reasoned with Norma Kay, gone to the RV, and gone back to the gym at 1:30. His explanation of the faked note was somewhat credible.

Chastity's story could be true: She'd gone to the Dairee Dee-Lishus and was there when Seraphina pulled up. They'd argued in the parking lot, argued in the road, and argued in the pasture before Chastity had gone inside the RV, leaving her sister in the Mercedes.

Joey's story, although less complex, could be true: He'd been fired, taken a ride on his motorcycle, toured the county, and returned to the tent after he'd calmed down.

Thomas Fratelleon's downright simplistic story could be true: He spoke to Malachi at 12:05 and then went to bed.

I tried to think if I was missing anyone. Bur Grapper was a suspect in a minimal way. He could have driven to the gym and waited until Malachi left, then killed Norma Kay in a jealous rage. Had Seraphina entered the gym at the worst possible moment? If Bur had strangled her, he'd have to have driven her car to the creek and walked all the way back to the high school to retrieve his truck. He'd barely have made it home by dawn.

A black snake slithered across the gravel bar in

search of a toasty rock or a plump, reckless rodent. Finding neither, it disappeared into the weeds. I recognized it as a water moccasin, content to peacefully go about its business—but aggressive and dangerous when provoked. As a kid, I'd provoked plenty of them on a summer day, just to watch my friends scramble out of the water, shrieking and cussing. All it took was a long stick and a steady hand.

"The next year I lost that point guard," Bur said, perilously near tears. He wiped his cheeks with a disgustingly crusty handkerchief, then tucked it underneath the cushion and took off like a Roman candle on the Fourth of July. "Him and his uncle went deer hunting over by Pineville. The next thing I hear, the kid's paralyzed on account of a goddamn bullet in his spine. He was the one I was telling you about who was shooting fifty-eight percent from the floor and eighty-seven percent from the line. What am I supposed to do? Amos thinks we can bring up this reedy kid off the sophomore bench, despite the fact the kid's flunking everything, including study hall. His eligibility's a joke. I know we're gonna face Greenland the week after Thanksgiving. I ask you— what am I supposed to do?"

"I'm real sure you're going to tell me, Bur," Ruby Bee said wearily. "What year are we up to, by the way?"

"Nineteen eighty-four. Greenland's got another damn six-foot-four center, and all I've got is one kid in intensive care and another one that can't tell the basket from a knothole on an outhouse door." He finished the beer and dropped the empty can on the alpine pile. "So what I do is tell Amos to get the kid enrolled in nothing but basic English and phys ed classes. In the meantime, I come up with this defense that's fuckin' impenetrable."

Ruby Bee was beginning to think it might not hurt that bad to be killed, as long as death was instantaneous. Wasn't there some international law about torture? If she was entitled to a final request, it would be that Estelle be roused and forced to listen to all the details—players, plays, good calls, bad calls, blind refs, technical fouls, intentional fouls, free throws, field goals, defense, offense—all of it. And she deserved it, having missed the first seventeen years of Bur's recitation.

"I ain't sure about this," Kevin hollered, looking down. "The ladder's extended as far as it kin go, and I cain't reach the roof unless I grab the gutter and swing over to the windowsill. The gutter's a mite rusty."

"Why are you waiting?"

"The windowsill's rotted, and the wood's liable to crumble if I step on it. I'm sorry, Mrs. Jim Bob, but I'm gonna be a father real soon, and I aim to be there to go fishing and plant a garden and read fairy tales at bedtime." He realized what he'd said and came close to losing his grip and slithering down a fast forty feet. "Stories like *Cinderella* and *Sleeping Beauty*," he explained in case she thought he was referring to male hairdressers. It wasn't as if he'd ever actually met a male hairdresser in his entire life, but he didn't want her to get ideas.

Mrs. Jim Bob had ideas, all the same. "Kevin, I am

telling you to step on that sill so you can attach the lights like I said. Stop discussing frivolous literature and do as you're told."

"Yes, ma'am."

My hands were shaking as I went into the tent through the back entrance. Out in front, the faithful were gathering, although curtain time was more than an hour away. The ushers were already guiding wheelchairs to the front row and helping people fill out those handy, dandy informational prayer cards. A hymn played softly on the stereo system. Outside, the tables were piled high and the vendors were eager to accept credit cards.

Malachi was staring at the fuse box as if admiring the configuration of the lights. He was in a pastel pink jacket and trousers. It struck me as the color of strawberry vomit.

"I want to talk to you," I said, tapping his shoulder. "Jesus went out into the wilderness for forty days and night, but forty minutes was all I needed."

"For what?" he asked.

"To realize that Joey Lerner is not responsible for Chastity's pregnancy."

Malachi's face began to resemble his ensemble. "Why are you saying this, Miss Hanks? Are you determined to cause Chastity even more pain at a time when she's coming to terms with her sister's death?"

"She's holding up," I said dryly. "A long time ago, as far back as last week, Thomas Fratelleon told me that Joey was a decent young man. Somehow or other, he's now guilty of impregnating a teenager—but nobody cares. He doesn't care. Chastity doesn't care. Thomas doesn't care. When you told me about it, you never so much as mentioned his name. Seraphina cared, but she's dead. Not one of the rest of you seems to believe Joey ought to do what used to be called 'the honorable thing' and marry Chastity. In the good ol' days, there were plenty of shotgun weddings in these parts. Hell, it was standard dress for the groomsmen. So why are you giving him a raise instead of insisting he acknowledge paternity?"

"Joey's a drifter," Malachi said, "and unwilling to accept responsibility for his immoral actions. There's no way I can force him."

"Sure there is. All we have to do is require him to submit a blood sample. In a matter of days, we'll have the results of the test, and if there's doubt, we can order DNA testing. Proving paternity is a piece of angelfood cake."

"Why are you doing this?"

"To solve two murders," I said. "You are aware that Norma Kay Grapper and Seraphina—your beloved wife—were strangled, aren't you? They died because they were prolifers strongly opposed to abortion. Talk about irony . . ."

"I don't care to talk about irony or anything else. In less than an hour I'm going onstage to do the Lord's work. I need time to prepare myself through prayer and meditation."

"You're not going anywhere in the next hour, unless it's to the county prosecutor's office. You're responsible for Chastity's pregnancy. She's a minor. You, on the other hand, are a felon. You're not only guilty of statutory rape but also incest if indeed you legally adopted her. And don't forget homicide, Mr. Hope. I'd love to pin it on you."

"You're accusing me?" he said. "This is an outrage. Don't you know who I am?"

"A real scumbag, in my opinion. How long did you think you could continue sending Seraphina off to hotels for the night before she caught on?" I gave him a chance to answer what was basically a rhetorical question, but he didn't seem inclined to do more than stare at me. "She was going to catch on real soon, because she was determined that Joey was going to marry Chastity and take a menial job in order to support her. He may be as decent as Fratelleon claims, but I have a feeling he's not a sacrificial lamb. All he had to do was demand that blood test I mentioned a minute ago. If he preferred, he could save the cost of the lab work by telling Seraphina the truth. It wouldn't sit well with her, would it?"

"God gave man a body as well as a soul," Malachi said as sweat beaded on his forehead. "He made us creatures of flesh. Just as we hunger for food, we hunger for sexual fulfillment. I could see what was in Chastity's eyes when she looked at men. I knew it was only a matter of time before she offered her chaste young body to the devil. She would be tainted forever after, branded as a sinner. I had to save her so she could take her rightful place beside me. She and I have been chosen. I planted the divine seed in her in order to bring God's offspring into the world. Don't you see that?"

He put his hand on my shoulder, but I knocked it away and said, "I couldn't possibly describe what I see standing in front of me, but I'm sure some choice phrases will come to mind. Until this is sorted out, the revival's canceled, Mr. Hope. It's over and done. I'm going to radio for deputies to set up roadblocks and turn people away. Then you, Chastity, and I are going to the sheriff's office for a long talk."

"You have no right to judge me. I am graced with powers you cannot possibly fathom."

"Well, you can try to arrange for me to be struck dead by lightning, but don't leave the tent. I'll be back in five minutes."

He was sitting on a carton, his face buried in his hands, as I went out the back exit and over to my car. It would take several strategic roadblocks to divert the expected multitude. I was trying to decide which would be the most effective locations as I switched on the radio.

"Don't do that."

I looked into the barrel of a gun. I hate it when that happens.

"Where can Kevvie be?" asked Dahlia as her father-in-law turned down County 102. She was sitting in the backseat, staring glumly out the window in hopes her husband might be walking alongside the ditch. Why he'd do that she din't know, but he'd been acting real weird lately. She took a candy bar from her purse and morosely ripped open the wrapper. "I called the supermarket, but they couldn't say where he is. He was supposed to come home for supper. Where can he be?"

"He's probably planning to meet you inside the tent,"

Eilene said, crossing her fingers. "The two of you can wait until the revival's over and then insist on having a word in private with Malachi Hope."

"Where can Kevvie be?"

Earl gritted his teeth and kept driving.

"I'm sure they keep the discarded eyeglasses in a box," Edwina Spitz said as she turned down County 102. "All you have to do is ask real nicely if you can have yours back for emergencies. Jesus won't mind a bit."

Lottie slumped down in the seat and sighed. "Maybe my faith isn't as steadfast as I thought it was. In any case, I'm blind as a bat without my glasses."

"And my ankle's swollen worse than a beach ball," said Eula, who was in the backseat, where she could elevate her leg. "If Malachi Hope doesn't heal it again, I may break down and take my pills."

Their conversation dribbled off as Edwina's car fell into line.

"This is ridiculous," I said, as angry with myself as I was at Thomas Fratelleon. Almost as angry, anyway. I was on the floor in the tiny bathroom of the RV, and in a most undignified posture.

He finished wrapping the electrical tape around my ankles, examined his handiwork, then stood up. "It is a bit ridiculous, Miss Hanks, but I don't know what else to do with you for the moment. I'm sorry that you'll experience some discomfort during the next three hours. However, I must return to my post in the van so that Malachi can perform his miracles. We don't want to disappoint all those generous Christians, do we?"

"You're asking the wrong person, Mr. Fratelleon."

"I suppose I am." He stepped over my legs and washed his hands while I glared up at him. If my wrists had not been bound and secured to the pipe beneath the sink, I would have given him something that would have kept him disappointed for a long time.

He dried his hands on a guest towel embroidered with a likeness of his employer. "I should be back as soon as my duties are concluded and Malachi begins his final appeal for donations. In the interim, neither he nor Chastity will have any reason to come in here."

"The man of God never has to answer the call of nature?"

"Malachi takes a childish pleasure in urinating in the grass behind the tent. As I was saying, while he's finishing up, I'll have ample opportunity to escort you to your car. We'll be on our way well before anyone emerges from the tent."

"On our way to the logging road?"

"We'll search for a more secluded one. I had no idea Seraphina would be discovered so quickly. I would have much preferred to have had several weeks to convince Malachi that she had abandoned him in order to resort to a more secular lifestyle."

"And abandoned her teenaged sister to his unhealthy sexual desires?"

"Seraphina never realized what was going on," he

said as he carefully folded the towel and replaced it on the rack. "But as you said to Malachi—"

"He told you?"

Fratelleon gave me a disappointed look. "He wears a microphone, too. How else could he cue the van when he felt ready to perform another miracle? I was monitoring various conversations earlier. The one you had with him caught my attention."

"You should have been listening to CNN," I said.

"You were perceptive when you told Malachi that Seraphina would have figured it out when Joey denied paternity. She was very close to it when I came out of the tent late Sunday night—or early Monday morning, to be accurate—in order to investigate the arrival of a vehicle and the loud voices. Chastity said something at the height of the argument that was incautious. Seraphina's disillusionment would have resulted in the one thing that could destroy the corporation—unfavorable publicity. If Malachi was charged with a sex offense, even his most zealous followers might suspend their regular contributions."

"You're breakin' my heart."

"When you're my age, you'll appreciate why I long for financial security. I must ensure that Malachi has the resources to build the City of Hope. It will generate millions of dollars, a modest percent of which will end up in my portfolio. If Joey has the sense to remain with us, he'll be a rich young man."

"And Malachi will have Chastity all to himself," I said. "He won't have to worry about Seraphina finding out that he's a crackpot, possibly a psychopath. How long do you think it will be before he decides he can walk on water and bring people back from the dead?"

"It's only a matter of time," Fratelleon said with a small frown, "but it will not concern me. I'll see you in approximately three and a half hours."

I tried to kick his leg as he stepped over me but hit the toilet instead. "It was a real stroke of luck finding the ignition key in Cory Jenks's truck, wasn't it?" I said to delay the inevitable as long as possible. I'm not claustrophobic, but I'm not fond of views limited to plumbing. "You knew from Norma Kay's letters that she'd had an affair with him. All you had to do was borrow the truck long enough to drive to the high school and kill her, then take the whistle off his desk and plant it on Seraphina's body to further implicate him. Were you afraid Norma Kay might stop sending checks if Chastity and Joey failed to get married?"

"Norma Kay Grapper took it upon herself to become involved in this. When she reminded me on the telephone that she could prevent her husband from selling the acreage to us if she chose, I knew I was going to deal with her sooner or later. As I walked back from the creek, it occurred to me that the key might be in the ignition. I decided to seize the moment. Until later, Miss Hanks."

Once I heard the front door close, I did some dedicated wiggling and writhing. The tape around my ankles refused to stretch, and the tape binding my wrists to the pipe was too tight to allow me to try to get any friction against the pipe. I kept trying until I was exhausted. As I rested my head on the floor, I heard the crescendo of music and applause that accompanied Malachi's entrance onstage.

I had less than three hours.

Two hours later my wrists were raw, but the damn electrical tape remained resilient enough to serve as a bungee cord. My buttocks were sore, and my forehead was bruised from being banged against the pipe. (Frustration had affected my depth perception.) The sounds of the revival weren't improving my mood. Every "Hallelujah" from the tent elicited a distinctly less reverent exclamation from me.

One was forming on my tongue when I heard the front door open. I craned my neck to look at my watch. I had most of two hours left before I could anticipate Thomas Fratelleon's arrival (and my subsequent departure). I had no idea what Malachi or Chastity would do upon entering the bathroom; anything from being freed to being peed on was a possibility.

I decided to get it over with. "I'm in here!" I shouted. "I need help!"

The door opened a few inches and an unfamiliar face peered through the slit. It had stringy whiskers, yellow-tinged eyes, and a toothless grin. "I shore din't expect to find a pretty filly on the floor in here."

"Who are you?" I said, immediately pegging him as a Buchanon but unable to come up with a first name.

"I'm Petrol Buchanon. What about you, honey pie?"

I licked my dry lips until I could stretch them into a painful smile. "My name's Arly, Mr. Buchanon. It's kinda hard to explain why I'm hog-tied like this, but I'd be real grateful if you'd be kind enough to find some scissors or a knife and cut off this awful tape. This floor's harder than bedrock."

He looked over his shoulder. "Is there anybody else here? I don't want to get caught. Over in the tent, Miz Twayblade's slinking up and down the aisles, searching for me, so I came in here to hide. I reckon I could have stayed in the house down the hill, but it was mighty boring."

"There's no one else," I said. "Please help me."

He returned shortly with a knife. Five minutes later I was massaging my wrists while I waited for LaBelle to connect me with Harve. Petrol was more interested in the contents of the refrigerator than my telephone call; I urged him to take anything that appealed.

I doubt many Buchanons have feasted on caviar sandwiches and champagne.

Snuffling like an asthmatic hound, Bur wiped his runny nose on his sleeve. "The ball was in the air when the buzzer went off. Five thousand fans on their feet, their guts tight and their eyes locked on the ball like it was a ballistic missile. You could have heard a rat fart in the locker room. I'm telling myself we're gonna beat the bastards in spite of—"

"Whatsat?" Estelle said, pitching forward. She rubbed her eyes, then gave Ruby Bee a confused look as she struggled into consciousness. "I can't believe we're still here. My neck's got an awful crick, and I'm so hungry I could eat a horse. If Bur's gonna commit suicide, why doesn't he just do it so we can go home?"

After what she'd gone through, Ruby Bee was well beyond feeling any compassion for Bur. The fat was in the fire, in any case, so she said, "You never did say why you're planning to kill yourself, Bur. You don't have to if you don't want to, but you ought to leave a note. I have a piece of paper and a pencil right here in my purse. You just spit it out and I'll write it down for you. Then all you have to do is sign it and you'll be all set to kill yourself. How do you want to start?"

He gazed drunkenly at her. "I ain't never written one of these before. I don't know how to start."

"Of course, you've never written one before," Ruby Bee said with a sniff. "If you had, you'd be dead."

Estelle leaned forward and patted his knee. "I'll be right pleased to help you with the wording, Bur, but you have to tell me why you want to kill yourself. Is it because you're afraid to spend the rest of your life bumbling around an empty house?"

"Maybe grief over losing Norma Kay?" suggested Ruby Bee, her pencil poised above the backside of a grocery list.

"Sort of," Bur said, plucking at his robe and hiccuping occasionally. "I drove her to do it, what with my orneriness and suspicious nature. I never once found any proof she was sleeping with anybody, but I couldn't make myself accept it. Sunday afternoon I called her a liar and slapped her so hard she fell against the counter. The next morning I'm told she hanged herself on a basketball goal. What am I supposed to think?"

"Wait a minute!" snapped Ruby Bee. "Are you saying that you think she hanged herself—and that's why I had to sit here and listen to the details of every last basketball game you coached since the year nineteen hundred and sixty-one? Bur Grapper, you are as stupid as cow spit. Norma Kay was murdered!"

"She didn't kill herself?" he said weakly. "I guess that's good to know."

Ruby Bee stuffed the grocery list and the pencil in her purse, then grabbed Estelle's arm and hauled her up. "I have never in my life spent such a tedious afternoon. You listen up, Bur—if you ever speak to me again, and I'm not saying you should—you'd better not say one single word that has anything to do with basketball. I don't know what I'll do, but you can bet the farm it won't be pretty. Come on, Estelle, let's go."

"Would you happen to know who killed her?" Bur asked meekly, then realized he was talking to thin air. Which reminded him of that crucial shot back in 1989, when thousands of hysterical fans began to chant, "Airball, airball, airball!"

If they hadn't, he most likely wouldn't have socked the referee.

Who had it coming.

Well, hell—maybe he would have anyway.

"I want everybody to shut up!" I yelled from the edge of the stage. "If you'll do that for me, I'll explain what just happened. I don't have any obligation to cooperate, though. You can read about it in the newspaper or catch it on the six o'clock news tomorrow night."

The overhead lights were on, and the speakers were silent. A thousand, maybe as many as twelve hundred, faces looked back at me, most of them hostile. I made sure there were deputies near the steps that led to the stage and then looked out at what Malachi Hope had seen at every revival: fair game. They wanted something from him, and he gave it to them. He got the job done and sent them away imbued with optimism that Jesus would take a special interest in their problems, that the doctor's troublesome diagnosis was wrong, that they would become rich and happy forever after. Amen.

If they emptied their wallets, that is.

After I'd explained that Fratelleon had been charged with two counts of murder and Malachi with child endangerment (did you really think I was going to tell the truth?), I announced that there would be no more services and no City of Hope. "Get your religion at your churches and your entertainment at Branson," I added, "and keep in mind the distinction."

"What about how Malachi cured folks?" demanded Dahlia, squeezed between her in-laws.

I'd prepared myself for the dubious reward of raining on their parade. "Is there one person in this room who can honestly say he was cured? I don't mean who thinks he was cured, but who went to a doctor and had it confirmed by a legitimate medical procedure."

Dahlia wasn't ready to give up fried chicken. "I saw for myself how a blind man threw away his white cane and walked down the steps on his own."

"Yeah," said a man across the room, "but I saw him drive one of those trucks into Maggody last week."

"I felt a tingle when Malachi squeezed my shoulders," cried a young woman.

I looked at the metal rectangle on which I was standing. "I'd imagine you did when you received a few volts. Malachi could have knocked the socks off you with this gizmo if that's what it took." I wouldn't have been there if I hadn't been assured that Joey and Chastity had been taken into custody, too. The former would be questioned, the latter taken to a temporary shelter while her fate was determined. The command post was unoccupied.

"How's your eyesight?" I called to Lottie Estes. When she shook her head, I looked down at the wheelchair occupants. "Any of you unable to walk into the tent without assistance?"

A woman crippled by rheumatism raised her hand. "This is my own wheelchair, but Malachi didn't call for Jesus to cure me. My husband brought me all the way from Springfield. This was our third night, and we were hoping . . ."

And so it went. I finally quieted them down and said, "The only miracle that took place was that Malachi made you believe in him."

As they filed out of the tent, I went behind the curtain and sat down on the flattened grass. How much crazier could life in Washington, D.C., be? Politicians and evangelists were of the same genus, if not species, and IRS agents probably fit in there somewhere, too. I could drop back into social circles in which the cost of layer grit was never discussed. I most likely couldn't find a decent chicken fried steak or a cherry limeade, but I'd survived culinary deprivations in a past life.

I stood up, walked up the aisle of the tent, and turned around to take a last look at the stage. The only hope Malachi had brought had been as short-lived as a politician's promise.

"Poof," I said, then went out to my car. If I hurried, Ruby Bee's Bar & Grill would still be open. I may have survived on canapés and cocktails, but at the moment there was a grilled cheese sandwich in my future. And an icy beer.

"I'll go to the clinic," Dahlia muttered as they drove back up County 102. "Malachi still could have cured me, you know. Just because Arly started sprouting off about how he's a fake doesn't mean he is one. There was something in his eyes that was real unsettling."

"How about a gnat?" Earl said, snickering. "Or a mosquito, or—" He broke off as he caught sight of the Voice of the Almighty Lord Assembly Hall. "Will ya take a look at that?"

All along the road cars and trucks were coming to an abrupt stop as the lights came into view.

"It looks like Noow Yark City," gasped Estelle.

"Don't it, though," Ruby Bee agreed.

"I ain't never seen anything like it," said Eula Lemoy, so awed her swollen leg slid off the seat of the car.

Lottie Estes felt as though she was gazing at a magical kingdom all illuminated in a diffused haze. For the moment, she was glad she didn't have her glasses. "Beautiful, isn't it?"

Mrs. Jim Bob stood by the rectory so she could soak in the mesmerizing splendor of the thousands of lights blanketing the Assembly Hall. A portable sign in front flashed the words: "Bingo! Grand Prizes!" Another sign above the door proclaimed: "Welcome!" Other lights looped among the sycamore trees and twinkled high in the branches. A loudspeaker played "Onward, Christian Soldiers" with so much spirit feet were tapping all the way to the low-water bridge. Right by the door was a shiny cotton-candy machine.

"Oh, my gawd," said a woman in a yellow dress.

Mrs. Jim Bob pursed her lips as she tried to think where she'd heard that particular voice. "It should be impressive. It cost over four thousand dollars—and that's not chicken feed."

"Four thousand dollars?" the strange woman said, her hand on her bosom. "Who's paying for it?"

"The mayor of our little town. He sold some property and can well afford it. Can we expect you to attend our Wednesday night bingo game?"

The woman recoiled, almost losing her balance as one of her heels dug into the lawn. "I can't rightly say. I'm from—from way down past—past Magnolia, and I'm just visiting kin for a few days."

Mrs. Jim Bob was about to mention that Wednesday evening was a mere twenty-four hours away when she was shoved aside by what felt like a stampeding buffalo.

"Look up there on the roof!" Dahlia screeched, waving her arm and jumping up and down. "It's Kevvie! You jest keep hanging on to the vent pipe until the volunteer fire department gets here. I'm so proud of you. This is a real, live miracle!"

Nobody offered a word to the contrary, not even seconds later when every light in town, from the streetlight at the south end of town to the V CAN Y sign in front of Ruby Bee's Bar & Grill at the north end of town, blinked out.

After all, the stars were real pretty, too.

The typeface used in this book is a version of Palatino, originally designed in 1950 by Hermann Zapf (b. 1918), one of the most prolific contemporary type designers, who has also created Melior and Optima. Palatino was first used to set the introduction of a book of Zapf's hand lettering, in an edition of eighty copies on Japan paper handbound by his wife, Gudron von Hesse; the book sold out quickly and Zapf's name was made. (Remarkably, the lettering had actually been done when the self-taught calligrapher was only twenty-one.) Intended mainly for "display" (title pages, headings), Palatino owes its appearance both to calligraphy and the requirements of the cheap German paper at the time—perhaps the reason it is also one of the best-looking fonts on low-end computer printers. It was soon used to set text, however, causing Zapf to redraw its more elaborate letters.